The Monsoon MARIGOLDS

SHEKHAR SRIVASTAVA

Invincible Publishers

First Printing: 2019

ISBN: 978-93-88333-89-4

Invincible Publishers

To Poonam and Brij, the only people who love me more than I do.

To my family that always stood by me in all times of ordeal and elation.

Acknowledgement

Writing a novel was not as tough as it seemed to me at a certain point in my life; it wasn't that easy as well though. This story that took me one year to complete was in my mind since the last few years but I would like to mention that some specific people and conditions drove me to pen it down—some indirectly, a very few directly. Taking a break to complete a novel was never an easy task for me. Hence, in this journey of completing it, I would like to thank all those people who continuously encouraged me.

The first and most important person I would like to thank is my mother who always puts more faith in me than I do, like all mothers do!

My inspiration for writing is my father who loved to write and whose unpublished manuscript still resides in my cupboard. The second being all the writers I have read in my life so far.

It would be unjust not to include those who discouraged me on this path—verily, there is nothing that drives you as much as the will to challenge yourself, to get up, and go against the tide even if it creates some impediments in the beginning. *And I am not being sarcastic!*

I would like to thank Mr Ajay Setia who worked as an anchor for my story to turn it into a novel. With his proficient stance, this book has become a reality for me.

Last but definitely not the least, I would like to thank my Lord—*Shri Radharaman Ji*—because of whose love and blessings, I am what I am today and will continue to be!

VOLUME 1

CHAPTER 1

Summer is the most dreadful season of Delhi–a city known to be a paradigm of cultural amalgamation comprised of almost all the cultures of India and many other countries–and sitting under its sky during dusk hours often becomes relieving for people, like it was for him.

It was a warm summer night and Siddhant sat at a table at a rooftop bar after the office hours got over, watching the night getting darker and the pandemonium and sound of the city augmenting. He watched the red and green stop-and-go traffic signal, and the crowd going by, from the parapet of the bar while waiting for his evening meal. He noticed a pretty teenager girl walk past his table and then lost sight of her. She went by once again waving her light brown hair, which he noticed had golden streaks, and then he caught her eye. She came over and sat down at the table. The waiter came up and Siddhant asked the girl in his deep voice after a moment or two, 'What will you have?'

'Campari' she said as if she had achieved something by getting herself a drink.

'Campari for me too,' Siddhant said to the waiter. She contemplated the possibility of him looking at her, which he eventually did.

'You from Delhi?' Siddhant asked.

'Oh yes, it's a fascinating city,' she replied with a broad smile.

'And I thought someone only from the farther cities could say that,' he said frivolously after a moment, not looking at her once again.

'Are you upset? Did I disturb you?' She asked. He seemed to be listening to her for the very first time.

'Oh I am perfect,' he said calmly.

'You seem to be a bit different.' Siddhant didn't reply to it for a moment, and then added looking at her, 'Why don't you go somewhere else for work? Some other work.'

'You think getting work is that easy?' She expressed after a pause. 'It's easier to get a drink and dinner like this,' she added and winked at him.

After gulping down a bit too much of Campari, she looked dazed yet more ambitious for her work.

'Why don't you take me somewhere? Some quiet place with fewer people,' She asked in a wobbling voice.

'Where do you stay?' He asked.

'Oh, no... not my place.'

'I asked you where you live?' He asked assertively. And she told, seeing the commanding in his deep voice.

'You want to eat something?' He asked then.

'I am not so hungry you see.' She looked unstable now but could walk.

'What's your name?'

'People call me Rosie,' she told him in her now confused voice.

Siddhant didn't care to ask her real name. He booked a cab and walked her down to the street. With a roaring sound, a cab stopped after two minutes in front of the building. He now gave her a two thousand rupee note which she kept instantly in her glittering golden clutch which looked bizarre with her little black dress. He opened the door of the cab and asked her to sit inside and closed the door as soon as she stepped inside.

'Tell him the location of your house,' he said, and showing the mobile phone to the cab driver, he added to the driver, 'I will be tracking the route. Drop her safely.'

'Thank you so much,' she said half-consciously but genuinely.

The engine of the car roared the next moment and he turned towards the parking area where he had parked his car. What she had asked him in the elevator resonated in his mind though. 'Have you ever loved someone in your life?'...was what she had asked to which he hadn't replied, as he didn't care about what a drunk, teenager harlot had asked.

But now, while walking, some other words from someone else too resonated in his mind–'*Your compassion could be the reason I was attracted to you. So much so that I did not realize it could be anything but love.*' Siddhant walked on, despondent and dispirited.

Delhi definitely is not only about people from all the parts of the country but also about many who are indifferent to the unbearable chaos and sounds of the historic city; people who can be called very lonely–more lonely than those who sit alone in a dark room–and chained to the cruelties of life.

CHAPTER 2

Mathurs, residents of a cooperative housing society in Noida, had always been a simple family of three members. Mr. Mathur, was a chief engineer at Power Corporation, a man of calm temperament who never had a tiff with anyone in his lifetime–except one night with his wife, when his only son Siddhant was a kid–to Siddhant's memory, until his tragic demise many years ago. Siddhant was in his first semester of Masters in Business Administration from Delhi University when one ruinous night Mr. Mathur succumbed to cardiac arrest. Mrs. Mathur was a housewife who once was an extremely social being but post her husband's death, she restrained herself and became quite a reclusive being who found contentment only in the happiness of her son. She had relocated to their hometown after Siddhant got his first job, she got assured that her grown-up son could handle his life well now. After a few years of living in a hospice and working for terminally ill patients–something that she had wished to do since long and found relief in after her husband's death–she had come to live with Siddhant.

Since the time when Mrs. Mathur had come to live with her son thirteen years ago on his twenty-forth birthday, they were never too expressive with each other, for both of them had never been too outspoken earlier as well. Although she could sense the vibe of love from her son for herself, she could sense the unsaid words as well, which relayed to her the hollowness of an unsettling relationship his parents had had and which had affected Siddhant and his childhood. He witnessed them arguing and fighting just once but always knew that they were never really happy together. His mother wasn't unknown to it and all she wanted was marital bliss for her son now. Unfortunately, she could not see that. After spending only a few months with her son after coming back from the hospice, she too was encountered with the ultimate reality of life. From then on, Siddhant lived alone in his three BHK apartment with everything he was left with a sense of bereavement, few extremely short fling encounters, and relationships of short duration made for carnal pleasure with women who would arrive in his life without any hiatus to be seen. The corporeal meetings that he would have in bed–or on the couch, in car, restrooms, and many other places–which were never driven by love, would take place with fervent fondness, and would end without any major conversation with the woman with whom he would have his body intertwined just before the storm of needs was over, with passion and momentum that was unmatched.

Siddhant, in his late thirties, worked as an associate creative director at an advertising agency in Delhi. At the workplace, Siddhant always tried not to be rigid with his associates. He was the last person in the office–or anywhere–to meddle with someone, but anyone who knew him knew it well that he was the last person to be meddled with.

The routine he followed had always been the same since the last thirteen years or so. He would get up at six in the morning, go for running and play badminton till eight in his society's club and after having his breakfast of oatmeal and boiled eggs and getting ready, leave for office by half-past nine. Sitting in his cabin for hours and doing work without speaking much to others had become his diurnal routine. He was not exactly a reclusive man at the workplace but the fact that he spoke less when it was not needed still had made those who were the selected ones to be called his close friends, the one who really could not meet him in his downtime.

***

Like every weekday, Siddhant was sitting in his cabin with his laptop open and his narrowed eyes on the screen and a pen in his mouth, indicating that he was thinking deeply over some plan. After a few minutes, a woman in a formal dress entered the cabin.

'Good Morning Siddhant,' she greeted him in her poised voice.

'Good Morning Pooja,' he greeted the lady asking her to sit on the chair across his table, without looking at her.

'So did you ideate something for that conference's plan?' she asked him about the plan that they were working on.

'Not yet, I am still working,' he answered her plainly, looking at the laptop screen.

'The team needs to submit them the presentation by today evening Siddhant,' she reminded him.

'I know Pooja. I remember it,' he said in his deep voice.

'I am sure you do,' she said quietly. She waited while he still looked at his laptop screen.

'Anything else Pooja?' He asked looking at the lady for the first time since she had come to the office today–Olive complexion, downturned eyes, and round lips with pink lip colour.

'Nope.' she said and then was about to say something but restrained herself and left the cabin quietly.

Pooja worked as an account manager in the same agency but was quite younger than Siddhant. She was in her late twenties but what she lacked in her age, she made up for in her sincere outlook towards Siddhant. She was not only his colleague but considered herself his close companion. Siddhant had never shown her any gesture that she could misunderstand for a reciprocal of the inclination that she had had towards him, but she genuinely cared for him and her emotions had reached to the level where she thought she was the only emotional support to him and the only one who genuinely cared for him. She had never expressed her feelings to him overtly but never concealed her care for him either. She had seen his anger and his softer side as well. In fact she could not express her feelings for two reasons, first being Siddhant's somber expressions, which he always wore like a skin, and secondly–and majorly–she wanted to wait for the right time. She wanted to make her presence certain in Siddhant's life, steadily.

In the evening when almost everyone had left the office and Pooja entered his cabin, Siddhant was still looking on his laptop screen doing something. 'It's nine thirty Siddhant, when will you be leaving?' Asked Pooja. Siddhant looked at the wall clock and replied, 'In a minute, you leaving?'

'Was about to,' she told.

'Wait then, I'll drop you home.' he said, to which she smiled.

In the car, Siddhant and Pooja had their regular talks, about work plans, what's going in the industry, new ad campaigns, presentations et cetera. He never spoke more than this to her but Pooja always asked him his wellbeing and things about his personal life sometimes. She was all that a well wisher could be, but she was nothing more than that to him.

'How is Raghu anyways?' Asked Siddhant enquiring about her younger brother who was in college doing B. Tech. and would always be out with friends without seeing his sister's face for months who lived in the same city, few kilometers away from his hostel.

'He is fine, mad as usual. I called him up yesterday and he surprised me like every time. Told me that he was in Lansdowne for trekking with his imbecile hippie-like friends.' she grinned. He replied with his normal lopsided grin. They continued their mild conversation until they reached Pooja's home. They wished 'Goodnight' to each other and she stepped out of his car and walked towards her apartment. Siddhant watched her, a pretty girl with aspirations for both her professional and personal life. A girl who knew about his past and the reason behind his despondency. Siddhant continued driving towards home.

***

The month of July was welcomed with windy and fresh atmosphere. The rain had arrived on time; first drops of rain on parched earth had brought a pleasant time for olfactory organs. The aroma of freshly cut grass and the sight of dark clouds were perfectly alluring.

Siddhant was standing in his cabin watching the light rain through the window with a mug of coffee in his hand. He looked while contemplating over something. Life had been a different journey to him. All his life, he always indulged in relations he was always frivolous about and today he was going to attend the wedding of one of those girls he once was involved with, Priya, who once wanted to marry him. For a moment, he thought if he and 'that girl' who departed from his life soon after his mother's demise were never meant to be together, and wondered if they really were never the kind of people who could spend their lives together.

'Hope I am not disturbing you,' expressed Pooja entering his cabin. He had not realised she had come until she spoke.

'Sit Pooja.' he said getting conscious.

'Brooding over something?' She asked sitting on a chair across him. He was still standing. She was aware of the person he was thinking about.

'Not at all,' he replied.

'You know Siddhant; this is one thing you can't do. You can't lie to me.' she smiled and opened the notepad she had just now kept on the table that she carried while entering the cabin. He didn't see any point in answering and kept looking outside the window.

'You know what I think Siddhant,' she said and stopped.

'What?' He asked without looking at her.

'I think you should spend more time with me,' she said jovially. He didn't say anything. She would get irritated sometimes at his silence when he won't reply to her on her encouragement for him to move on. When he didn't say anything, she thought it best to stop saying anything for now. She didn't want to push him too much. She kept silent and asked after a few minutes.

'And could you tell me why you won't be able to come tonight for the dinner we are planning,' she asked. She and their few friends-cum-colleagues were going out for dinner the same night about which she had texted him last evening to which he had bluntly refused to come for in turn.

'I told you I guess. I have to be somewhere else,' he said at last in his deep voice.

'No. I don't think you said anything. You simply texted NO,' she complained.

'I might have forgotten to,' he said calmly.

'And where are you really going tonight,' she asked rather commandingly. Siddhant looked at her this time. Siddhant had never allowed such liberty to anyone in his life, except one. He couldn't acquire such insinuation from her for her caring act. He never had allowed anyone to come and cross the wall he had erected around himself.

'And why do you think I need to lie to you Pooja,' he said. She got embarrassed.

'Okay.' she said after a while.

He looked at her for a moment in the same manner and then looked outside. She got up and said calmly, 'Take care Siddhant.' and left his cabin. He still stood there.

***

The evening had brought with it cold, fresh wind and the sky looked beautiful while the sun sank beneath it. Siddhant was still sitting in his cabin. Pooja had left the office for the day and he was about to head for the farm where his old friend was getting married tonight.

***

Priya looked beautiful and poised. At a farm in Chhatarpur where her wedding was taking place, she was sitting on a wedding settee with her husband. The settee was settled on a higher stage, which was set up on the farthest end of a huge hall, which looked like a typical wedding arrangement being done in any Indian wedding. It was an archetypal Indian wedding scene with huge chandeliers and floral arrangements hanging up on the ceiling of the hall and the vibrant multicoloured foliage decoration, which included jasmine, marigold and orchids. Siddhant went straight to the marrying duo and wished them with a bouquet. The stage was adorned with lilies and orchids, which looked resplendent. Priya's face looked surprised and pleased at the same time when she witnessed the face she had seen years ago. She felt happy to see Siddhant but showed curb in her movements; after all, she was surrounded by many guests and family members. But she had to respond when Siddhant congratulated her and her to-be husband.

'Congratulations on a new beginning,' he congratulated to the wedding duo with a meek smile.

'Thanks a lot Siddhant,' said both Priya and Siddharth, the man she was getting married to.

Priya introduced both of them to each other telling Siddharth that Siddhant was her colleague at her previous office and they had met after years on this day. Siddharth nodded gently. It was not the occasion for them to speak of anything more than that.

Siddhant sat on a table, which was embellished with orchid flower centerpieces and recalled his past affair with Priya. An affair that was serious from her side. Not too cautious of such brief affairs, Siddhant always knew that this relation would not end in a life-long relationship when Priya confronted him. It's a fact that Siddhant never even gave her any objective to think so. In fact, he had always been very attentive to make a girl realize how serious he exactly was for a relationship and always made it sure that a girl he is in a relationship with is aware that he is not up for a life-long bond. But Priya still thought she could make him change his mind; she could not. He was never interested in marrying any of those girls he had ever been in a relationship with, except one.

He still remembered the day when Priya had wept in front of him when she had asked him why he wasn't ready to continue the relationship with her when he once again had finally told her that he had deep respect for her but he could not think of what she was pressing him to think of.

He was right and she knew it. He had always made it clear to her, but her anguish didn't allow her to comprehend that that day. She left his life even before her service agreement was over with the company on a medical basis, never to meet him again. He thought it right for her so that she could move on. He was happy today that she had moved forward and was turning over a new leaf with a man she found suitable for herself.

The whole hall was filled with exuberant guests involved in joyous chit-chat wearing glittering, opulent looking outfits. It all looked ironical to him how he was involved in such a ceremony today while hating such associations. He was thinking about the same when a feminine voice brought him back to the present.

'Hey, you are Siddhant, if I'm not wrong?' Asked a young girl to him. A young girl who looked loaded with jewelry and saree which could have weighed more than her own weight was standing near him, a bit surprised to see him.

'Sorry, do I know you?' Asked Siddhant gently.

'Of course not, but I know you. I am Naina, Priya's sister,' she told Siddhant. Siddhant thought that Priya might have told him about her years ago, but neither he remembered her nor had he ever been so keen to know about the family of girls he was ever involved in a relationship with. So he just nodded.

'Priya told me all about you. I mean she discussed with me everything since our childhood,' she said.

Siddhant got a bit clueless as to what to say as he couldn't know what to say to the sister of a girl with whom he once was in a fervent fling and who was getting married today which he was attending. But neither did Naina wish to discuss anything of that sort; she knew all about them after all. She changed the topic.

'She was very dubious if you would come when she dropped you a message yesterday on Facebook,' expressed Naina. He smiled.

'How are you doing? How's life?' She asked.

'Oh I am doing well. And I am happy for Priya and her new beginning in life,' he told her with a smile. Naina waited for a moment looking at her sister meeting the guests far on the stage and said quietly, 'She was kind of lost for a long time after...you know.' Siddhant didn't say anything and looked at the flower centerpiece while she also didn't want to look into his eyes, as she felt a bit awkward discussing that.

'But I am happy she is happy now, Siddharth is a nice guy, he really cares for her a lot,' she told Siddhant smilingly looking at him. He also smiled looking at her.

'Okay then Siddhant, it was very nice meeting you,' she smiled broadly. He reciprocated and she left him sitting there looking at Priya.

Siddhant had met Priya five years back in the interview cabin of his agency. She was a girl in her early twenties. A young, vivacious girl who hid her jitters with her confident smile. In a brand new white formal shirt and navy blue trousers, which she surely was wearing for the first time, she looked captivating to Siddhant's senses, which he kept fastened at the workplace. She looked like a petite kitten that had her paws hidden behind her innocent countenance, which Siddhant thought he had seen. He was attracted by her personality and her vulnerability that he had sensed in her. Within a few months, the cordial relationship had reached Priya's bed and under a comforter in Priya's home when she was alone in her house one weekend. Half drunk and driven by the carnal desires, they reached the room and after undressing each other they forgot every formal limit they were bound by inside the office premises. It was in the morning when Priya formally proposed him after they had explored each other better than many couples.

'I love you.' He was lying stark naked in the bed with eyes closed and she was keeping her head on his chest.

'You are the best man I have ever seen in my life,' she said with a smile.

'How many of them have you seen,' he mocked with his eyes closed. She smiled and kissed his chest. Such meetings under the comforter became a normal routine for the next few months for them after which he started getting anxious about her requests to accept her formally and take the relationship to the next level. He, who had neither accepted her proposal nor denied the physical intimacy, finally told her to stop thinking of him and move on when she had asked him to meet her in the day time and at a public place–a rare occurrence.

Siddhant never realised what her life was like after they parted ways, or when he made it crystal clear to her that she never was the one he could spend his life with–which is what he would tell every girl, sometimes before and sometimes after his brief dalliance with them because the only lasting alliance he could ever have was with a girl who was far away from his life. He actually never gave it a thought, how any girl might have thought, after he parted ways with them, leaving them with the same impassivity with which he would enter their lives. Not that he had realised it just a few minutes ago what Priya went through. He was just thinking–without deducing any statement.

He looked at her while she was smiling and meeting guests, burdened with heavy jewelry and wedding dress. She looked at him while meeting others and smile was still on her face. He smiled suddenly at her. She looked at him for a moment and then someone else was there to greet her. Her smile looked full of beauty and peace to him. She was a nice girl, she had always been, and he was happy that she was getting the companionship of a man who was better for her.

CHAPTER 3

The morning was quite warm with a bright sun shining in the sky. Had it been Delhi, nobody, without knowing the exact day and date could call it a month of December. Miles away from the Indian capital, sunlight was falling on the windowpane of a bookstore situated on the sporadically crowded street of Udaipur. Glancing over all types of magazines, from fashion to food, looking for almost half an hour, Siddhant at last got a book he thought he would like to read–a novel by Ernest Hemingway–and was about to leave the store after the billing was done for the book.

The moment he was walking out of the doors, at that very moment someone had entered the bookstore and was walking up the staircase. He suddenly came across her. She saw him and he saw her too; they crossed their ways and within a fraction of a second they realised that they knew each other. Familiar face, they both thought; seeing each other after many many years, they turned towards each other.

Their appearances had changed, both of them thought; but they knew and recognised each other as well as they could, had they looked same as they were thirteen years ago, when they had last seen each other in Delhi.

Devyani, a woman of his age, did not have light curls anymore but smooth, straight, mid-back length auburn hair and her face looked grown up; mature yet more elegant and beautiful, Siddhant perceived. She wore a casual outfit, which made her look different from what she looked years ago. The man looked a bit more different, she thought. He looked leaner than before; broader and muscular, but leaner. He wore a polo shirt and chinos. He had thick, heavy stubble now. Siddhant looked different now, lankier, she noticed.

'Hi,' said Devyani first, while they looked at each other.

'Hello...how are you?' He asked, surprised at meeting 'her' after so many years.

'I am...fine, perfect,' she answered with a smile.

'What are you... doing here?' He asked.

'Oh, I'm here for Rhea's wedding,' she answered plainly.

'That's great to hear,' he replied calmly. They smiled and stood there for some seconds and then Siddhant asked her–in a serious tone with a serious looking face–something for which he was almost convinced the answer would be negative.

'Coffee? If you have time...' He asked and she waited for some seconds before nodded her head in agreement.

After half an hour in a nearby cafe, they seemed to be little lost if not uncomfortable sitting across each other after so many years, as if they were not supposed to be there but time had plunged them into the situation.

'You look lean,' she said after some time without looking at him, with a smile.

'I have grown old,' he said and smiled.

'No, I don't think so,' she said.

'You look the same,' he said.

'I believe I have grown weak and old,' she smiled.

'Weak! That's one thing you never were,' he said looking into her eyes.

She spoke after a minute, 'I wish I could stay in Delhi for some time again.' He didn't say anything for a while and then asked, 'Where do you stay...or have been all this while?'

'Mumbai.'

'How's your dad?'

She gazed at him for a moment or two and then said in a low voice, 'He's no more.'

'Oh, I'm sorry,' he said quietly and asked after a few moments, 'What happened, if I may ask?'

'Cancer of the esophagus,' she replied glumly. He didn't say anything and then asked about Rhea.

'So, Rhea is happy?' He would always change the topic if she won't like it, she thought.

'Yes, she is very happy,' she said with a smile that again came on her face.

'You still like that?' He asked her indicating towards the black coffee she was having.

She smiled and said, 'You remember.' He too smiled.

She then said securely without looking at him, 'This beard suits you.' They smiled again. It seemed as if they were away from each other for just a few days.

'You still live there?' She then asked.

'Where else would I go,' he expressed. The cafe had the noise of people sitting in it though it wasn't disturbing. 'That home has a connection with me it seems. Tried to relocate somewhere else but...' he added in his deep but undisturbed voice.

'So who else... I mean who else lives...?' She did not know how to ask if he was married or with someone or not. His phone rang but he silenced it. She gazed at him.

'I never got to know anything about...you,' she said.

'I saw you many times,' he said. She looked at him in surprise.

'At places we had been to,' he added and they laughed lightly.

'How come you are here?' She asked.

'I just wanted to spend some time with myself. I was tired of...' he didn't complete himself.

'Are you happy?' She asked and looked caring but somehow tried to hide that.

'It is quite a question,' he said and smiled. 'So when is she getting married?' he asked about Rhea.

'She has time, some seven-eight days,' she answered.

'And after that...' he looked at her to know.

'Mumbai...of course,' she said, looking dull. 'Why don't you come tonight and meet Rhea, if you have no other priorities,' she asked while hiding her curiosity to know his answer. 'She'll be happy,' she added.

He smiled and said, 'No Devyani, it doesn't look good. It's a big occasion for your family, your aunt. I don't want to create trouble.'

'There won't be any trouble. They will be happy if you would come, I am sure,' she explained in her soft voice and invited him to the palace hotel she was staying at with family and relatives. She couldn't force him, but she wanted him to come.

He waited for a few seconds and then said 'Okay', but he wasn't sure if he would go. She, however, was sure he would come, for he had said to her so. A sudden tune made them a bit conscious of their surroundings. It was someone's call on her phone from the palace. It was someone from the family who asked Devyani where she was, he figured from her conversation.

'You must go, they must be waiting for you,' Siddhant said quietly once she had answered where she was and had disconnected the call.

'No, it's okay. I have time,' she replied.

'But they must be waiting for you.' She now felt clumsy to say no. 'Okay,' she said quietly.

They walked towards the main door of the cafe and when they were out and her cab was there to take her to the palace, she said in a low voice, 'We will be waiting for you,' and walked to get inside the cab. Her gait was still the same.

Siddhant stood there still. He didn't know what phase of life it was. But it was reality that they had met today after thirteen years, and that too with such cordiality. He, however, did not tell Devyani about his colleague who had asked him to settle with her a few weeks ago, when Devyani tried to ask him if he was involved with someone. He just did not want to tell Devyani about Pooja. His mind and heart asked him not to.

He had told Pooja that he could consider her proposal in the time to come but couldn't promise anything. He had thought about Pooja's proposal that if he would ever get married to her, it would just be for the sake of being with someone–nothing more, nothing less.

CHAPTER 4

While sitting in the balcony of his hotel room, Siddhant looked still. He had come to Udaipur only because he wanted to be away from everyone for some time, literally everyone. But little did he know that he would be meeting a person whose presence had always made a conspicuous effect in his life. Devyani Sinha was the girl he had met years and years ago. All his life, Siddhant had always been a very determined person. Determined about his relations, what he believed in, what he refrained from, and almost every other thing that concerned him. But the only person whose existence had changed the course of his life, his basic nature to look at things in general and relationships in particular, was the one whom he had the worst relationship with. Not that he held her responsible for that, but since last thirteen years, his life WAS being decided by the very events that took place in his life because of the only girl he ever loved. Although he never wanted to confront that fact but he knew it.

He was a person who was always determined but it was also in his disposition to rethink about actions that he would take. And that's what he was thinking about now. Why did he even say yes to meet her tonight? Why did he not lie to her that he was busy today evening? Or why would he lie? Couldn't he tell her directly that he didn't want to come for dinner?

And the very next moment he was embarrassed. He was not a teenager. He was not a college goer. Why was he thinking so much over a petty dinner?

And now, he thought about how it would be to be around her even if it was a matter of just one evening.

CHAPTER 5

At around eight in the evening, Siddhant was at the palace in his black dinner jacket he had bought just an hour before coming to the dinner. They were all sitting in the dining hall of the palace and the guests were not completely unknown to Siddhant. Devyani's aunt, Rhea, and Devyani were there who knew him. Devyani sat opposite Siddhant at a long table, which was laid with fine dine cutlery perfectly positioned over it. Devyani was happy that Siddhant had come and so was Rhea. Everyone else too seemed to be happy to meet Siddhant as a guest and Mr. Bedi found excessive pleasure in meeting Siddhant and had found a great gentleman in him.

'I didn't know your friend was such a charming man Devyani,' said Mr. P. N. Bedi who was Devyani's uncle, her second aunt's husband and a famous gossipmonger who would blatantly say anything to anyone when he was high on alcohol. Devyani didn't know what to say and everyone else chuckled. Siddhant gave a formal smile and said nothing.

'I am glad Siddhant is here and Siddhant, you have to be there on the wedding day,' said Rhea. He smiled and nodded.

'Oh of course, but you should have come here earlier Siddhant,' said Mr. Bedi.

'So Siddhant, where do you work in Delhi,' asked Mr. Bedi's son Aditya who was Rhea's age. Siddhant answered him.

'You know Siddhant I had a friend who was exactly like you, a gentleman. His wife was such a mess I tell you, left him because she wanted to do something in her *career* you see,' Mr. Bedi said. 'These women behave so rebellious sometimes,' added Mr. Bedi and left everyone silent for a moment. Mr. Bedi did not realise the fact that an estranged couple sat there.

A lady, of Devyani's aunt's age–with a bony face, open hair and chunky jewelry in her ears and neck- who was sitting quietly till now replied him on this.

'It's not rebellious Pushkar, it's just that whenever a woman wants to do something of her choice or wants to go professional, people either call her rebellious or worst, insensitive and morally corrupt,' said the lady in her heavy voice with a smile covered with narcissism. Both Devyani and Siddhant stopped for a second and looked at each other. Devyani wished this topic had not been raised on the table. Everyone else was also silent. The lady with a heavy voice was Rhea's paternal aunt Mrs. Khanna–her father's sister.

'Oh what are we discussing, I am getting married and you all are discussing god knows what,' said Rhea just to change the topic. Everyone laughed.

'No actually Rhea-'

'Oh uncle! Please stop now,' said Rhea and stopped Mr. Bedi in the middle.

'Then tell us how did Raghav woo you, it's hard to woo Rhea you see,' said the lady with heavy voice laughingly. Rhea smiled shyly.

'Oh she's blushing...so it's true he sang a song for you in front of your office to propose you? With all the band people and everyone? Oh so kiddish and cute,' the lady stated. Rhea was still smiling.

'Oh these girls love men who can sing I tell you,' said Mr. Bedi. 'Siddhant my boy, I must tell you, you should also sing for your love. Or you also sing as if a scarecrow has come to life. Oh my friends would tell me that,' he added and laughed. He was the only one to laugh on his lame joke cracked in a drunken state.

'Siddhant is not that bad a singer actually,' Devyani said and smiled looking at him. He too looked at her. They all discussed other topics while having dinner for a while which again was directed towards Siddhant and Devyani.

'Devyani, make sure Siddhant attends the wedding. You can even force him,' Rhea smiled and said. She was happy that Devyani and Siddhant had met after so many years.

'Don't worry Rhea, if he has told he will come, he will.' smiled Devyani looking at him formally. He looked at her, then downwards on the table.

After dinner, Siddhant and Devyani were sitting on a bench in the open garden where they sat after a brief walk, away from others. There was nothing to be talked about between them they thought.

He took out a pack of cigarettes from his jacket's pocket and put one cigarette between his lips and asked her when he was about to lit it, 'You mind if I?'

'No,' she said softly.

'Weather is delightful here,' he said while smoking.

'Hmm...better than Delhi.'

'Delhi is not a place to be at in this weather.'

'When did you start this?' She asked him. He wasn't expecting it and looked at her.

He replied after a pause looking at her, 'Thirteen years or so.' They looked at each other briefly but neither of them said anything.

And then he said, 'I think I should leave now.' They got up and Devyani walked him towards the gate.

'I was thinking if we could have lunch together till the time we are here,' she said suddenly but not abruptly while he didn't expect that. 'Not here of course,' she added when he looked at her while walking.

'Okay,' was all that he said plainly, after looking at her for a moment.

***

Sitting in the cab while going to his hotel, he thought how he could never say no to her and even after regretting his decision to meet her for dinner tonight, he had again agreed to spend time with her.

CHAPTER 6

Siddhant was in his hotel room. His body was tired; his mind, restive. He was reaffirming it to himself again that he had met her today and then he thought of the day when he had met her for the very first time.

***

Tanya was a vibrant, ballsy girl who was Siddhant's friend, companion and confidant since the time they were doing their graduation from the same college. She was a social animal; always ready for parties, drinks and had never been absent when anyone needed her. However, the reason she was a bosom friend of Siddhant was neither subjected to their nature nor their ways of living and seeing life. It was because they knew each other more than anyone else in their lives. They knew that deep down; they were practical yet modest beings never giving a wide berth to people who needed them for help, or them in their lives. Dusky complexion, light curly hair and an extremely charming personality of Tanya had many admirers. One was of course her boyfriend Aahil–a tall, good looking guy who looked as if he had an air of superiority but it was never seen in any of his gestures–who was into his family business and had met Tanya when they had a meeting a year ago at an event where people from the magazine's office that Tanya worked for were also present. Celebrating her year long relationship with Aahil, Tanya had decided to throw a party at her apartment, where all her friends and close colleagues were joined by Aahil's friends.

Amidst the loud music, cocktails and a bunch of party animals who were carefree and drunk, Siddhant was having a conversation with Aahil plainly in the corner of the hall near the balcony. He was not very fond of Aahil. Neither were they friendly. He was having a fun chat with Tanya and her colleague Gautam when she left the chat in the middle to rush towards the door to receive someone as soon as the doorbell rang.

The boring conversation amongst the party chaos was getting more boring when Siddhant saw Tanya meeting the newcomer with utmost warmth and cordiality. She air-kissed the cheeks of the guest who was behind the open door and welcomed the guest inside when Siddhant realised it was a girl–a girl of probably Tanya's age. Siddhant had known almost every friend of Tanya but had never seen this girl. He was still listening to Aahil's boring future business plans while Tanya was walking her guest towards them.

'Hey guys, meet Devyani, my cousin from London. She landed here yesterday from Mumbai. And Devyani, meet Siddhant, my close confidant,' said Tanya gleefully. 'He is Aahil. And he is Gautam,' she added and pointed her hand towards each of them. Each of them greeted her.

'Hello,' said Devyani to everyone in a very soft, low pitched, perfectly articulated voice which was quite rare to hear in that apartment where a bunch of drunk people had run amuck by now. While only after a few seconds, Tanya ushered Devyani towards some of her colleagues leaving the three men again with their boring discussion about Aahil's family business, Siddhant was listening to him tepidly but simultaneously he had another task as well. Now after every few seconds he was looking towards the bunch of girls Tanya was gossiping with. He was of course looking for the new guest. Siddhant knew that it was not just a boring talk of Aahil that was making him lose his interest in talking with him; it indeed was the new guest of Tanya.

Siddhant Mathur had dated a few girls in his life. Most of the times, girls would propose to him, ask him for a date. And some of those girls were really blessed with such elegance and beauty that anyone would wish to end up marrying them. But Siddhant was never too keen on carrying such relationships forward for more than a few months. He was a tall, suave, good looking man. Lean yet muscular, he kept himself in shape with running and playing badminton. He was far from running after women. Still, he had been in relationships with some very charming girls. But today, even he was losing the balance of not looking towards a woman so intently. It was true that he had never seen a girl like Devyani. He never had an idea of what a perfect woman looks like. Today, however, he realised as if he was learning to know so. Her olive skin, oval face, dark brown hair with light curls, light brown almond-shaped eyes, well-shaped nose and bow-shaped lips; everything was enchanting and making her more of an enigmatic fairytale character to him. She was wearing a beige colour flared cocktail dress with short, beaded sleeves. The way she smiled with her dusty rose lips was enough to mesmerize all the boys in the party. And then, Siddhant realized that the voices of people had lowered down. Music was still loud but almost all the men in the party now looked at Devyani. Everyone was charmed and Siddhant realized that he was not the only one.

'So, do you know her?' Asked Siddhant abruptly interrupting Aahil while he was still saying something.

'Sorry who?' Asked Aahil.

Siddhant realized he sounded clumsy and continued 'Oh, I mean I never knew Tanya had a cousin in London who was coming.'

'You mean Devyani! Yeah, she is some distant cousin. She was in London for last four years. Her family lives in Mumbai. She's here to stay with her aunt,' said Aahil. 'Worked with some famous fine artist there I guess,' said Aahil staring at Devyani. Siddhant realized that Aahil had also joined the club of guys in the party who couldn't take their eyes off her. He changed the topic.

'So what were you telling? You are planning to expand?' Asked Siddhant to make him take his eyes off her.

'Oh yes, actually I am...' continued Aahil.

And Siddhant continued looking at the new guest. This time, more vigilantly. He didn't want others to see him gazing at her awkwardly the way he had just now noticed Tanya's boyfriend.

It was four thirty in the morning when all the 'party animals' were lying like bundles here and there in whole apartment–on the couch, bed, even on the floor, resembling empty bottles of wine they had gulped down like there was no tomorrow. Aahil had left an hour ago. Siddhant was taking a nap on the armchair near the balcony when he heard a bottle being kicked, which rolled on the floor, and he came to his senses. Devyani was taking Tanya–who had passed out after emptying a bottle of vermouth–to latter's bedroom putting Tanya's hand around her shoulder, holding her waist from one hand and Tanya's hand around her shoulder with another hand. Siddhant saw her struggling and reached to her instantly holding Tanya easily, taking her to the bedroom.

They sat near her bed on the rug. Yes, he was not a guy to run after women but today the case was different. He felt like speaking to her–about anything, anyone but just didn't want to ruin this time he was having with her. Devyani, however, looked indifferent to the presence of Siddhant.

'It's routine for her to pass out, don't worry,' said Siddhant just to initiate the conversation. She reciprocated with a smile in a very formal manner. He felt embarrassed; he was not a guy to give up so easily but he had never made any attempt in his life to initiate a conversation with a girl like her, because he had never met anyone like her.

'So you are into art,' tried Siddhant again. Unfortunately, she again reciprocated with a smile, which was way too fake. More than that of Aahil's which he would flaunt most of the time. He again started, 'So you don't speak much to strangers? I mean I don't see a reason for giving me smile all the time.' She hesitated a bit this time but expressed in a poised manner, 'It's not like that. What am I supposed to speak to you about? I don't know you.' She smiled again and started doing something on her phone. Her soft voice was perfect, as perfect as an operator's but with a pleasance. And that very voice pinched him. He still didn't give up. He kept on gazing at her silently. She got a bit surprised and looked at him for the first time with her own choice. He looked at her intensely with half-smile. She looked at her phone again, and after a moment or two, looked again at him saying, 'I hope you didn't find me ungracious. I was just being candid.' She smiled this time with a real smile. He smiled with a pinch of laughter and looked in a different direction and then again at her, 'I am glad you cared for what I must have felt,' and laughed this time. 'I am kidding...I was just trying to make you feel comfortable,' he added, and his voice had a sense of seriousness this time.

'So you are Tanya's associate at work?' She asked.

'I work in an ad agency. Tanya and I were in college,' he answered. She nodded politely.

'I hope you didn't get an impression that I was going to be flirtatious with you,' he said after a few moments with a mischievous smile. She laughed for the very first time but with the same self-restraint. After a few moments, she tried and got up.

'I think I should leave.'

'You sure?'

'Yes. Actually I am new here and I don't want dad to be worried. He is a bit apprehensive about me,' she added smilingly. She tried and fixed her ankle strap heels by lifting her right ankle up, backwards. She looked at her leg backwards with her hair waving on her cheeks. She was only an inch shorter than Siddhant with her heels, he realised. And she WAS the most beautiful girl Siddhant had ever come across.

He escorted her to the elevator once she was done covering Tanya with a quilt and asked Siddhant to look after her. He somehow felt irritated on what had happened. He didn't want her to go. He didn't ask her how to contact her; he didn't want to look or sound desperate either.

Tanya woke up at one in the afternoon when everyone had left except Siddhant. They were on a cleanliness drive to make her home look like home. He was helping her clean utensils while she was applying dishwashing gel on plates. He had waited for Tanya to wake up. He actually wanted to know all about the girl he was becoming more and more curious about, but that was obviously not the reason he had stayed back.

'You never told me you had a cousin in London,' interrogated Siddhant rubbing the plates dry.

'Devyani? There was nothing to tell. She is my distant cousin. She has some plans here of art exhibitions I think,' Tanya answered.

'What kind of girl is she? I mean is she a regular foreign return bragging about it?' he asked rubbing another plate dry.

'Devyani? not at all. I mean we are not in touch since many years but still; she's not like others. Actually I had met her just once years ago and called her as she is new here and her dad asked her if she would like to meet me. I mean any other chick of her immediate relation in the family might behave boastfully but she won't,' said Tanya. 'Oh, I mean her father is a big man, an influential bureaucrat. In fact she has a long list of bureaucrats in her family. Her dad was my dad's distant cousin-'

'You said she's not like others,' he snapped.

'Yes. I mean she is more of a 'humanitarian person'. Last time I met her was the occasion when she was doing something for...I guess some old-age home. Doesn't like blowing one's own trumpet. She likes being reclusive doing things she finds peaceful.'

'And what's her take on life. You know what I mean. Is she committed or...I can't believe she's not.'

'Well, I...just a second! You- Siddhant Mathur–are you trying to tell me you are falling for my cousin?' she asked lazily cleaning the plates. He didn't say anything. She turned with utter surprise leaving her sponge she was cleaning utensils with. He was still rubbing utensils dry and smiled without looking at her.

'You have already?'

He looked at her and smiled broadly and stood there. 'I don't know. But there is something about it. I just...I just feel it won't stop here,' he said quite plainly.

'Wait a second, you think it is possible?'

Siddhant gave her a questioning look raising his eyebrows.

'Dude, she is the daughter of one influential bureaucrat. Don't you think it's a bit too much?'

Siddhant shrugged his shoulders with raised eyebrows smilingly.

'My dear Sid, I truly believe you are debonair, you may live in the world where girls are crazy for you and you can get any girl you wish to but trust me, she won't accept anything like that,' said Tanya walking towards him and then toward the sink again, mockingly, making fun of him.

'Okay I agree. I agree. But still, I can't let it go like that,' he said calmly. She turned and looked at him and sighed. He didn't discuss that again as she still seemed to be in a semi-conscious state to him.

At around four thirty in the evening, they were done with the cleaning of the house and were having coffee when Tanya's mobile rang. It was an unknown number.

'Hello,' said a voice from another side when Tanya received the call. It was a soft and low-pitched voice. Tanya reciprocated after knowing it was her new cousin who had just come to India.

'Are you okay now Tanya?' Asked Devyani.

'Yeah baby I'm perfect. Not to worry. Hope you reached home in time.'

'Yeah, I reached in time,' she replied.

After a moment or two, Tanya disconnected the call after regular polite enquiries about each other.

Siddhant knew that it was Devyani's call but he didn't ask anything about her this time and kept on reading the magazine he was holding, to Tanya's surprise. She thought he was just kidding while talking about her cousin in the afternoon and it was nothing but a regular appeal of a girl that makes a guy go gaga over her sometimes but perceived that he was still not over her when he was about to leave and they were still discussing her drinking habits.

'...But you're a limit lady. You just don't know when to stop,' said Siddhant in a complaining overtone to Tanya while wearing his shoes.

'Don't you think this is the nth time you're reminding me of my forgetfulness baby?' She asked him smiling sarcastically. He didn't say anything as if he was still thinking about something. He got up, hugged her while she was still lying on the couch lazily and reached the door. When almost outside the door and about to disappear from her view, he suddenly turned around and, 'By the way, when are you throwing such a party again with such distinguished guests,' he winked at her with his mischievous smile and slammed the door hastily. She knew it now that it wasn't just a 'regular appeal of a girl that makes a guy go gaga over it.' Siddhant, after all, wasn't from a species of guys to think about girls this much, he didn't pay heed to such matters much, and above all, she knew him very well. She knew it now that he wasn't done with it and he definitely wasn't going to give up so early since it was the first time he himself was discussing a girl with her.

Uncertain about his attempts, she closed her eyes and lay down on the couch.

CHAPTER 7

The restaurant was not very crowded which made them comfortable with the vicinity. They sat on the corner table and the rays of sun penetrating the glass window were drowning their table. She wore a long green coat with a white top inside, paired with blue jeans, with her hair straight and open.

'When did you come here?' She asked.

'Two-three days back. You?'

'Three days back.'

'How has it been since then?' He asked after moments.

'Good, nothing special,' she answered.

There was a brief pause between them. The waiter came over and asked for their order.

'Risotto di funghi,' she said while Siddhant ordered lasagna.

'You and your bizarre choices,' purred Siddhant on her food choice once they were done with the order. She got surprised and looked at him and then laughed a bit. She realized he was talking about her food choice; they both laughed. After some time, the waiter came over and Siddhant concentrated on his lunch; he didn't want her to feel awkward about this afternoon rendezvous.

He was having his meal while she gazed at him the way he ate. The moment he realized, he asked her what was wrong and she replied with a smile and said 'nothing'.

'Sometimes I think whatever happened was good,' he said calmly after a moment, looking at his glass of water with glistening water inside it.

'Do I need to reply?' She asked with a smile that contained the tiredness she carried in herself about what he had just now said.

'Oh no, no, not at all. I just expressed myself,' said Siddhant with a mouthful of lasagna.

Till the time they finished their lunch, there was nothing much that could be spoken. Neither of them said anything about leaving. The solace in the now almost empty restaurant gave them some peace it seemed. He felt as if time had been stopped in his life before this moment and now, today, he felt as if life had come to life, not exactly because of her but he couldn't comprehend the actual reason either.

'What are you thinking?'He asked when saw her looking at him. She waited for seconds.

'Thinking that...can separation end the bonds,' she said quietly. It was neither a question nor a resentful remark straight from the heart. It was the reality of life that came out of her mouth.

'I neither know where it was broken from...nor am I aware where it is still continuing from,' he sighed. He really didn't know the answer.

'Would you like to have anything else sir?' The waiter who had come to their table asked them.

'Negroni. You will have something?' Siddhant asked Devyani.

'No thanks,' she replied.

'I hope the weather remains this way till... I am here,' he expressed once the waiter left.

'It will be. Till the skies are clear,' she replied.

'Oh I am sure.'

'When did you start drinking?' She blurted.

'This?' He asked directing his thumb towards the bar of the Italian restaurant.

'Yes'

'Around the same time,' he said glumly. She knew what time he had referred to. They again didn't look at each other.

'Till how long will you be here?' She then asked.

'Not sure.'

'Won't you stay till the wedding?'

'Your drink sir,' the waiter interrupted. He didn't say anything for a few seconds.

'You know me Devyani. I mean you know me that much,' he sighed. She had started looking at the glass of water with unblinking eyes.

'Anyways, forget all this. Tell me do you still read at nights? Still ask anyone to read out for you with that irritating lubricating eye drop in eyes?' He asked her cheerfully. She laughed now, but with some tension still on her face.

'No wonder those lenses,' he said with a smile. 'So now tell me, where are you taking me to lunch tomorrow?' He teased her.

'There's a café I have heard of, in the opposite direction of the palace, few kilometres away from the main city. Nice place for readers I've heard', she said looking at him.

'Café...reading...away from others...you sure you want to come with me?' He teased her again and they laughed.

The afternoon was spent well between them. Even with her consistent requests to leave her outside the restaurant to go alone, he dropped her at the palace. She wanted him to come inside the palace but he didn't.

The only thing that remained constant between them today was some conversations left amidst the actual spoken words, some eye contacts being broken the very next moment that they were made in, and the silence which was still…there.

***

The sun now looked like a red ball in the evening sky and Siddhant sat in the balcony of his hotel room. *Till the skies are clear…*she still uses ambiguous, equivocal phrases he thought. But he would never reply. But is that sufficient? Because he knew that she knew what he understood and what not by just looking at him. This was one thing he hated about himself, she knew him maybe even better than he knew himself. But this was the very same thing she once believed she had achieved in her life. But that was not sufficient for them. No. Never, because that's the reason they separated years ago and met like this today.

The only thing that Devyani was still thinking about, sitting amongst her relatives in a huge hall inside the palace where wedding preparation was being done, was about her estranged lover's remark this afternoon…*No wonder you wear lenses.*

'Hey Devyani, will you please have a look at the wedding bespoke of mine?' Asked a lady of Devyani's age and she accompanied her to another corner of the palace.

She didn't remember telling him that she now wore lenses. And moreover, he looked into her eyes –at least only into her eyes– just for a few seconds throughout the day.

CHAPTER 8

Siddhant Mathur always knew what to do. Not only about Devyani but in his life too. He knew what he had to do yet he was unpredictable for others around him. Even Tanya sometimes couldn't tell what he would do in certain situations, in spite of the fact that she knew what kind of a person he was. He had innate vitality in his character which was subtle unlike that of Tanya's overt one. He knew what he needed in life. Not a firm believer of love at first sight, which seemed more like a Bollywood movies' romance to him, he believed that there are certain characteristics in humans, some unknown phenomena that makes people think about someone without any connection, incessantly. That's what exactly was happening with him as well. He didn't know if this was what people called love. He didn't know if this was the feeling girls had had when they told him they loved him.

But the desperate urge to meet Devyani had made him forget all this for now and his only focus was to know what he exactly felt about the lady he found so perfect and for that, he needed to meet her. Not more than a week had passed when the day arrived. It wasn't a party like he had asked sarcastically to Tanya but a meeting in the late afternoon at a café in Connaught Place.

'Don't know what I am doing here with you,' Tanya almost whispered. 'I don't know what she would think of me once she gets to know I called her so that an idiot like you could meet her,' said confused Tanya to Siddhant, who was sitting beside her at a table for three in a café. She had called Devyani telling her a lie that she wished to ask her something about her aunt's interview– who was a politician–that she wanted to take for the magazine she worked for. He smirked at her and didn't pay any heed to what she said. He had a more important thing to think about. He was actually desperate for the first time to see someone in his life.

And the door opened. She entered with the known elegance she had had. She wore an off-shoulder knee length blouson dress of peach colour with blue floral print over it. She looked more than what Siddhant had expected. He managed not to look wanting while she walked towards them after looking for them just for a few moments, in her black cone heels.

Both Tanya and Siddhant got up to greet her. 'I am so sorry to have kept you people waiting,' she said calmly and eloquently in her low and soft voice.

'Oh please don't mention that. No need of formalities dear. By the way your dress looks chic, going somewhere?' asked Tanya while they settled down.

'I actually planned to visit some old relatives and friends today but I dropped the plan. I would go if I get time,' replied Devyani.

'Anyway, you know Siddhant right?' Asked Tanya.

'Oh, of course, we met at your residence,' answered Devyani looking at Siddhant giving him a polite smile.

Tanya's phone rang. It was Aahil. She asked them to excuse her and walked towards a corner. It wasn't anything planned but it was a great opportunity for Siddhant to be with Devyani for some time. He couldn't let it go.

'So you have friends here?' Asked Siddhant.

'Yes, very few actually,' replied Devyani.

'Don't you have any plans to visit the city or nearby areas like many foreign returns have?' Asked Siddhant with a naughty smile moving his hands making a 'hands up don't shoot' gesture when she gazed at him.

She waited for a moment looking at him and laughed. It was the first time she had a genuine and comfortable laugh. He felt triumphant. She felt comfortable now in his presence and he could sense that.

'I have no plans as of now,' she said with a smile mixed with laughter.

'Ahhan...My friends tell me I could become a good tourist guide for NRI's,' said Siddhant jokingly with serious facial expression, as soon he gulped down his vanilla latte.

'Oh I am sure, but I have no plans to experience such a voyage Mr. Guide,' replied Devyani with a smile and one raised eyebrow, moving her head and added, '*And* I am not an NRI.' Each of her movement was enchanting. Siddhant couldn't help but fall for her with every passing moment. 'Oops! My bad,' he uttered. She was not an alien to his presence now. She was comfortable and it was crucial to Siddhant as he had realised by now that it definitely can't stop here and has to move forward. He thanked Tanya in his heart but that was when she arrived playing a gooseberry.

'Hey guys, I am so sorry. I need to leave ASAP. Aahil needs to see me right now,' interrupted Tanya to their conversation which had just started. Devyani looked perplexed; Siddhant, partially delighted, partially devastated. He didn't want Devyani to leave the café as Tanya was leaving.

'I am so sorry baby, but I just have to leave you see,' said Tanya air kissing Devyani's cheeks.

'It's okay. Take care,' replied Devyani with a formal smile. She didn't want to disturb Tanya by shooting questions on her. Tanya left with a blink of an eye. They sat there with an awkward silence. Siddhant couldn't let her feel that awkwardness.

'Why so worried. I mean I am not gonna kidnap you,' he said to cheer her up.

'No actually, my driver dropped me here and is on leave for the day and I don't know the ways here. It becomes a bit clumsy when you travel alone in an unknown city, although it's not too far,' she said and added, 'And I didn't want to create a nuisance for Tanya either.' She had spoken smilingly and hesitantly but still, calmly, without forgetting her etiquettes.

'Well that IS a problem....' said Siddhant as if he was really worried, 'unless you trust a gentleman who can drop you home, if you don't mind,' added Siddhant looking at her raising his eyebrows questioningly. She smiled and looked the other way.

'I don't want to create a nuisance for you either,' she then said plainly.

'Oh you may call it nuisance but trust me, only a man can tell how great a pleasure it is to have a lady like you to serve,' he said trying to be flirtatious with her for the very first time in a very cheesy manner, which he realised immediately. She felt embarrassed but more than that, relieved.

Siddhant opened the door of the car for her to sit and smiled. She got inside and sat with ease. The engine roared and they headed towards Prithviraj road where her aunt lived who was into politics.

'So you live with your aunt here?' Asked Siddhant.

'Yes,' she replied.

'For how long, if I may ask. I mean you are here for some of your art work Tanya told me, so will you relocate permanently or....'

She didn't say anything for a few seconds and then spoke, 'I am not sure. Let's see.' There was a pinch of tension in her soft voice. She seemed to be partially lost in a thought.

'My friends told me I could become a good driver as well, by the by. So you don't need to be so worried,' mocked Siddhant while driving. It brought her a smile again. She smiled not because she found the joke funny. It was more because she felt comfortable with him. In fact, she felt good in his company, and she felt good that he tried to bring her smile back. She directed him towards her aunt's bungalow and he stopped the car the moment she said, 'Here it is.' The car stopped outside the gate of a white coloured bungalow, which looked quite pristine in its look, partially inspired by Lutyens' architectural style. Its gate was a few feet away from the car.

'Thank you very much Siddhant. I was worried. Thanks for making me comfortable. And please don't mind if I behaved a bit clumsily,' she said in her soft voice with an eloquence which sounded more pleasing with the tone she had used. Siddhant couldn't help but smile looking at her face. She smiled back. She opened the car door, got down and closed the door when-

'Devyani,' called Siddhant sitting on his car seat. She turned around and looked inside through the window. His head was leaning back on the seat as if he felt very much complete and comfortable.

'Yes?' She asked with her regular polite smile. He waited for a moment, looked downwards, looked at her again and asked, 'Would you mind if I ask you to spend some time with me over brunch.........one in the afternoon tomorrow?' And before she could say anything else but, 'I...Siddhant...' he continued, 'And you won't get disturbed or behave clumsily this time.' There was silence except some cars' sound from the nearby streets. He was serious this time. He was neither joking nor making a flirtatious attempt. His eyes had the intensity his voice had command. She waited for a few seconds without looking confused and then said, 'Okay,' in a voice which sounded most soothing today, with a smile which looked serene in the dying light of the sunset.

***

Siddhant was outside Devyani's aunt's bungalow before the time the next day. Leaning his back on his car's door, he waited for her. He had tried for the first time to 'look good.' Not that he was careless of his looks, this was the first time he was conscious about it. Wearing a light pink shirt with rolled up sleeves, khaki trousers with a brown belt and pastel coloured espadrilles, he looked well dressed with his classic side part hair and stubble on face. He looked groomed. Suddenly his phone rang, he picked it up and it was from some bank providing loan. He disconnected in a moment, checked a few messages and kept it back in his trousers and looked towards the gate when he saw her coming.

In a beige chiffon top and white A-line lace skirt, she was walking towards him wearing pastel coloured pumps and holding a blue clutch in her left hand. Siddhant couldn't yet become accustomed to the delight he felt every time she would appear in front of him. She looked as gorgeous and confident as she looked in their last two meetings. Or maybe more, he thought.

'Hello, hope you're doing well,' he greeted.

'Hope you too. I hope I did not keep you waiting,' she said smilingly.

'Not at all, it was a pleasure,' he said with a smile while opening the door of the car, waiting till her hands and hemlines were safely inside it. He got inside the car and they were off for a cookhouse and bar he had booked a table at, away from the hustle and bustle of the city.

It was not the most coveted eatery to be at but somewhat different from the traditional places to have a good Sunday brunch experience. And it was new and Siddhant believed it could be a bit reclusive today, unlike other places on Sunday. Interiors with lush plants, antiques, rich upholstery and chandeliers made the ambience rejuvenating. Once they were done with the order–Whole Wheat Pasta in mushroom sauce for Siddhant and Panzenella for Devyani–it was the time for him.

'You must be wondering why I asked you out for today,' he asked with a charming smile he had had.

'Actually no, I have been experiencing this all this while since I stepped into my teenage,' she mocked and said in a shy manner.

'You must have I am sure. But what would be crucial to me would be to know how many of them did you agree to go out with,' he asked slyly. She smiled slyly. He tried to change the topic; he didn't want her to be uncomfortable or shy for the time that they were there.

'Don't worry. I just felt like being with you. I mean, I just wanted to know...more about you,' said Siddhant, 'Sometimes you just need to satiate the urge to meet some people and spend time with them...as much as you can,' he said looking at her without blinking his eyes. She was looking at him. She had experienced men asking her hand in marriage by only the third meeting with her multiple times. But this was a different thing. The way Siddhant looked at her while speaking was a different experience. And to her surprise, she was feeling more comfortable with the way he spoke to her. He again changed the subject although he knew she wasn't uncomfortable.

'You lived with your relatives in London?' He asked.

'Yes. My cousin and I were there, we worked for an artist there. You live with your parents?' She asked.

'No. My father passed away years ago,' he said, to which she muffled, 'Oh, I am sorry.' ' Mom stays in hometown serving the hospice that she feels relieved working for. Making me a lone wolf,' he added.

'That's really nice. You know, I too worked for an orphanage nearby our home back in London. Feels good to work for the underprivileged,' she said.

Their meal had arrived. While having the meal, they discussed briefly the reason why Tanya had left the previous day in such haste. Aahil wanted her to meet one of his clients to have them featured on the magazine that she would work for. He obviously had not told her about it and had just called her immediately.

'What are your plans for the day?' He asked once they were done with their meal.

'Nothing much, what about you?' She asked. This was the first time she had asked or initiated something from her side.

'I just wanted to go for a drive, to a solitude place, only if someone could accompany me and disturb my reclusion,' he said in a flippant manner looking at her. He had asked her.

'Well, I won't mind disturbing,' she said mischievously. She was comfortable and liked being with him. He was steady and not what she was accustomed to–boys asking for an affair, tying the knot and other such proposals.

As soon as the car moved out of the parking, she said with a willful half-smile, 'Well I just wanted to clarify if I am not giving you any objective to think that it is something more than just spending some time with you.'

'Oh no, not at all. I would just think you are trying as much to know about me as I desire to know you,' he said while starting off the car, looking at her with a doting smile. She liked his manners. She liked that he wasn't the kind of guy who would open his heart up telling a girl what he felt.

'It is nice to go out with new people sometimes...what do you think? I am sure that is the reason we are here,' she said looking at him.

'If you say so,' said Siddhant jerking his head and giving her a mysterious smile. She stared at him. What went in his mind was definitely a mystery she thought. She still did not find what he felt for her.

'Why else do you think I agreed to come with you?' She asked him curiously. He waited for a few seconds, as if thinking how to put what he felt.

'You know Devyani, there are few things that we don't understand. There are a few questions we don't have an answer for. There are a few instances...when we do what we feel like but deep down in our mind and heart, we realise it later what the exact reason was for doing it...' he answered philosophically. He didn't look at her while driving and speaking now and looked serious.

'Oh god, I didn't know my consent to come with you was that deep,' she said just to make him say something else in the context, but he kept silent.

Just the moment when she looked the other side out of the window, he started 'So what do you think about us Indians, coming back after years? Wish you didn't have any pre-conceived idea about us.' He asked half smilingly.

'And why do you think I would have such an idea Mr. Siddhant, I am as Indian as you are,' she said emphasizing her statement with her big brown eyes.

'I must say I'm Impressed,' he said making an expression appreciating her quote.

'And anyway you are the first person whom I am spending time with after coming back,' she said. He didn't reply.

'What are you thinking now?' She asked.

'I am thinking that how is it possible,' he answered with a question.

'What is possible?' She asked.

'You know when I saw you at the party that day. I thought of you as an ultimately gorgeous lady who is a boastful foreign return who might find it below her dignity to speak to everyone. And today, you are spending time with me just because I asked and you think spending time with new people is a great idea,' he teased her.

'That basically means you are judgmental Mr. Mathur. And by what means you think I look boastful,' she asked playfully.

'Well, I supported my statement. I called you ultimately gorgeous,' he said looking at her coyly. She blushed and looked the other way and suddenly back at him trying to tease him, 'I hope you are not trying to woo me by that because that was too regular and not going to help.'

'Of course I am trying to woo you but how does that mean that calling you ultimately gorgeous lady would be too regular,' he answered quickly. She didn't have an answer. 'And anyway, I could probably have a girlfriend. You won't know that,' he continued mischievously.

'Oh why not, spending Sunday with a girl and taking her out without getting any annoying phone call really suggests that you could probably have a girlfriend,' she said quickly with her perfect eloquence and they suddenly burst out laughing.

The chit chat continued while they headed towards a solitude place and she finally found herself inside the vicinity of a solitary resort on the outskirts of the city, which had a huge garden of mud ground that was next to a widely stretched complex that was made to look like a rural establishment. By this time, they had got to know the ordinary details about each other and she told him that she was in London for only a few years and had completed her schooling here in a boarding school in Dehradun. It was half past five in the evening and she couldn't feel more at peace since the time she had arrived in India. It was silent with the sounds of some birds and peacock coming from a far distance.

It was the last week of February and the sun was not too harsh. They walked some yards on a stone pathway and stopped near a place where the establishment ended and the muddy ground of the resort started. A table was laid there. He thought she would like to sit there but she walked towards a bench, which was quite away from the table and where they could be left completely alone. He followed her and they settled down. She looked as if she was alone and then she said 'Thank you.' He gave her a questioning look with raised eyebrows. 'For bringing me here, I mean you could have taken me anywhere but you chose this place,' she said looking at him and they laughed the next moment at her 'anywhere' remark. She took a deep breath while laughing and added, 'I mean you could take me to some other good place but you chose this.' He nodded his head playfully, still smiling. She had liked his smile; it was effective and indeed impressive.

She gazed at him, suddenly realized it to be awkward and looked the other way, changing the topic, 'London has beautiful sunsets. But there is something different here,' she said calmly in her soft, soothing voice.

'I am pleased you liked it.'

She continued after some moments in her pleasing voice which sounded both relieved and relieving, 'Such moments always remind me of...of something. This purity...nothing artificial... nothing to care about...nothing to think about.'

Siddhant was gazing at her while she looked towards the sky, but not only at her beauty now. He tried to know more than just her physical appearance. There was no formality between them now. He didn't prefer initiating the conversation now and waited for her to express what she felt.

She wavered and said, 'Sorry I got a bit lost.'

'I am glad you expressed yourself,' he replied with a loving smile.

'I didn't expect I would feel such relief today.'

'Told you so,' he said smilingly.

She smiled and said, 'Let's walk.' They got up and started walking in a desolate garden away from the bench crossing the small artificial mud huts made to create a rustic ambience. Devyani was not as introvert as he had perceived initially, she just took time to be comfortable with him, and it didn't take long.

'You never told me about your people, your family, parents,' he asked.

'My dad is in Mumbai,' she said briefly and then stopped.

'And you mom?' He asked after a few moments.

Siddhant's phone rang and it was Tanya. She had called to know Devyani's whereabouts as her phone was out of reach when her aunt had tried. He told Tanya about her and disconnected the call after a few moments.

'Sorry. It was Tanya asking about you, your aunt must have asked her,' he said.

'It's okay,' she said. Siddhant didn't want to continue asking about her mother, he didn't find it of any use right now.

'Coffee?' He asked.

'Sure.'

'Or leave coffee, why don't you try that *kulhar chai*,' he asked indicating towards a boy who was selling tea in earthen cups. She gave a questioning look raising her eyebrows in surprise.

'You must try it, one doesn't get it in London after all,' he said mockingly.

She laughed and said, 'I know. I've seen it in my childhood.'

He passed her the *kulhar* and she sipped her *chai* and said, 'It's good actually...I remember having it once when I was a kid... with my mother.' She stopped as if she had said something accidentally.

He looked at her and asked her now, 'You didn't tell anything about your mother. Is she here or...?'

She looked at him. Her expression dulled with a faded smile on face. 'Is it important to know?' She asked. He gazed at her.

'Of course not,' he replied to make her forget the sullen emotion she had felt just now.

She looked the other way and they started walking again. But she didn't look offended or pessimistic about the mention of her mother and that was the reason Siddhant kept mum, waiting for her to speak when she said, 'She left us when I was five. Actually dad asked her to.' There was a pause. They stopped near a flower-bed abreast the edge of the wall of the resort, which had many marigold flowers in the plants that shone in the setting sun's light. They could look towards the farmland next to the resort garden and the setting sun, which had started sinking beneath the sky now. And then she added, 'One day, when I was fifteen, still in the hostel in Dehradun, I got to know from dad about her demise. Someone from her home had made him a call to tell.' There was a silence around them. Just the sound of the windmill from a faraway land could be heard. She looked towards the setting sun; her face looked cold, red in its light. The small sterling silver pendant with engravings, which sat around her neck, shone in the dying light of the sun. Awe had transformed Siddhant's face while he gazed at her. He didn't expect something like this coming. It looked like her eyes hid her life's stories. She looked most beautiful to him at this moment. Not because she looked so pure in the rays of the sun, but because of her inner emotions, her deep eyes telling a story, and because her moist eyes had made Siddhant more vulnerable for her.

She looked completely different to him. She looked beautiful but not in the way she always had. Her beauty looked serene to him, pure and real. It was not just about her olive skin and beautiful light eyes. Of course not. She was much more than that and he had anticipated it since he had started brooding about her after their first meeting.

'I'm sorry I couldn't have known that,' he consoled her in a low voice and apologised for reminding her of something that made her looked dejected.

She became conscious as if she had woken up from a dream and said, 'No, actually I am sorry. I...I shouldn't have just expressed all that,' she said embarrassingly but her almost perfect voice eloquence appeared back. Her face had turned red.

'Please don't say that, it's perfectly alright,' he told her. 'Let's sit inside, you must be feeling cold,' he added, and they walked inside an artificial mud enclosure which was made to be looked like a rural hovel. As soon as they sat at one table, Siddhant realized that Devyani still wasn't over the fact that she had shared with him something that she shouldn't have; she looked embarrassed. He stared at her while she was still looking elsewhere, trying not to look at him.

'I won't ask you to forget what you said a few minutes ago,' he said. She finally looked at him, a bit surprised. 'After all, you spoke about your mother and you shouldn't be resentful, even if you shared it with a person you met only a few days ago,' he added in his deep voice, looking with intensity in his eyes and care for her on his face. She felt nice about his words, she was feeling comforted now. 'But if you are really feeling uncomfortable, I won't force you to be here, I can drop you home-'

'No,' she said suddenly. 'I am fine now,' she added after a moment and gave him a smile.

It was seven when they left for Devyani's home. On the way back home, Devyani didn't speak much and neither did Siddhant force her to. She was comfortable but embarrassed by the fact that she had shared her private life with a man she had met just a few days ago. She looked at him once. He looked calm while driving. All this while, Devyani was also wondering that how she–a girl who was mostly reticent–could be so comforted that she shared her past with a man, got embarrassed about it and was comforted by the same man, and that too all in one day; in fact within just a few hours. She had never shared anything about her mother with anyone else and this fact also had given her the reason to feel so embarrassed and confused. He was probably the first man in her life that she had felt so comfortable with, she thought. But the question was why? And that was why she didn't speak much. Siddhant however didn't wish to make her more sheepish and thus spoke very less, apart from telling her about few landmarks of the city that they would pass, in his normal deep and serious voice with a caring smile, just to make her feel as if nothing weird happened from her side and also to diminish the probability of her feeling uncomfortable due to the extreme silence in the car. She had obviously sensed that and liked that too. She couldn't expect any other man in such a situation to be as tender as he was. Still thinking about Siddhant, her feelings and her mother, she suddenly realized that they were already outside her aunt's bungalow the moment Siddhant stopped the car. It was nine and no one was there to be seen. Street-lights and triple light lamp on sides of the gate were the only sources of light.

'So, here you are,' Siddhant said. He was still looking serious but gazed at her and smiled. Devyani, however, now wished to express her gratitude for whatever Siddhant had done for her.

'Siddhant, you know I...I really want to thank you for today. Thanks for taking me to such a nice place where I could find peace,' she said in her soft voice looking at him, curving her mouth into a smile. He was now looking straight outside the car sitting straight with a very unpredictable look and intense eyes. She couldn't say why he looked that way, as if was in a deep thought, she also looked straight and tried, 'It was really very nice spending time with you-'

'I love you,' he said in his deep, serious voice, still sitting straight looking outside.

Silence fell in the car. Surrounding which was already silent with just the sound of crickets and a few cars, which ran far away from them felt to be more noiseless. She looked at him and he too looked at her after a second, still serious. After just a few moments she laughed briefly, looked out and said, 'Oh god, I can't believe you just fooled me.' There was still no reply from Siddhant. She looked at him and found him still staring at her. She got a bit restless now and looked downwards.

'I had no desire to make you feel clumsy Devyani, but I couldn't help but express to you what I feel,' he expressed in his deep voice. 'After struggling hard not to tell you, I had to say that I haven't seen a girl like you...ever,' he added. He sounded serious and assertive.

Devyani looked at him; he was looking at her, his expressions a bit mild now. She started telling him seriously but was interrupted, 'It's not possible for me. I am not a person who would indulge in affaires like this and-'

'In that case, will you marry me?' He asked in a commanding voice. It was another shock for her. She kept staring at him. She opened her mouth after a while saying, 'Siddhant, it's really awkward for me but...I hardly know you and....' she tried when he said, 'How much time do you want to know me?' he asked confidently. It made her answerless again. She controlled herself, gathered a will to speak and told him, 'It's not possible Siddhant, I am already committed to marrying someone else.' Siddhant did not say or ask anything to her for the first time. 'I am sorry if you believe I should've told you this. I didn't think it was necessary,' she added elegantly. She looked at him and found a flicker of frustration in his eyes. She couldn't look into his impressive, authoritative eyes and looked downwards scratching her clutch just to look a bit normal.

'Well the damage has been done then, I must say,' he smirked ingratiatingly looking at her.

'I really am sorry if my behaviour made you feel...'

'Do you wish to marry him...the guy you are committed to...'

She spoke after a pause, 'It doesn't matter. I won't question the decision of my dad.'

'So you don't wish to marry him,' he declared.

'I said it doesn't matter Siddhant,' she raised her soft voice a bit. 'It is my dad's right to think of my well being and...and under any circumstances, I won't deny him that,' she added in a trembling manner, her eyes seemed to be a bit teary and her voice shook. Siddhant realized that and suddenly moved towards her and said poignantly, 'Devyani, Devyani...I can't...I don't want to see you like that, I never meant to. I am sorry I got you into such a situation.' He looked downwards and asked, 'What do you want me to do?' He expressed at last in the most caring manner she had experienced. She looked at him; his eyes were glistening as if wet. She was really unsure of what she wanted to say, and when he himself asked her of her wish, she thought for a few seconds. She was sure that this relationship is not acceptable. She thought for a few seconds and then said in a firm voice and a very determined manner, 'I don't want you to come in my life again if you love me-'

'That can't happen-'

'Even if that results in a tormented and wretched life when I am already marrying someone else?' She ended with an asserting question looking at him.

Silence fell in the car again. Siddhant stared at her, his eyes looked most unguarded now. They both looked into each other's eyes, only a few inches away from each other's faces.

'Alright,' he said quietly while looking into her eyes. He had controlled himself; his eyes did not look that unguarded now. He moved back and got out of the car, went towards her side of the door walking around the bonnet and opened her side of door in a gentle manner, without looking at her. She got out and looked towards the gate of her house. He closed the door gently and moved to get into the car again from his side but stopped and looked at her again who looked at him now. Her face had deep feelings, which were hard to understand in the triple street light lamps on both the sides near the gate of her house. He moved again and got inside and she started walking slowly towards the gate. The moment she reached the gate and the watchman opened the gate for her, the engine of his car roared and she waited for a moment and then turned back. Neither his old, green Renault Duster nor he was there. She started moving again, walking on the gravel leading to the main door of the house when a thought hit her mind it seemed. She turned back again; the watchman was sitting outside the gate near his cabin and nothing else was there to be seen in the streetlight. Trying to pacify her mind, she slowly walked again and went inside.

CHAPTER 9

He hated waiting. He hated waiting when he was supposed to meet anyone out of necessity, but he could bear that with a hidden disgust. But whenever he had to wait for someone he really wanted to see, he couldn't bear it. He was waiting for Devyani for the last thirty minutes in the café. With two cappuccinos and something hidden inside his mind, he tried and kept his calm.

The door of the café opened and she entered. Crop top with palazzos pants, a Pashmina shawl on one shoulder, and nude stilettos. She stopped and looked around for him, found him gazing at her and walked hastily and sat across him. Before anything else, she apologised with a smile, which anyone could say looked too fake.

'I am so sorry. You see this wedding shebang and everyone-'

'So you forgot that someone might have been wasting this noon,' he scoffed, playing with the paper napkin kept at the table. Her smile faded.

'I couldn't leave,' she sighed.

'Is that what you have to say really?'

She didn't say anything. He hated it. He wanted her to retaliate to speak more of her mind. But she'll not reply and he knows that. And he hated why was she so benign all the time. Why was she so tolerant.

'Speak up for lord's sake. I'm talking to you,' he said in a low, infuriated voice. She didn't say anything.

Moments passed by. This is why he hated it, because her silence was always more powerful than his words. It always had been. After almost five minutes of silence and probably his realisation that he was sitting in today's reality and everything was not as he had thought, he sighed.

'I am sorry Devyani. What to do with this habit of mine? You know my foibles,' he said calmly. She waited for a few seconds the then replied calmly, 'Habits can still go. Sense of belonging... seldom leaves.'

'Listen Devyani,' he held her hand and said, 'till the time we're here, I promise I'll not bring anything to you that disturbs your mind...I'll not let anything make you upset.' His voice was composed and swelled with affection; she realized and looked at him. Since the day she had met him here in Udaipur, it was the first time when she had seen him like this. His countenance was not having any sign of disturbance resulting from anything that disturbs one's state of mind. He looked like Siddhant she had known years ago. She smiled looking into his eyes. She saw his square face with hollow cheeks, prominent jawline, almond shaped deep eyes, somewhat thin lips and his aquiline nose, for the first time so closely since she had met him here. He smiled too and this smile was also something that she had seen years ago.

'Shall we go somewhere outside?' She asked him.

'Of course. Wherever you say.'

***

How calm was that smile he thought. After thirteen years, that smile had again entered his life. So what if it was only for a few days. He had forgotten how his mind was so receptive of her smile. The satisfaction was always missing he thought. But till when? Next few days? But why was he even thinking about the number of days? Who was she to him now? Or maybe he thought what was 'he' to her now?

'You like it here?' He asked her watching some local bards singing and playing their string instruments on the street. She had felt so good and relieved here that she had forgotten that she was away from all her people and relatives. Or maybe because she was there with him.

After a while, they found themselves walking on a silent street pavement together and found contentment even while they both were silent. That silence indeed was not in vain, it gave them some relief, some unknown sense of calmness.

'You didn't ask me about my life Siddhant?' She said calmly while walking.

'I didn't see a reason to Devyani. You were always the right person.'

'Right person?'

'You always knew what to do. You always took decisions that were correct and just. And you aren't a person who'll compromise on what's right. So I am sure you are doing more than...well. So...'

'Hmm...'

'Didn't you...marry?' She asked quietly but hot hesitantly.

'You mean remarry?' He laughed and she looked at him. 'Na...I didn't.' They were never married but she knew why he said 'remarried'. The bond that they had had back then, only needed the formality of tying the knots. They always treated each other like a husband and a wife and sometimes even called themselves so.

'Why?' She asked out of concern and not curiosity.

'I didn't know actually that I loved you so much,' he laughed again. 'I realized when you left that you're the only one who can tolerate me,' he added.

'Be serious Siddhant,' she asserted.

'Okay, okay. You see Devyani, I realized when you left that I can't marry anyone. Maybe I am not the one who should marry. I think I am the most imperfect man to get into relationships,' he sighed.

'You know that's not true.'

'No. See, I haven't been able to...do justice to anyone in life when it comes to relationships,' he emphasised.

There was an awkward silence now. He realized she didn't like what he had said. But till how long will he lie and not speak his heart to make her feel comfortable. He didn't want to disturb her but then he had said what he had felt, which eventually made him feel bad, as she felt bad.

'Okay, I agree with whatever you say. But don't be upset Devyani. I... I don't want to see you like that,' he said with a sense of responsibility that he would always have while speaking to her when she would be upset. She smiled again but now she also felt bad about him. Till how long she will stop him from expressing. Why was she forcing him to control himself? She had no right to disturb a man who was not wrong, who always cared for her. She was the one who left him with a reclusive life with no one around and now when he spoke his mind after so many years, she still controlled his feelings? She didn't feel good but she indeed felt relieved in his company. She liked it.

'Okay forget all this, tell me how did you feel when you met me after so many years?' He asked with that same youthfulness she thought. 'Didn't you think who's this old, lean, once would-be-husband looking man?' He added. She smiled.

'No, it's not like that. In fact you look good with this beard. You look so wise,' she said looking at him. Her voice was as normal as her face was. She looked happy and he, satisfied that she was normal now.

'So I didn't look wise back then right?' He chuckled. She laughed.

'I really... missed this smile...' said Siddhant looking at her. They had stopped now and she too was looking into his eyes now, which she had missed all these years. The weather was changing a bit now. Cold winds were making people more active now as people wished to get inside homes and shops.

'May we go somewhere? The two of us... if you have time?' He asked. He was neither smiling nor frivolous now. He looked serious; his eyes intense.

'Siddhant...' she hesitated but couldn't complete.

'Why? Trust has toppled from the *EX* boyfriend?' He teased her.

'Please Siddhant, you know...'

'Okay... I'll not say anything. But a coffee won't bother your self-respect, would it?'

'Siddhant, please...'

And the café that was in the corner of the street pavement they were walking on was their last destination of the day.

'Please don't misunderstand me Siddhant. But you know how it is,' she explained.

'Sorry?'

'I mean I said no to you when you asked...'

'Oh it's really okay Devyani, you know that.'

'You know I trust you.'

'I know, and you don't need to be so apologetic really. And besides, not every man gets to have coffee with his ex-girlfriend in such romantic weather,' he laughed.

Both of them tried to become as normal as possible for the next half an hour in the café. The small winter day was getting over in Udaipur and it was Siddhant who proposed to drop her to the hotel.

The car stopped outside the palace hotel when the sun was setting. The sun looked reddish and the hotel's outline looked ethereal as if a destination from a dream has come to life. Devyani still sat on the backseat of the car with Siddhant while the chauffeur was at the driving seat.

'Thanks Siddhant,' she uttered.

'For what Devyani?' He smiled.

'For giving me this time. All this while, after a long time, I felt really good.'

He couldn't stop himself from looking into her beautiful brown eyes. He turned to the driver.

'Would you mind going out', he said to the driver.

The driver opened the door and stepped out, leaving hesitant Devyani looking at Siddhant.

Siddhant looked at Devyani. They were only a few inches away from each other; Devyani felt uneasy when he started getting closer to her till he kept his hands on her left cheek. She, by now looked incessantly into his eyes. 'Siddhant...' she murmured in a low voice.

He kept his thumb on her lips. He had felt the warmth of her breath after ages; she had felt his lips from such closeness after years. He moved closer and felt those bow shaped lips with his like they always belonged to him. With each passing moment, the passion of the moment was only getting more intense with no sign of the feelings getting diminished. He made her forget the hesitation she had had. She felt what she had missed and he wanted to posses those lips more than before. His actions could say that better and she surrendered herself as if the swelled up feelings made her do so. They were holding each other like they once used to.

After many minutes of sense of possession and surrender, they parted and looked into each other's eyes. At that very moment, her countenance changed. The sense of passion diminished behind the sense of guilt. He still looked at her face, her eyes. She looked the other way and the look of guilt was taken over by that of bewilderment, and then she looked sombre. He, who was until this moment still taken over by his passion, now tried to speak to her.

'Devyani...listen to-'

'I have to go,' she snorted before he could say anything, opened the door of the car and left without looking back.

He still sat there looking at her till she was not visible and entered the palace walking on the stone pathway with lush green grounds on both sides. His countenances were now full of distress but sans any look of guilt.

So this was it, he thought. He met her and lost her once again. He couldn't even keep her with himself for a few days. Was it the last time he had seen her in life? Probably.

CHAPTER 10

Two weeks elapsed from the night when Siddhant had told Devyani what he felt and had got somewhat devastated by her reply. He still could not think of the ways to overcome his feelings. He felt sick about how powerless he felt for the fact that he couldn't take things forward. Such was his reverence and tenderness for Devyani that he didn't want to disturb that and it made him sicker. Initially, Tanya thought that it was a basic, strong infatuation that was making him feel what he did. But when he looked more and more doleful each time he met her, with a sombre face, fake smile, and stony-eyes, she knew it was something of grave importance. She knew him for years and had never seen him the way she saw him now. She had called him up at her apartment and was persistent with her opinion that this had to happen.

'Look I told you this the very first day Sid. She has her own people, her own life. I told you I didn't know much about her and had no idea she was here for some wedding shit,' she added to her opinions about Devyani. He looked at her plainly like he was since the last thirty minutes without saying a word.

'Listen, I am leaving for Mussoorie next weekend with Charu and all and you HAVE to come. You will feel good,' she informed.

'Don't be irritating now. I can handle it myself,' he said finally in an irascible manner.

'Oh that I can see very well but I would rather like you to handle it *there*,' she argued.

He was silent looking outside the window.

She was still doubtful but decided to say nothing so that the chance of his coming couldn't be bridled altogether by his irritation at the moment.

She turned around to go to the kitchen to keep the plates kept on the dining table.

'Tani,' he called her in a low voice. She turned back and there was a sign of a smile on his face.

'I'll come,' he said firmly looking at her.

She kept the plates back on the table and went to him and hugged him tightly.

'I knew you would come and I'm sure everything would be normal once again,' she said lovingly. She was happy that it would make him pacified again. But she didn't know that he had agreed just because he didn't want to upset Tanya. She cared for him and he had been very discourteous and thankless to her since last few days. He, at last thought, that she might be right, no matter how hard it would be to look happy when his mind was tormented.

While Siddhant was still coping with Devyani's answer from that night, Devyani seemed to be normal, at least to Tanya whenever they had a word after that night.

On a morning, two days before Tanya had to leave for Mussoorie *en masse,* Devyani called her for a regular chat. Initially, Tanya had thought that her frequent calls after her meeting with Siddhant that day implied that she also was interested to know how he was doing, but when Tanya never mentioned anything about him and Devyani never asked, Tanya thought that it was just a normal chat that Devyani would initiate as she didn't know anyone else in the city. However, when Tanya mentioned about her jaunt with friends to Devyani by the by, she sounded a bit lost. In the afternoon, when she and Siddhant were having lunch together as their offices happened to be just fifteen minutes away, she didn't mention to him about Devyani's call. But it had to happen. Tanya's phone rang.

'Hello Tanya,' said a soft voice from the other side.

'Hi Devyani,' said Tanya.

Siddhant stopped for a moment while having a spoonful of *rajma chawal,* but again concentrated on eating as if didn't hear the name. Tanya kept on talking.

'Yes,' then paused. 'I don't mind but see you don't know anyone so...' she continued. And at last added, 'Me, Siddhant and some friends you don't know...okay, no problem...okay bye, take care,' and she hung the phone and sat idle for some moments. She stared at him as if she had committed a mistake. He looked back at her when he didn't see any sign of movement in her even after disconnecting the call. He looked at her now lifting his eyebrows, questioning her.

She started, 'See I didn't know this could also happen but...'

He changed his expression and seemed to be emphasising on a question with eyebrows still lifted.

'It was Devyani and she wishes to come with us to Mussoorie for god knows what reasons. I mean her dad can arrange a trip for her to any exotic location she puts her finger on, on the world map,' she said, irritated.

He smiled sarcastically looking outside the window of the restaurant they were sitting in, towards the moving cars outside. He didn't know if he was supposed to be happy or embarrassed or disgusted or anything else.

'Okay, should I ask her not to?'

'To worsen what has already been messed up?' Blurted Siddhant.

'But why should you have an issue even if she's coming? I mean it shouldn't really bother you considering that you already are determined on coping with it?'

'Oh yes, coping with it with her being constantly in front of my eyes, right?' He said mockingly.

'Okay then, I'll be telling her we aren't going, simple as that.'

He waited for a few seconds and then said, 'No, actually let her come. I won't have an issue. You are right, considering I know I have to deal with it.'

'You sure?'

'Yeah,' he said wearing a broad, fake smile. Tanya still gazed at him, confused, while he seemed to be normal, and they resumed finishing off their *rajma chawal.*

***

Tanya and Siddhant joined Charu, Karan, Om and Pallavi on the Delhi airport. Devyani was to reach Mussoorie on the evening of the day when they were to arrive there in the afternoon.

Charu and Karan had been in a relationship to the surprise of most of their friends. Charu, a gracious theatre artist was in love with Karan, a Casanova who worked in a BPO and was surprisingly, equally loyal to her. However, it was his whimsical flirtatious behaviour that sometimes irritated Charu. Completely opposite to them were Om and Pallavi who were neither in a relationship nor wished to. They were just friends like they all were in the group. Pallavi was a chirpy girl who was like a twin to Tanya and Om was a singer who would always carry his guitar wherever he would go. Albeit it was his flawless singing and adroitness as a guitarist that had made Pallavi fall for him once; she had soon realised that it was just an infatuation at the time of their college days. They were all more than familiar with Siddhant although they once were Tanya's friends only. In fact Om and Siddhant would get along very well with each other and were much like each other. Pallavi had now developed a secret crush on Siddhant, which she couldn't keep as a secret as once when she was drunk, she had confessed about it to Tanya when they were alone. It was a group of people who were compatible with each other and were carefree in each other's company but what was bothering Siddhant was Devyani's imminent arrival to the cottage they had reached in the afternoon.

It was incomprehensible to him why Devyani wished to join the group of Tanya and friends to Mussoorie even after knowing he would be there. He wondered why would she be around a man who had proposed her for marriage a few weeks ago and moreover, whose presence could bring her a 'tormented and wretched life' ahead? And the second reason that Tanya had wildly conjectured was out of the question to be considered even for a moment, which implied that she might have developed 'some sort of fondness' for him. It in fact had irritated him the most. Devyani wasn't the kind of girl who would come all the way to a certain place to tell him her side of the story. She could have told him over the phone had she become fond of him weeks after his proposal. And he couldn't deny that she was marrying a guy with her own choice. But whatever it was, at least he had a chance to meet her once again, which he had not asked for but could also not defy, as he had been curious about it.

March's third week was soothingly cool in Mussoorie when they reached there via taxi from Dehradun airport, passing the snaky roads on a bright and sunny day. It was a huge cottage–where they all had reached in the afternoon–with a stone pathway leading towards the reception area and a garden with lush green ground and foliage on both sides. There was a stone pathway leading from the other side of the building of the resort, to its huge backyard, which had benches around its boundary walls and from where the quaint hills shrouded by clouds were visible, rousing and quiet.

They all went to their rooms but the wait for the evening was most coveted for Siddhant, although it wasn't as special as it would have sounded to him a few weeks back. They all were sitting in the backyard's corner where some tables were laid and that was when Tanya went out to receive Devyani and led her back.

It was six in the evening and Siddhant was sitting on a bench facing the opposite direction from where Devyani came, accompanied with Tanya. Tanya introduced her to Charu and Karan as they had met her for the first time having been missed her party that day and she sat on a chair beside Pallavi facing Siddhant now. She greeted him with a brief smile to which he nodded. They were having their conversations when Karan, who was already taken aback by Devyani's beauty and poise, directed the chit-chat towards her.

'I however never knew we were to be joined by such a damsel,' said Karan gazing at Devyani to which Charu rolled her eyes.

'Stop it Karan, she's not going to be flattered so don't try,' said Pallavi mocking him.

'I'm just praising the beauty girls,' replied Karan.

'But I must say we are pleased to meet you Devyani,' said Pallavi.

'Same here,' said Devyani in her normal polite manner.

'I guess we met you at the party that day, although it was a brief introduction,' said Om to Devyani to which she smiled and said, 'Yes'.

'God you are so eloquent and polite, I wonder you are Tanya's cousin,' Pallavi mocked Tanya and everyone laughed. It was of course hers and Om's second meeting with Devyani so they all tried to make her comfortable.

'Better than you baby, who was thrown outta your house last week when you stayed with me,' said Tanya to Pallavi adding to the humour.

'But how come you didn't make me meet her Tanya?' Questioned Karan.

'Because you were busy watching my play that day my love,' taunted Charu.

'Lucky as hell,' he replied widening his eyes to which she hit him by her elbow.

'I work in a theatre group actually,' told Charu to Devyani initiating the conversation. Charu was a girl with grace and charm that was eminent. But she couldn't deny that Devyani's presence had bemused her too along with the others.

'So you have a boyfriend back in London?' Asked Pallavi drinking her beer which kind of appalled Devyani. Siddhant also looked at Pallavi and Devyani now.

'Why can't you people get over this bf-gf drama all the time,' said Tanya handling the situation.

'Oye, I was just asking okay?' Pallavi defended herself. 'And besides British men always give me sleepless nights', she said in a ribald manner with a wink.

'She is not completely wrong by the way,' Karan defended Pallavi winking at her. 'I mean I say same for the women of London,' he added.

'Better stop or I will give you a real sleepless night,' Charu defended Devyani.

'It was a simple question baby,' said Pallavi.

'Cut it out or he'll soon ask what your mother found in your room that made her mad that day,' said Charu and they all burst out laughing. Devyani didn't know anything about it and Karan initiated letting her in on the humour, 'You now Devyani she had in her room a few vibra-'

'You asshole,' said Pallavi and threw a beer bottle at Karan but missed.

'Shush! You should come on in Devyani, you must be feeling tired. Why don't you freshen up!' said Charu and took Devyani inside with her. Before going in with Charu, Devyani and Siddhant looked at each other at the same time. She looked as much of an enigma as she had looked the first time he had met her. She walked inside and they sat there till nine when they all went to the dining hall.

'Don't mind what Karan says, they all are like that all the time. You just be comfortable,' Charu comforted Devyani as soon as they were inside the room.

'Oh no, I am fine,' smiled Devyani. Charu tried controlling her laughter but burst out laughing and told Devyani when she looked at her in surprise with a smile, 'Actually he's right. Her mother really found two vibrators in her room while cleaning her room up', she laughed again and added, 'And that too switched on, buzzing under her bed mattress.' She again laughed and Devyani too laughed but with a usual restrain and poise she had had.

Devyani went inside the washroom and they all met again in the dining room at night and their regular chitter-chatter continued till late night, which Devyani didn't participate in as she went in her room. She in fact waited for the morning, with sleep still away from her eyes.

***

They all were ready for trekking the next morning by seven with their bagpacks and Siddhant although was not interested, didn't want to be a killjoy and hence agreed to join them. They were still having their breakfast in the backyard of the resort when Devyani who did not look ready for trekking said in a very low voice, 'Tanya, actually I am not feeling well to go for trekking and would like to stay back if you don't mind.'

Everybody looked at Tanya when she asked, 'What happened baby, are you alright? I can stay back if you want me to.' Everybody was still looking at Tanya as she, Pallavi and Karan were always up for trekking every time they could go for it.

'Oh no, please don't, you may go. I can take care of myself,' said Devyani.

'I can stay back,' an unexpected voice came from Siddhant side. Everyone looked at him, as he was not very eloquent since the time Devyani had arrived there. But to everyone's surprise, Devyani didn't ask him to go with them. They all looked towards them and Tanya said, 'I think that would do.'

They all left within a few minutes. Before leaving, Tanya kissed Devyani's cheek and told her, 'It will take time for us to return baby, maybe tomorrow morning, so take care.' Devyani nodded.

Devyani and Siddhant sat there. There was a silence although not awkward. They were mature enough to get over the things that couldn't work. Siddhant was looking towards hills when she broke the silence in her soft, confident and low voice.

'How is life?'

'It's good. Nothing special, how about you?' He expressed very plainly.

'Perfect.'

He nodded and she waited for a minute before speaking again.

'Are you upset with me Siddhant?' She was not formal this time. She was a confident girl who didn't believe in circumlocution.

He didn't expect it from her for the kind of restraint she always possessed in her disposition.

'Why should I be?' He asked normally looking at her.

'I mean did I hurt you that day?'

'No. I was just a bit shocked at what happened. I didn't expect it to end up the way it did,' he replied plainly.

'You think I should have told you all the things before,' she asked. He waited for a few seconds.

'See Devyani, I don't think you should be worried about what you should or shouldn't have done to me. You should be happy in your life with decisions that you make,' he said in a manner that she got confused how to take. He sounded caring and uncomplaining to her.

'Did you wonder why I came here?' She asked after a minute.

'Hmm... I did. Although I think that we just had an encounter, which I didn't expect to happen. That shouldn't stop you from coming here,' he said.

'Does that mean you're not upset with me?' She asked in a deep voice.

He looked into her eyes. He felt helpless once again though he tried not to.

'I never was Devyani,' he said and smiled.

'Shall we take a walk?' She asked and they started walking towards the end of the boundary of the lawn from where they could see both hills and the valley between rocks and hills.

'I wanted to talk to you Siddhant, from the day we were together that day. I felt it all really went wrong,' she said in a relaxed manner while walking.

'I am sure you don't mean you did anything wrong that night,' he blurted.

'No, not that. But I believe you were the one person, I realized that night, that I could call my friend since the time I landed here. But sometimes, things are not in our hands,' she said calmly.

'You still can,' he said the moment they reached the boundary of the lawn and they looked into each other's eyes.

She then looked heavenwards, 'I wanted to speak to you, but had no idea what to say or how would you react. I called Tanya up many times but she never mentioned you, so neither did I.'

'What did you want to call me for?' He asked.

'To tell you all these things that I am saying now.'

'You haven't come here to tell me all these things, have you Devyani?' He asked her calmly while looking in the direction in which she was looking.

'No. But I won't be lying if I say that you were one of the reasons I came here for.'

He looked at her while she looked towards picturesque hills. The innocence in her voice and eyes had stimulated the love he had tried hard to conceal. He kept on looking at her guiltless and calm countenance when she continued, 'Did you know I lied to Tanya about not feeling well today?'

'Yes,' he said plainly, looking again in the direction she was looking in. They stood there in silence; his hands were in his jeans' pocket while she had folded hers.

'Don't you want to know why?' She asked.

'I am still trying to figure that out.'

'Do you remember what I told you about my mother?' She asked. His silence meant yes to her.

She continued, 'She died a few kilometres away from here.' There was always something about her to make Siddhant astounded, and that had happened just now once again. He looked at her and she continued, 'She was from here, daughter of a farm worker. My dad married her against the will of his parents but could never witness a happy life', she said. 'He abandoned her and all that I know about her is that she breathed her last somewhere in a village a few kilometres away from here,' she added.

Her eyes were wet, her voice sounded burdened with restlessness though her face hid that. The frustration inside Siddhant that had been swelled up in last many weeks was nowhere to be felt now. All that he could feel now was his strong will to know her and her enigma, more than ever.

'You alright?' He asked fondly.

'Yes,' she said quietly, looked into his eyes, and added, 'I want to see the place where Ma breathed her last.' He looked into her beautiful eyes and then she expressed, 'I knew that you are the only one I could ask this from. Will you help me Siddhant?'

There couldn't be a question of saying no. Devyani Sinha was much more than how she looked, behaved and the kind of elite social stratum she had belonged to. She was probably as ordinary and humane as any other girl could be. The petty yet humanly desires she had hidden behind her beauty had touched the most vulnerable part of Siddhant. They looked at each other; Siddhant with utmost fondness in heart and firmness on face and Devyani, with a vulnerable expression.

CHAPTER 11

Siddhant entered his hotel room in utmost disgust and guilt. Guilt was for the decision he had made that day to have lunch with her till the time he was in Udaipur. He shouldn't have accepted the overture. What did he think? What will such meetings lead to? A 'friendship'? A fucking friendship was what he wanted? Was he a teenage jerk? Was he so vulnerable when it came to women and their companionship? That he agreed to be with her for some days? What a waste.

There are a few people who are very resolute while taking any decision in life and don't think of its impending repercussions, but as soon as the decision is taken, they start feeling not twice but many times as to why did they take that decision? Was it okay? Was it worth taking? Why did they do so? Siddhant was one of those people and was indeed determined in life for long-term decisions but when it came to relationships and taking small decisions on the path to reach that relationship's goal, the problem of rethinking would occur with him almost always. Or it is better to say that in the case of one person particularly, he would always get carried away and would think again and again after taking any decision. And he was enraged to the core over his decision.

Knock on the door of his room disturbed him while he was changing. It was Hitesh, one of the staff members of the hotel, which he was staying in. Hitesh had been no less than his personal attendant since Siddhant was there in Udaipur and served him as if he were serving Siddhant since long and knew him too well.

'Good evening sir, do you want anything sir, coffee?' asked Hitesh entering the room with his almost fake but polite smile. He was a young, lean, short man in his early thirties who always seemed to find extreme fulfillment in serving Siddhant.

'No Hitesh, and please don't disturb me now till the time I don't call for you,' Siddhant sassed.

'My apologies sir, have a nice time sir,' said Hitesh in his low and soft voice and left the room, closing the door.

When he was about to close his eyes lying on the bed, Siddhant's mobile phone rang to his utter annoyance. He took the phone from the side table and it was Pooja. He received the call.

'Hello,' he said.

'Hey! Where are you Siddhant? I've been trying to reach you since morning but network issues. How are you?' she asked in her poised and caring voice which Siddhant hated the most at the moment.

'I am fine Pooja, hope you too are doing well,' he said calmly.

'Everything is perfect here Siddhant. Your work is missed,' she asserted.

'Okay Pooja, I am in the middle of something right now,' he said to avoid her attentiveness and added, 'And I had told you I did not want to be disturbed here right?'

'Alright alright. I'll not bore you. Take care Siddhant,' she said.

'You too Pooja,' he said and hung up the phone.

The more he wanted to be away from the continuing mess of his life, the more he would always get into it, he thought. And despite trying hard to inflict his state of mind on Hitesh and Pooja, he again went back to what had happened an hour ago in the car. But he tried convincing himself now; after all, he was not a teenager actually and it was a fact that only one person always disturbed his state of mind. But he told himself that it was a chapter of his past which had knocked his present one fine day and it was gone now and he had nothing to complain about it because he shouldn't. She came and she had gone, why should he worry so much. Let bygones be bygones. It's time to think about the present, he thought.

CHAPTER 12

At around ten, in her high heel ankle boots and a knee length dress, Devyani was walking to and fro in front of an emporium on mall road when she heard the honking of a Royal Enfield across the narrow lane in the bustling crowd of the road. Siddhant in a helmet and aviator sunglasses was looking at her with a humble grin. She smiled broadly and almost ran towards him across the road.

'Ready?' he asked her vehemently. She smiled and sat behind him and they set off for a village near Chamba, around a hundred kilometres away from Mussoorie. The village was a small one, a name she had heard only once or twice from her dad. She was going to see the place she always wanted to, where her mother belonged, where she lived, met her dad and ultimately left the world from. It was a lifetime experience for her; some unanswered questions, some unknown facts, she had begun her journey with all of those with a man she found a great man in, a man with whom she had shared some of her life's most obscure secrets, and with a man she felt most comfortable and safe with, probably more than anyone else apart from her dad.

Siddhant was full of life again with her. On the snaky roads of Mussoorie, the cold wind blowing against his face made him feel tranquil and complete with a girl he had been sulking about since a few weeks. Valleys, farmlands, and river canals on one side and colossal rocky hills on the other side of the road were making it a beautiful experience for Devyani and the dangerous paths on the way and the cold wind were giving her goosebumps. She had grasped Siddhant's shoulders firmly although she felt hesitant of what he would think initially but when he said loudly, 'It's okay,' she grabbed it tightly. She liked the way he understood her without her saying anything almost all the time; she liked his simple, benign gestures.

The herd of sheeps, village belle walking with buckets and pitchers of water, girls going to school crossing the shortcuts on their way made Devyani feel so connected with the surroundings that she felt she was not here for the first time, but was a part of this place. That was obvious for it was her root.

Macaques, mules and so many vehicles and foreign pedestrians, all made her more and more relaxed and satisfied with what she was doing.

They rode for almost three hours when after enquiring with a few villagers, they got to know where was the exact place where Devyani's mother might have lived years ago. They arrived at a desolate old piece of land where no sign of any establishment seemed to ever exist. There stood nothing but a small kiosk around the corner of the land where a vendor sold tea and snacks.

Devyani stood there looking everywhere she could get a sign of a house but was disappointed. Siddhant asked the old vendor but what he told was more disappointing to Devyani.

'I have been running this shop for the last six years but never saw a home here. My father used to tell me that there was a home of an old farm worker but he died a few years before I started my kiosk. Municipality dazed the small house as nobody was alive to claim the land. Since then, nobody but you have come to ask about them,' the man said and then added, 'Were you related to them anyhow?' This was all that the old man said in his typical Hindi accent that people from rural hilly regions have. Siddhant moved his head in no and went to Devyani who was standing a few meters away listening to the man. Siddhant tried to say something to Devyani but decided not to say anything for now.

They sat on a bench there for a while as Devyani had wished to. A School'S bell rang across the valley and some girls came out of the building in their blue uniforms. Devyani looked at them and thought that maybe her mother had attended the same school. She looked down the road and at the distant hills, which might have been seen by her mother as well, she might have walked over the same path once. There was no home, no sign of her mother's existence there, yet she felt complacent. She felt lighter now; to her surprise, the warmth she was getting from that land was enough to make her feel the presence of her mother for her whole life. She looked at the land where her maternal ancestral house once might have stood, and then she got up.

It was two in the afternoon when they left the place and were coming back to Mussoorie when the weather changed suddenly and it started raining hard with freezing wind. Siddhant stopped the motorbike at the turn of the snaky road near a tea vendor kiosk, which was on the corner of the turn and they ran under the canopy, partially wet. There was a man slumbering on a bench inside the small shop, which was a part of his kiosk. Siddhant went to the man waking him up to get some tea who got up lazily and started making it. As soon as the man gave Siddhant two plastic cups of tea, he went back to sleep. Siddhant walked to Devyani who was standing under the edge of the canopy where the jet of water was falling incessantly from the canopy. He moved the cup towards her but she stood there, deep in thought.

'Devyani,' he said but she didn't reply. He kept looking at her.

'Life is so strange Siddhant,' she said finally. He listened to her.

'All our life, we keep on trying to find compassion and love, but give no value to it once we get it,' she said and stopped for a while. 'My dad didn't value Ma's love for him and when she died, he was never the same again. I never saw him smile again,' she added. She sounded as if the entire burden had been lifted up from her life. The rain was falling making sounds. She looked into his eyes and kept on looking for some time before realizing and breaking the eye contact.

'I wanted to thank you Siddhant, for everything that you did. I never thought I would be able to come here. When I got to know you will be here, I don't know why but I just knew it was time,' she said calmly and added, 'I just wanted to see this place once, before getting married to someone.' The atmosphere got tensed with her talking about her marriage. He looked downwards and kept the plastic cups on a small bench. She wanted to confess some more things to him. He looked serious and innocent, looking downwards while she looked at him and said, 'The guy he has chosen was never my choice for marriage Siddhant.' This was the moment that made him somewhat elated from inside although she never mentioned that she wasn't going to marry him, and he looked at her. She was looking at him.

'I'll be marrying the man of my dad's choice just because dad wants that and you know how he has been since Ma...and I really can't make it tough for him...It shouldn't matter what I think I guess....' she told him, in a low voice while speaking her last sentence. They were looking at each other and were only a few inches away. She knew that it was more than just reverence that she felt for Siddhant at this moment. She somehow wanted to feel him more closely. She felt submissive to her mind and heart and looked at his face. Their faces moved towards each other so slowly that they didn't realise that they could now feel each other's warm breaths in the cold weather. Their mouths now exhaled white vapours in the cold weather and were so close that they were about to be touched. Devyani's eyes were half closed now looking at his lips and so were his. It seemed they didn't want to think about anything else right now and had surrendered to what came from inside. They could have succumbed to the turbulent feelings they felt at the moment when a car honked and passed by noisily and brought them back to their senses. Their faces were still so close to each other that they couldn't completely come out of what they felt at the moment. Breathing heavily, Devyani realized what had happened. She opened her eyes and looked at his face from such closeness, kept on looking, and suddenly moved backwards. She was confused, embarrassed, and couldn't believe what had just happened. However, it was Siddhant for whom the situation was more difficult. After coming so close to a girl he always wished to come more close to, it was difficult for him to go back to normal. He already had controlled himself for many weeks but it was not in his control now. They realized the rain had stopped. They stood there in silence when Siddhant said quietly, 'I think we should leave.' He took off his jacket and gave it to her as the weather was bleak and she was cold. She took his jacket slowly. Siddhant didn't say a word more and waited for her while sitting on the bike. In his wet t-shirt, almost every part of his lean torso looked visible. She went slowly to him and sat behind him. The engine of the motorbike roared and they set off for Mussoorie. Dark clouds made the weather bleaker and the same roads that they had covered before seemed different. This was the first time when Devyani realised how it feels to be around a man to whom one can be sexually attached with. She didn't know what she exactly wanted but now, even holding his shoulder gave her a shiver down the spine. His muscular torso, which was almost visible in a flimsy, wet white t-shirt made her go restless. His back would get pressed with her bosom while he rode on the curvy roads; it made her feel so tensed from inside as if there was a violent tempest that was forming inside her. They didn't speak a word on their way back to the resort. He parked the motorbike as soon as they reached and escorted her to her room and stood outside the room just to tell, 'I'll send someone for help. You might need something hot to drink,' and left. His deep, concerned voice sounded different to her today.

They didn't speak with each other for the whole evening as Devyani kept herself closed in her room and Siddhant slumbered after having as much cognac as he thought he needed.

She knew that something had happened to her. She wasn't the same girl who had arrived in India a few weeks back. She was realising with each passing moment how it feels when someone wants to get as close to someone as possible. But she also knew that it was not just the carnal pleasure that they sought from each other.

She wanted to know Siddhant as much as she knew herself. There was something about him which was making her restless. There was something behind his great reverence for her, which she could actually feel now. There was something about that lopsided grin and that mischievous, mysterious smile that she had seen on their meeting the other day. The commanding voice and intense eyes had something that was penetrating her. She lay down in her bed and thought all about him. She knew yet hid what had happened to her.

CHAPTER 13

Siddhant took a hot shower which he needed badly and read the first chapter of the book he had picked from the Udaipur bookstore three days back. He had pacified his mind and was about to sleep. The day was not bad but the events of the evening had exhausted him. At around ten at night when he was just about to hit the sack keeping his book on the writing table, the bell of the room echoed the space. He opened the door and it was Hitesh again.

'I am so sorry to disturb you again sir,' he said in his same polite voice complimented by his almost fake smile. 'But someone dropped a letter for you. A boy from the palace hotel near the lake had come to give it and told it to be of extreme importance and to hand it over to you right now,' he added and presented the letter to Siddhant. Siddhant looked at the letter with a shadow of confusion and anxiety on his face and took it from Hitesh and said, 'Thank you.' As soon as Siddhant closed the room's door, many thoughts flashed in his mind as to what could it be? He sat on the sofa near the bed and opened the note. He could still identify the perfect cursive handwriting the note was written in.

Hi Siddhant,

I am sorry I will not be able to come tomorrow for lunch. I wanted to inform you in advance. I hope you will understand. Besides, I wanted to invite you to come here for dinner tomorrow.

I will be expecting you.

Regards,

Devyani

What was this? He thought for some minutes. Forget about what was in her mind but she still wanted to meet me now? Why? And what's the point in sending a note? Couldn't she call? Once again he was in the middle of what he was trying to free his mind of. He was again at a crossroad. Will he again take a decision that he will regret? But what if the decision won't put him in any such situation to invoke guilt later? Now he had started to think the other way round. What if this time, his situation may put him in a normal condition and not a guilt-invoking one? And he had a reason to think so – no point of criticism for the evening but an invite! He although wanted to give it a thought once again this time. He switched off the lights and closed his eyes, although sleep deprived now.

Couldn't she call if she was so intact from the point of criticism? She could, any other person could, but then she was Devyani. There was nothing she would do like ordinary people. And he could not forget that she always called herself an old school who would write things down instead of speaking sometimes. And she was the only woman Siddhant had ever loved.

CHAPTER 14

Tanya and others were back to the resort by nine in the evening, disappointed and frustrated. Bleak weather had ruined their plan of trekking.

Next morning, they all set off for sightseeing and walked over the slant lanes of the mall road. Charu, Tanya and Devyani were walking together while Pallavi was with Siddhant a few meters behind them. Karan had taken Om to a nearby bar. To some extent, all of them knew that there was something brewing between Siddhant and Devyani and that's what Pallavi was more inquisitive to know about. While walking with Siddhant, amidst the casual conversation about girls in his life and boys in hers, she inquired to him about Devyani.

'How do you find her anyway?' She asked suddenly.

'Who?' He asked.

'Her of course,' she said while checking a stole outside an emporium directing her gaze towards Devyani for a moment, who was standing outside a store across the lane, diagonally to Siddhant and Pallavi. Siddhant didn't say a thing but Pallavi continued touching stoles with her palms, 'She is pretty, I mean beautiful...very beautiful, but somehow she looks fake to me. As if masquerading to be someone she's not all the time you see.' And she looked at Siddhant who now looked at Devyani who was looking at different stores across the street, standing outside the store that Charu and Tanya had stepped inside to get something. She was a confident lady and couldn't let her behaviour get affected by anything that happened inside her mind and in her personal life, he realized. Or maybe she behaved as she genuinely was–real only in his presence and a regular elite foreign return in everyone else's, he realized a moment later.

'Are you okay?' Asked Pallavi.

'Yeah I am fine...so are you buying something?' He asked looking back at Pallavi to change the topic.

'No, not my type,' replied Pallavi and they had just started to move forward again when Siddhant got alarmed.

Devyani was still wandering outside the store but now almost in the middle of the road. She looked towards the huge hills visible over the stores' canopies and upper storeys. She was witnessing the mammoth hills when suddenly she heard honking and looked down the road in the middle of which she was standing. Her eyes got wide, her eyelids and jaws got tightened and she got almost numb; fear crossed her face. She was a feet or two away from a rashly-driven XUV when she felt a hard hand around her wrist that grasped it tightly and pulled her in the direction opposite to the store that Charu had gone inside of. A car drove with over speed and within a few moments, vanished around the corner, leaving all the pedestrians shocked for a few seconds. Devyani found herself in Siddhant's arms. She was panting heavily with open mouth and looked into his eyes. He was still holding her tightly with his one hand around her waist and another on her upper back making sure she's safe. His eyebrows were down and drawn together. His face muscles were tightened, but he looked fearless and determined. Their bodies were next to each other and she could feel his chest pressing hers, his legs touching hers and she now realised that she was holding him tightly around his shoulder with both her hands.

'What happened?' Charu and Tanya came almost running out of the store they were shopping at.

Siddhant released her from his grasp although her hold was still tight around his shoulder for a moment. They separated in a moment and Siddhant replied firmly, 'Nothing, someone's car got out of control.'

'I am sorry guys it was my fault. I didn't see it coming,' said Devyani in her soft voice within a moment. She was normal now and behaved with as much civility as she always carried in her mannerisms.

'It's okay baby, these moron new drivers I tell you,' said Charu.

'Let's go to the bar guys,' said Pallavi, asking them to join Karan and Om in the bar a few meters away. They all headed towards the bar when Devyani looked at Siddhant and said, 'Thank you', in a very low voice, which could be heard by him only, to which he just nodded. She looked at his face, which was still tensed and resolute.

After visiting nearby tourist attractions for the whole day, all of them were tired and just wished to sleep after they were done with dinner. The night was sleepless for Devyani and lying in her bed before the dawn hours, she was thinking about her Ma and dad. Her mind had digressed from the present now and she thought how guilty her dad was for not understanding in time the love that her mother had had for him. How unfortunate his life had turned out to be for not knowing the value of something he had had and how he never found that again. Could it be different altogether had her dad been more caring about her mother's feeling?

Sun had still not risen fully above the sky which looked reddish from the windows of her dark room. Devyani woke up from her brief slumber and got up to look outside from her room's windowpane when she saw Siddhant was standing far in the backyard facing the rising sun. She was resolute in her mind now and wanted to go to him. She opened the door quietly and reached to him walking slowly on the gravel and then the grass and stood next to him. Everything was silent as it was too early for anyone to be up. He realized she was standing next to him in the chilly hour and still looked straight after looking at her briefly. She too looked at him and then towards the hills.

They stood there for some moments without saying anything but neither of them was either uneasy or uncomfortable in each other's presence. They looked as if their silence also meant something to each other. The white vapour was being exhaled from their mouth. The hills and the sky looked serene. And then something most unexpected happened to Siddhant when he heard a soft voice.

'I love you,' Devyani had said in her soft but not low voice, without looking at him. They both were looking in the same direction.

He couldn't believe his ears and looked at her. After a moment or two she looked at him and he turned towards her. She turned towards him and said again more confidently with glistening eyes, 'I love you.'

His face brightened and in a moment he had forgotten all the frustration swelling up inside him since the last two days.

She moved towards him slowly and touched his face with her hands for the very first time. Her soft fingers ran through his eye and nose, moved towards his cheek which she touched with her palm and then moved her fingers towards his lips. She wanted to feel him but he still showed restraint. She felt good touching his face, which was now tightened with the feeling that was passing through him. She removed her hand now and moved closer to him with her face towards him and their faces were closer than ever. She touched his face again, his lips with her fingers and with an urge to touch his lips with hers while her eyes half closed, her face reduced the distance when he said quietly, 'Are you sure you wanna do this?'

She stopped for a moment, opened her eyes fully and looked into his eyes and reduced whatever distance between their faces was now left. She touched his lips with hers. Their lips met and she felt like melting in his arms touching his lips. After a brief feeling of warmth from his lips, she moved her head back and looked at his face again, from eyes to lips.

The fervent fire of their ignited love had reached its pinnacle inside them. Siddhant circled his one hand around her waist tightly and took her head in the other and the violent storm of their feelings that had been swelling up since a few days had destroyed all the barriers they were making, willingly or unwillingly. He felt her soft lips and then felt her more, and more.

Everyone in their group knew by early morning what had brewed between Ms. Sinha and Mr. Mathur. They were all correct when they sensed something between them. The atmosphere looked more enticing to Siddhant and Devyani now, calm yet romantic, serene yet tantalising.

They were left back at the resort as their group didn't want to disturb them and they left for a nearby valley as Devyani had suggested Siddhant to.

They were sitting in the corner of the road on an edge of a slope, parking the bike on the roadside pull-off. There was nothing like before between them now.

'I just don't want it to get over,' said Devyani who was holding Siddhant's upper arm while resting her head over it with closed eyes. 'I don't wanna go from here,' she added in her soft voice.

'Me too,' said Siddhant whose elation knew no bound. He was with the girl he wished to be with at last, alone, engulfed by the surreal beauty of nature.

'Did you know that I lied to you that day that I was committed,' she looked at him and asked playfully.

'What?' he said with a grin. She laughed and then said, 'There is a guy though, but I never wanted to marry him and I haven't even met him. And that's the reason I was lost that day when you asked me about my plans here. I was here because dad wanted me to meet him so that we could know each other and could probably get married, but not so soon. Dad is in no hurry.' She then stopped and added after a few moments, 'I just wanted a simple life, with whoever I would get married to. I didn't want my dad to go through any trauma and separation. That's why I said whatever I said that night.' Her smile had faded now and she said, 'I don't know what would happen once he gets to know about us.'

'Don't worry, I will handle everything,' said Siddhant holding her face in his palms and she kissed him. She wanted him to be around her all the time now. She wanted to melt in his arms and hugged him tightly.

'I love you Siddhant, I just don't want to be an inch away from you, not even for a moment,' she said hugging him more tightly. He was caressing her back and planted a kiss on her neck while saying, 'I never knew you were so expressive my love.'

She looked at him now with her hands still encircling his back and shoulder and said, 'It is just a beginning my love, you have no idea how expressive I can get.' Her bawdy expression and enticing eyes were enough to make him crazy and he pulled her close to himself in a more alluring manner than before and all that they could hear the very next moment was the sound of their passionate expression of love they needed the most at the moment.

***

After a week, when Siddhant, Devyani and all others were back from Mussoorie and Devyani had told all about Siddhant to her dad and aunt, she was still dubious as to what would happen. She had told her dad, as she didn't want to meet any man of his choices. It was true that she knew her dad but his less expressive voice over the phone couldn't let her guess what was in his mind as he neither approved their relation nor disapproved it.

Devyani was a confident girl who was firm and determined in her life. But when it came to her personal life, she had never thought of defying her father, neither did he defy her actually. There was a nice father-daughter relationship between them but she knew that he could get stern at times. He was a bit over-possessive about Devyani as he had had a bitter experience in a relationship in his life as well and he never wanted her to go through the kind of trauma he had gone through. It was his fault and he could never come out of that guilt. And that was the reason he was overprotective about who Devyani would get married to and what she would do in her life. He wanted her to achieve her ambitions and lead a life she deserved. And for that, he could get as stern as possible and wouldn't hesitate to be as stringent as he could get. Like Devyani, he also had two different lives. For people who didn't know him, he was a stern, reserve and reticent bureaucrat but for Devyani, he was a doting yet a stringent father. In a similar way, Devyani was a girl with formal etiquettes, elite background and snobbish looks for everyone who didn't know her; but for those who knew her, she was a humble, ordinary girl who found solace in petty things and had dearth of love and compassion in life as the only person she could call her family was her father and who also never had much time to spend with her.

Mr. Sinha was as unpredictable as Siddhant Mathur was. And this was the reason she was apprehensive when his father wanted to meet Siddhant and had called him to her aunt's residence over dinner on the evening he was to land from Mumbai. He was loving, yet rigid, ambitious, and willful, and that was the reason for her worries.

Siddhant and Devyani were sitting in a restaurant when he asked her, 'Why are you so worried?'

'I am not worried, I'm anxious about what would he say.'

'And why is that? Would a mere denial make you change your mind?' He asked in his deep voice.

'No, but that would definitely upset me,' she said quietly.

'Look, I'll manage everything,' he solaced her in his assertive tone, holding her hand.

She looked at him and said quietly, 'I don't want to lose you.'

'You will not. Trust me.' His commanding voice had generated a sense of confidence in her but she still was anxious about what would happen once these two men would meet. These two men, who were the only people she had had in her life she could love.

***

The most anticipated evening had arrived and they were all settled down for the dinner on a dining table in Devyani's aunt's bungalow.

Mr. Sinha, his sister Anubha–a conceited lady who took pride in her family tree as well as her stature in the city and its political corridors–her daughter Rhea who was in her teen-age, Devyani, and Siddhant were all who were present there on the table. Siddhant had reached on time and brought with him a bottle of Cabernet Sauvignon, a bouquet of white lilies and some chocolates. He was firm when he met Devyani's father and her aunt the first time; his handshake was firm with a gracious smile on face while greeting them. He was not the one who could be nervous but Devyani indeed was, but didn't look so. It was a formal meeting with all the basic knowledge being shared with each other, which mostly involved Siddhant telling them about his background. Mr. Sinha was a sophisticated man with a white lock of hair and had deep eyes and cold voice.

They were almost done with the dinner when the domestic help was serving the desert and when Mr. Sinha asked in his cold voice, 'You know Siddhant, I wish my daughter doesn't feel resentful marrying you after some time.'

An awkward silence fell. Devyani looked tensed and looked at his dad and then Siddhant. Siddhant looked at her and assured her with his look that he can handle the situation.

'Your daughter is a smart woman Mr. Sinha I don't doubt her decision. I wonder what makes you do that,' Siddhant said wittingly.

'You think she would be able to have a lifestyle she has been brought up with?' Asked Mr. Sinha snobbishly in his cold voice.

He looked serious this time. Siddhant realized it was an attack on his integrity.

'On the other hand Mr. Sinha, I would like to give her what she has been missing all her life. You see, I believe in giving her a *life*, don't know about its style,' Siddhant said in his deep voice looking into Mr. Sinha's eyes. Devyani chuckled inwardly at his witty retort. She looked at him and had liked the way he had conveyed his message in a subtle manner. Mr. Sinha, however, didn't say anything this time and the dinner was over within half an hour and Siddhant left the house.

Next day when she met Siddhant, they were already arguing on what Mr. Sinha's take would be on this matter.

'What makes you think he'll deny Siddhant, he was quite fine last night, finer than he is normally with...'

'With people he thinks are below his social stratum?' He said upfront.

'You know it's not like that Sid, he was fine, please...and I guess he liked you,' she said politely.

'Or you *hope* he did.'

'Siddhant, I know him, and tell me why are we fighting when I haven't spoken to him on this matter.'

'Because I want to know what would you say once he *officially* tells you to walk out of my life,' he said plainly.

'And what if he doesn't?'

'Then I would believe he is not as big an elitist as he looked to me.'

'Siddhant, he is my father. Please.'

'I don't see another reason to discuss him right now.'

Silence fell and they didn't say anything for some minutes. Devyani was more uncomplaining in life. She spoke first, keeping her hand on his, which was on the table, 'Everything will be fine.'

Siddhant's face looked tightened, he looked at her; frustration was mixed with fear to lose her.

'What if he-'

'He will not,' she didn't let him complete his worried query.

They didn't say anything to each other on this matter any more and sat there.

Devyani knew her father and believed or somehow convinced herself, that he would never deny her happiness and he knew her happiness lied with no other man but Siddhant. She was here to meet Dhruv, her father's friend's son who was in New Jersey currently. She had ambitions in life but all that mattered to her now was the man sitting in front of her. She wanted her dad to know that; she was yet to know what was in his mind.

Siddhant was right to his utter misery. Mr. Sinha was as determined in his decision of defying Devyani's wish to marry Siddhant as Siddhant's determination was to marry her. Siddhant's proletarian background, his lifestyle, his future, everything didn't seem to match that of Devyani's in his opinion. More than that, he didn't find him to be compatible and a good match for his daughter and that was the topic of discussion between him and his daughter in his study where he had announced his decision to her the next morning.

'Why him? And why are you in such a hurry to marry Devyani?' These were his words when she first asked him about his opinion. She stood there without saying anything in reply to his cold words.

'I wanted you to come here so that you could meet Dhruv. I didn't know even if *he* was suitable for you. I wanted to give you time so that you could move forward in life after finishing your studies,' he added coldly. She still didn't say a thing.

'If I am not wrong, you had your own ambitions and goals, what about those? You want to ruin all of those and your life by getting married like millions of other girls in this country do?' He added.

He waited for a few seconds and then continued in his stern voice, 'How could you disappoint me like this Devyani. I never expected this from you.' She stood there.

Devyani was silent but not guilty. She was his daughter only and knew what to say and ultimately spoke firmly in her low yet resolute voice, 'Dad, my ambitions were for my happiness, but what I wish to do now is for my bigger happiness in life. Whatever I was doing, I was doing for our happiness, but I never knew I would meet Siddhant here.'

'So? You decided to marry him?' He blurted. She did have an answer but she didn't want to say anything to hurt him.

That was all that took place between Devyani Sinha and her father that day. She was not verbose but had told him clearly what her priority was now. She sounded clear to him and he didn't say anything more, as he wasn't willing to hurt her, the same way she wasn't. And this conversation had to be discussed with Siddhant as soon as she could.

Next day, at lunchtime, Siddhant had come to a restaurant near his office building to speak to Devyani about what had happened, as she hadn't told him the same over the phone.

'Well, he is quite right, isn't he?' He asked and took his medicine that his doctor had prescribed him the last year after diagnosing his high blood pressure. She raised her eyebrows, frowning. She wasn't in a mood to make a joke of her life.

'No, I mean I'm not too keen to marry so soon if he doesn't want you to,' he explained to pacify her. 'We can wait of course,' he added seriously this time. She gave him a grumbling look. He knew the next moment what she wanted. She wanted to marry him and it was not a hastily made decision. All her life, she mostly had a forlorn and gloomy atmosphere around her and now, when all that was about to be scattered, she didn't see any reason to procrastinate it. He also wanted that but had his own reasons to delay it for a while. He wanted his career to grow further.

CHAPTER 15

Around six months elapsed and the relationship between Devyani and Siddhant bloomed in all the ways it could have. The plan to marry albeit had still not bloomed. There was no hurdle to be seen in spite of Mr. Sinha's stringent reluctancy as it was the very first instance in the Sinha family when Devyani seemed too affirm to take a step back in her firm decision. She never argued with her father, she never spoke in the tonality that was not ideal for a daughter according to her. She never interrupted her dad. She did all this not because she had any fear or apprehension but because Devyani, since the age she had entered adolescence, had created a wall around her, which she never broke under any condition. A wall that always showcased her in a certain peculiar, regulated, and controlled way to everyone around her, even her immediate family that included just her father. She had made it a very intricate part of her existence to behave in a certain disciplined way and never believed in pushing the situations and matters. In her opinion, things that were destined to happen would always happen. However, it was still not clear what was about to happen. But both of them were not worried as Siddhant too thought that they had enough time to be with each other before turning into a man and wife despite becoming not only mentally and physically attached with her but also accustomed to her presence so much that he had started considering her his wife already. The extreme attraction that he had felt for her beauty and charm had become secondary to the bond that he felt was natural with her and the way she became a part of his life. She was the only woman he had loved this much apart from the natural love he had for his mother. Her presence had changed him and he had quit smoking too on her insistence. He wanted to share all this with Tanya too who once had thought that all he was mad about was her beauty and 'that's it.' However, he couldn't do so as the distance between them had increased, and the priorities too, owing to their busy work schedule. Tanya had shifted to Dubai a few months back as her seniors thought that she could do well there and it could also be good for her career. The magazine's Dubai office had put loads of responsibilities on her shoulders and they couldn't converse and share much now, as they would do earlier when they both lived in the same city. Before leaving too, her presence had decreased after the arrival of Devyani in his life.

But between what was happening and what future had stored for them, another major incident took place at around this time. Siddhant's mother it seems had the same fate as her husband had had. On a ruinous night when Siddhant was sleeping in his room, he heard the sound of glass falling on the floor, from his mother's room and when he entered the room, he found her lying on the floor enduring the excruciating pain; her eyes were dilated. She was rushed to the hospital.

However, after two days, she left Siddhant all alone. Devyani was by his side all this while and was the only one he could share his agony with. After the mourning days were over, it seemed to Siddhant that he was probably wrong; he should marry Devyani soon.

***

Devyani Sinha had a strange notion since her childhood about humans and the events that take place in everyone's life. She always believed that there is a pattern or rule god applies to humans. In that pattern of her understanding, she had derived one day while lying in her hostel bed when she was around twelve, that in this universe, since the very beginning of its creation, some people experience ups and downs, some experience all the happiness all their life, some struggle with misery till their last breath, some enjoy wealth but never achieve mental peace, and so on. However, what she thought about herself was even more disturbing to her own self and she never believed in sharing it with anyone. Now she didn't feel the need too, as the advent of Siddhant in her life, according to her, was the very first incident in her life when she had felt the vibes of positivity around her. Such was the intensity of this vibe that she felt that the time of darkness was over in her life. The time of being reclusive and surrounded by people who least cared about others–even about their parents, spouses, and children was over. She could at last break the jinx of living the life that offered her anything she could buy with wealth but could never let her open her heart and forget the derivations that she had deduced a long time back.

For Siddhant, it was more than evident that Devyani would be as firm as she always appeared to be, to spend her life with him in the years to come. Unlike his many other relationships, he was mistaken.

One afternoon, Siddhant's mobile vibrated and he ignored it for he was busy on a phone call with a client. When the call was over, he hurriedly checked his mobile for he was sure it was her; it had three missed calls. He called her back instantly. In a brief conversation, Devyani asked him to meet her in a cafe in Gurgaon and eager to meet her, he reached the cafe in DLF Cyber City before time. Sitting on the table next to the glass wall and looking outside at the front of a Chinese restaurant, he had been waiting for some fifteen minutes now and the hot caramel mocha was not helping in being a good company. Siddhant's irascibility was starting to brew when she arrived.

Late by twenty minutes, she entered the cafe in a loose-fitting navy colour belted dress that defined her waist. Her dark brown hair with light curls and navy colour of her dress made a great contrast.

She walked to him hastily with her usual perfectly calculated smile which she always made sure did not go up till her eyes making a crinkle on her face; however, it was not as genial as it had always been when she was with him. He got up, walked towards her, hugged her, and kissed her lips. Any irascibility brewing inside him–even if it was because of her–could vanish as soon as he would see her, and he knew that. As soon as they sat, the first sentence that initiated the conversation was from her.

Siddhant realised that she looked frail, dull, and pale, and he could clearly see that.

'I am sorry I am late. Hope you're doing well,' she said.

'Of course I am but what's with you,' he asked.

She hesitated for a moment and then said firmly, 'I wanted to talk about something...promise me you won't be upset and won't let it affect you.' She kept her hand on his. He got confused and kept looking at her.

'What is it?' He asked.

'See Sid, I...I have been thinking about our relationship since last many days...in fact weeks now,' she said after a brief pause and then stopped for a minute.

'Tell me what is it?' He asked.

She waited for a few seconds and completed herself and this time more firmly and to finish the sentence fast, 'I don't think we are compatible to be together Siddhant.' He didn't say anything and just looked at her for some moments before speaking.

'You are kidding right,' he asked then.

She gazed. He was sure she was not kidding and above all, he knew that she was not of that kind. Humour was never a part of her disposition.

He who was sitting on the edge of his chair to listen to her now relaxed his back and looked outside. He never had any idea it would happen or what to say exactly if any such situation ever arises.

After a minute of silence, his numbness turned into disturbance. He was not angry, he was not irritated, and didn't feel betrayed for a second. He didn't know what he felt.

'What happened? Is it your family?' He asked looking at her and again moving a bit forward.

She spoke before he could complete, 'No, no, no...it's me. Siddhant I really don't think we should be together.'

'What for?'

'I don't have a reason Siddhant. You know me. You are the only one that I have ever opened my heart to. You are the one who will never compel me to justify will you?' She said not angrily but with a bit of raised volume.

In the most dreadful situation also, a part of his inner self was getting softened with her words. Because he knew that there was nothing wrong between them even if everything was not perfect according to her. But there were questions and she knew it.

'I never said I didn't adore you. I am not saying it that I don't like you. But I can't keep it a secret either that whatever happened between us happened maybe because I never found anyone like you,' she expressed herself warily. 'Your compassion could be the reason I was attracted to you. So much that I didn't realise it could be anything but...love,' she added. He was flabbergasted. She continued, 'I think we don't have anything in common and there's no force to pull off this bond. Will you be happy with such a bond?'

He was now getting composed. Partially because his ego was placated with her consideration that will *he* be happy with such a bond. And partially because in the past six months, he had become accustomed to her presence but at the same time, this fact had also curtailed the passion which he had had for the first few days of meeting her that had incited him to get her and had made him insecure with the thought of losing her. He was disturbed but with each word she spoke, he softened, for he had instilled a sense in himself to understand the situation from her side too. But his mind betrayed him, as he was still not sure.

'What am I supposed to say?' He expressed looking at her hands, which she now kept on the table.

'I think we should move on,' she said calmly. He looked at her.

'Will it be easy?' He asked her.

'It has to be. You are a great guy Siddhant. The way you understood me and made me realise my own identity is something that I'll always be grateful to you for,' she expressed.

It was over. They both were less tensed now. He sighed and she still looked at him. There was no point in keeping a bird caged that was introduced to deliverance.

'I'll not stop you. Although I can't, still I won't persist,' he said calmly to her with a sense of liberating her. He gave a fake smile to her; only because he realised she wanted him to.

She finally looked relieved. The waiter arrived and broke the silence asking them what they will have.

'Two vanilla latte with chicken and mushroom pie,' she told to the waiter and said to Siddhant smilingly after the waiter left, 'I'll have what you were having the first time we met after the party.'

'So you're celebrating the breakup,' he expressed with a restrained smile.

'Siddhant...'

'I am not saying anything,' he expressed.

'You know I always knew you will understand me. I know you are smiling right now just to make me feel comfortable but you will realise in the time to come that it was good for both of us,' she explained herself. He gazed at her with a faded smile and they sat without saying anything for some moments. He then spoke.

'So, Devyani Sinha, you are a free bird now. What are you up to? Back to London or getting married or traveling the world,' he asked after a while.

'Oh nothing yet. I'm just going to relax. It's the first time I am feeling I have my own time,' she said. She looked happy.

'But you are definitely going to be with someone.' His insecurity was overtaking his calmness.

'That's not important. Yet it is,' she said. 'I don't know if he will understand me as you do,' she pondered without looking at him. He didn't say a thing. Their order had arrived.

She added carefully when the waiter left, 'And I think we shouldn't be in touch Siddhant.' He looked at her. Not because he had thought they would be in touch but because she had mentioned what he had yet not started to think about.

'Don't misunderstand me but I don't want you to be disturbed, or our lives to be disturbed because of this. You see it will be difficult if I am married and still in touch with you,' she added and they both gazed at each other. He then nodded and just said, 'Hmm.' They ate their lunch.

After half an hour or so, they decided to leave–the cafe, their relationship, and each other, forever.

Outside the cafe where the sun was setting now and the sky looked painted with the hues of red, orange and blue, they were about to say goodbye for they never knew if they would ever meet again.

'So, here we are. It all seems to be so...I don't know,' she said looking at him.

'Hmm,' he said looking at her with utmost affection but with no sign of weakness.

'How will you remember me in life Siddhant?' She asked looking into his deep dark eyes. The whole surrounding, which had many people, seemed to be quiet to him. The resplendent sky stretched over the skyscrapers and the glass buildings surrounding them reflected on the other buildings' glass walls as well as in their eyes.

'As a soul unscarred from world's harshness,' he said quietly.

She smiled and replied, 'I will always remember you as a man I had deep respect for.' They smiled and then she left after kissing him on his cheek and hugging him. He saw her walking away in her beige colour pumps towards her car till she reached near it to get into it. She turned back and waved her hand with a usual smile before getting into her BMW. She was far now. He waved his hands and smiled, glassy eyed. She got inside the car and he turned his back and walked towards his car, silent and numb.

He had lied. He will always remember her as the fragrance of marigold flowers, which he had sensed for a very brief time and will never forget.

CHAPTER 16

The showdown at a cafe in Gurgaon was surprisingly not as depressing as Siddhant would have thought had he foreseen any such event. He was stronger than he had thought, he realised. However, it was a bit disturbing. The reason being, his seriousness for the relationship that he anticipated would transform into a conjugal one. But how could it be efficacious for whole life out of which he had lived only twenty-four years and out of which he had spent only a few months with her, even lesser than many of his previous relationships?

Days elapsed with the arrival of some lazy mornings, sleepless nights, fatigued afternoons, and a disturbed routine to follow. The day after his meeting with Devyani, he practiced the same routine of getting up at sunrise, going for jogging, having breakfast, and then leaving for office. However, the incontrovertible thoughts kept on running in his mind, which he thought were normal and which he would overcome in the days to come. Getting up in the morning to see her messages and calling her on his way to the office were being missed. The calls from her in the afternoon–which were reduced in number from the initial phase of the relationship to the last week of it–were not missed much though. At nights however, Siddhant preferred spending time with his friends after he realized that his home was becoming haunted after his mother's absence from the house and Devyani's absence from his life. But he knew that it was transient. He was realising that things were getting back to normal.

By the end of the month, the quarterly assessment at the agency added a new thing to his life. His promotion to a senior profile was nothing less than a bolt from the blue and an addition to his finances with a handsome increment was one of the events which he thought would turn some new pages in his life.

He was more relieved. However, not because of the rank and increment, but because of the new roles and responsibilities that he was now qualified to look into. It will increase his working hours and lessen the time he had had in his personal life. The most disturbing habit that he thought he was developing would vanish with this new change, he thought. The habit was really disturbing him actually.

After two weeks of ending the relationship–this is what he called it rather than consent on her decision–he had now started seeing his mobile phone every now and then. Even he did not realise what hormonal misbalance had persuaded his mind to think that there might be a text message or any other type of message from DS, the name he had saved for Devyani in his phone. This habit started taking shape one fine morning when he got a call from an unknown number. On the morning of the fifteenth day of his confrontation with Devyani, while he was taking shower after jogging, he realised that he had heard his phone ringing. He turned off the shower and stood still with his hand in his hair with which he was applying shampoo on his head, and tried to listen. There was nothing. After five minutes or so when he was rubbing himself dry, he again heard his phone ringing and this time it was clear. Coming out in his room, he took his phone to find out that there was a call from an unknown number and he received the call.

'Hello,' he said.

'Hello,' a soft female voice replied from the other side.

His heart skipped a beat although he knew that it was not the voice he had thought it was. It was less soft with that eloquence missing.

'Is that Ashish?' She asked.

'No it's Siddhant,' he replied, which he instantly thought was needless to tell yet his mind had betrayed him and he had told his name without a reason, with an expectation which even he was unaware of.

'Oh, it's wrong number then, sorry,' the girl said and hung up the phone.

He stood there with the phone in his hand with a feeling he thought was that of resentment, which he was unable to discover why he felt. He checked the call log and realised that there was a missed call from the same number he had just now received for only four seconds, five minutes ago. It was a normal occurrence he thought again and then started getting ready for the office. On that morning while sitting on his desk, he didn't realise why all of a sudden he felt an urge to check his phone for any message from DS. At first, he thought it was just an after-effect of the wrong number he had received in the morning but when it happened three more times till the afternoon, he had already started getting vexed vibes. He had checked his phone four times in total till two in the afternoon just to see if there would be any text from *her*. There was nothing. He realised on the same afternoon that it is quite juvenile of him to practice such a thing. However, this habit didn't vanish. In his disturbed sleep, he would quite often check his phone at midnight or even at hours before dawn. He was still assertive that it would be over with time and especially with the occurrence of any crucial event in the upcoming days, like a jaunt in the hills where he found solace, or something else.

The much needed and favoured beam of serendipity however came through the mist of gloom in the form of a sudden advancement in his professional life. With a step up in his finances and his profile to the level of seniority, he thought that nothing is missing and things would go down well with him soon. Basically everything was going to be good according to him and was getting better with every passing day. He thought it would all be over now; however, it was just a mirage his mind had begun to create and which was going to last for only next few months.

An office party was organized at a plush cafe and lounge in Connaught Place after a few months from the day of announcement of the increments and promotions. In the glittering lights of the bar and amidst the cacophonous music of the live performance of a rock band to which many were dancing, Siddhant was sitting on a barstool at the bar counter. He was not talking much to anyone since the evening and after giving a fair impression with a corporate smile to his colleagues to convey that he was as normal as they were, he sat alone and was having his third bourbon and wasn't bothered about the loud music. With the departure of almost everyone he had a good bond with in his life, alcohol had entered like a loyal life partner, always there when he was in need. It was around nine when most of the office people packed the lounge; Siddhant was not leaving despite a desperate will, in his attempt to look and behave as normal as he aspired to be. Also, he thought that the torment brewing in his mind could only be subdued by involving himself in ear-splitting places packed with as many people and serving as many types of whiskies as possible. While he was gulping down his bourbon, a girl arrived and sat beside him. He just took a glance and ordered another bourbon for himself while she ordered absinthe. Siddhant heard her as she was just a few inches away and her voice seemed to be loud and clear with a pinch of huskiness. He looked at her once again and they smiled at each other this time. She was wearing a maroon above knee length dress. She wore matching stilettos and beige handbag. Her hair looked glossy in the lights of the bar. She was dusky, pretty, and looked a nice, decent girl with beautiful lips.

'I'm Trisha,' she initiated the conversation.

'Siddhant,' replied Siddhant with a smile.

In the next half an hour, they were at the door of the room of a hotel they had decided to go to. As soon as the door was locked, they unchained their vigour while stripping each other naked fiercely. Siddhant held her tightly from her back and sat on the edge of the bed while she sat on his lap. He opened the chain of her dress and removed it in no time while kissing her neck. In the blink of an eye, he removed her pink strapless bra which she was wearing under her maroon dress and begun brushing his lips on her bosom while strengthening his hold on her back from one hand and rubbing her rounded rear from over her seamless panty which had lace panel, from the other. She had removed his polo shirt by now, pushed him on the bed and had started kissing his chest vigorously. While he caressed her round and dusky breasts, which were hanging downwards, she suddenly reached his left nipple and bit it lightly, to which he promptly reacted and insisted 'don't do that' in a low yet stern voice. She moved towards his neck and was getting more aroused. Siddhant now lay down still, without reciprocating. He all of a sudden found himself to be out of this engagement now. The wrong chords were struck out of nowhere. It was the second time when she reached his nipple–this time the right one–and kissed it when his disturbed cognition overtook the passion he was feeling a few minutes back. With a relentless push on her shoulder, she found herself on the other side of the bed. The push was not the part of the coupling, which she realised both by the intensity of it and his annoyance. He had yelled while getting up and thrusting her–'I SAID DON'T DO THAT.'

'What the fuck is this,' she bellowed after sinking in what had just now happened, with her hand on her breast in fear and amazement.

Siddhant regained his senses. 'I am sorry,' he apologised and tried to help her get up. 'Look I am...I am outta my mind. I shouldn't have been here'.

She looked at him for a second and rebuked, 'You jerk'. She collected her clothes from the floor hurriedly and dressed herself up.

'Should I drop you somewhere?' He said sitting on the edge of the bed now.

She looked at him even more surprisingly this time and then her expression transformed into that of disgust. She left the room immediately carrying her beige handbag.

Siddhant sat there. He, by now had inferred one more thing about life. He had understood that there was nothing like a differentiated existence of personal and professional life. It was all one. No one could justify any of the activities of life by saying that certain behaviour subjected by personal life won't have any potent outcome in professional life or vice versa. Life is one no matter if you have a professional side of it or academic side of it or 'no activity' side of it; it all affects you. And if any aspect of life is disturbed–especially the personal one–life would envisage some bizarre, erratic, vexed, or dispiriting repercussions.

He had discovered one more thing today, that what he kept ignoring inside himself calling it a transient ordeal was not a mere memory. It had become a very part of himself.

CHAPTER 17

With the number of people decreasing in Siddhant's life, the count of whisky increased substantially. Prostitutes, one-night stands, unprofessionalism at work, and uncalled brawls both at the workplace and in his personal life were now becoming a part of his very existence. He was running away from his own identity, which was connected with Devyani and didn't allow himself to feel close enough to anyone to express his vulnerability. He surrounded himself with people who were unknown to him and were least interested in his well-being. The weekends were still his biggest enemies even after six months and he didn't stop to rest or to keep his mind unoccupied to think over anything that he was hiding from. His health deteriorated enormously with over-consumption of alcohol and with each passing day, his condition worsened. According to him, he was successfully going away from her, but in his hiding, he was accumulating the disturbance, which ultimately resulted in dementia.

One evening, while sitting in a bar at late night, he came across a pretty girl who accompanied him to his apartment where he looked very disturbed sitting on the couch while she was in the kitchen to get herself and him some water. She sat beside him, kept the glasses on the table and asked him a personal question, something he had avoided since last many months so as to escape his helplessness and to avoid Devyani.

'Are you okay? It seems you are going through some problem,' she asked politely with concern but never expected a very detailed answer. But he realised that someone was really caring for him and still was there when he felt that he was all alone in the world and in his apartment. He was of course drunk; he couldn't be blamed for it on being asked by a girl who was there only for one night.

'She left me,' he uttered quietly without looking at her.

'Sorry?'

'She left me,' he said and looked at her with his shiny red eyes. 'She left me. What would I do?' He asked looking into her eyes.

'Your girlfriend?' She asked out of courtesy, carefully now.

'She left me. She promised me she would never. We had promised to marry, to have children, to go on a honeymoon... and then a second honeymoon...and then to have a grand golden jubilee and then...to die together.' He had expressed himself and stopped.

He continued after a pause, looking at the wall of his house now. 'Everything is gone. I am finished.' He wept now as if he realised after six months that she was finally gone. His eyes looked wide.

'Okay,' she said and tried to pacify him at last by holding his shoulders. 'Everything will be fine. Let's go to the bedroom. You need rest.' And she was taken aback the next moment when he all of a sudden sat on his knees in front of her and held her with both his hands and expressed himself more overtly.

'Why would I rest? What rest would I do? She meant everything to me and she left me,' he almost shouted. 'I loved her more than anything else and she suddenly left me. What is left for me now, tell me? Tell me what's left? Who should I live for now? who should I work for now? who should I rest for now? I don't know what I am now. I am losing myself. I am losing my mind,' he added. 'Can you bring her back? Will she never come back?' He asked looking at her intensely in a high-pitched voice. She was all alone with him in his quiet apartment and was terrified now.

'You are hurting me,' she yelled.

He kept gazing at her for some moments and then left her suddenly, stood up, and moved backwards. 'I am going mad. I am going mad,' he said quietly and then laughed hysterically.

'Oh now I am going mad for you. I am mad now, I know. I know. And I will never find peace anywhere in this world. And I know it more than anything else,' he said in a high-pitched voice. 'I was a fucking fool to let you go. I was an asshole to control and hide my emotions.' His laughter transformed into distress and he sat on his knees now.

She stood up now and was horror-struck as she couldn't gather the courage to move towards the door and unlock it as he was sitting on the way to it. He looked at her after a minute, still sitting on his knees. His eyes were red and wet and looked chilling to her.

'Who are you?' He asked very surprisingly now as if he was stunned by the presence of a stranger in his house.

'Please let me go,' she almost cried now. He stood up.

'Don't cry don't cry. I don't know how...how come you arrived here,' he said and then asked her suddenly, 'How come you arrived?' He then said himself, 'You must have gone astray. Yes,' he said it sincerely now, with lack of sense, and looked at the floor.

'You should go,' he said and then suddenly asked looking at her, 'You have a lover?'

She didn't say anything and was pressing her calves against the couch behind her.

'He must be waiting. Don't cry don't cry. You should go.' He walked towards the door and opened it for her and looked at her. His eyes looked ghastly and sick. She walked very carefully with her handbag pressed against her chest in a defensive body language.

'Go go go go go fast,' he whispered and she crossed the door in extreme fear and ran towards the staircase to avoid waiting for the elevator. He shut the door behind her.

He walked silently and sat on the couch where the girl was sitting a few minutes back. He had finally encountered the phantom that had been stalking him since last six months. He was already heavily drunk but walked to the cabinet and took the Paul John single malt bottle out of it. He took the ice out of the freezer and made himself a drink. He contemplated over something and then gulped down the drink.

He uttered then, 'What would she be doing right now?'

His head had started to ache badly now and with extreme dizziness, he couldn't control his body and fell on the couch and hovered in the thoughts as to what she must be doing right now? Where was she? Where was he? What time of the day it was? How long has it been since she had left him? How old he was? And whether he was dead or alive? If he was old enough to die and was breathing his last in his old age? Or he had been just dreaming of all these events of the past year? But the very next moment he realised that Devyani was not a dream. She was real. Levitating in thoughts as if floating in the endless space, he was still now.

***

The next morning brought new air for him. It was Sunday and he got up at around twelve in the afternoon. Despite being drunk the last night, he remembered everything and pondered over it for half an hour, still lying in the same position on the couch. The doorbell rang and he opened the door to find the maid standing there.

'Where were you *bhaiya?* I've come and gone twice since morning,' complained the maid and walked inside and then to the kitchen after picking the glasses from the table. She was the only person whose presence had been constant in his life and who had been coming since his mother was here.

He took a long shower and had a medicine after that. Until evening, he was thinking about last night and whether he was really losing his mind. In the garden cum park of his society, he was sitting on a bench in the evening, all alone, seeing the kids playing and swaying on the swings. Some teenagers and adults were playing badminton on the other side of the park. He was still thinking about how he is going to recover from what he had encountered finally. His head still ached. He was terrified of his behaviour last night and he felt not only sorry for the poor girl but also guilty and ashamed. He came out of his thought with a thud on the ground and a loud wailing of a small kid who had fallen from the swing. He kept sitting there without moving to help the kid and thought if someone would come and help the poor kid when his mother, who was standing away, talking with another woman, came running to him.

She consoled and caressed him. She took the kid in her lap and was brushing his knees and waist, which were hurt and smeared with mud.

'Nothing happened my baby. Mamma is here, you don't need to worry,' she convinced him, adored him, and hugged him.

She stood up after a few moments with him still hugging her and crying, and walked towards their home. She looked tensed although the kid wasn't hurt that much. It was the motherly affection that had made her anxious and worried while consoling him. And they disappeared inside the building on the right hand of the bench on which he was sitting.

Love was incurable and unavoidable. Call it a disease or a blessing he thought. And above all, one couldn't escape from it. There were forms of love that were always attached to man from birth till death. He also had some, even if the people were not around. He had no explanation to console or convince himself but he decided that his mind was not going to be controlled by the madness anymore. With the sinking sun, he had many thoughts going on in his mind. He had to live, and he had to live scarred yet normally. He stood up and before anything else walked slowly towards the grocery store; he felt famished and wanted to eat something.

The showdown at Gurgaon had left him scarred for the next thirteen years.

CHAPTER 18

Only a few days were left for Rhea's wedding and the whole palace hotel glittered with lights; merriment was in the air. The palace's chief dome and other small ones shone with the lights and décor that was put up for the wedding. Pillars of all the archways were woven with flowers and lights along with the resplendent shades of silks draped around the pillars. The regal wedding suited the family's stratum.

The colossal garden–in which all the décor and arrangements were glittering in lights after sunset–had guests who could be seen sitting on tables that were set in the garden sporadically. Siddhant was, however, waiting for Devyani with eagerness standing near one of the many beautiful fountains in the garden. Someone told him when he enquired about her that she still was inside the palace.

After a few minutes, he saw her walking down the boulevard towards him where he was sitting alone in the garden.

'Thanks for coming Siddhant,' she said when she reached him. He smiled.

'I had to come. I had to talk to you about the evening and something else too,' he expressed.

'Of course, tell me,' she said. And before he could say a word, a man arrived to greet him.

'So he is the man you wanted me to meet,' said the man cheerfully. A man in his late thirties, taller than Siddhant, looked decent and charming in his British cut navy coloured suit.

Devyani, looking surprised at his sudden appearance, expressed happily, 'Yes, he is the one I was talking about.'

'Well it's my pleasure,' expressed the man and extended his hand towards Siddhant while adding jovially, 'I am Robin Shah, proud husband of this beautiful lady here.'

Siddhant took his hand and said, 'Siddhant Mathur.' That's all that he could say with a restrained smile.

'I know I am disturbing the old friends but this lady is in much demand here I guess and everyone at the dinner table is looking for her, so I would request you, mister Mathur to join us please,' Robin expressed his wish.

'Of course,' said Siddhant quietly and they walked down the dining hall, which was inside the palace across the archway.

The colossal dining hall which could have been the place of some royal meetings in the past had a long table set with numerous chairs, alluring floral arrangements that included white and pink carnation centerpieces, and traditional candle holders over it. The towering walls of the hall had traditional stone carving with exquisite fresco artwork and *jharokhas*–overhanging closed balconies–which looked regal in all senses. The lofty ceiling of the hall had stupendous chandeliers that glistened the ambience.

On the table sat Siddhant across Devyani who was beside Robin on one side and Rhea on the other. While the dinner was being served, the conversation was going on. However, Siddhant was least interested and most of the time was nonchalant. After the dinner was over and Robin was busy with other guests and men, Devyani and Siddhant were sitting in the open lawn of the palace with no one around them.

'When did you get married?' He asked casually after a while.

'Six years ago,' she said calmly.

'Why? I mean sorry. But...why did you ask me to come today? To tell this? To...-'

'I just wanted you to meet him. Nothing special,' she said and he kept looking at her. 'And Siddhant, I want you also to move on. I can see that...what I did...or what happened between us really affected you beyond what I could foresee. But now, all I want is to see you happy with someone,' she added.

'So you wanted me to come and tell me that you're married now and sleeping with someone else? And I should too? Because the good, elite, and beautiful Devyani Sinha can't see me like this? And what if I love you Mrs. Whatsoever that man is?' He said all that in one go firmly, without realising the contraction on her face. She sat still and looked like a blind being seeing the ground of the lawn. Some minutes elapsed.

'It's good. It's good Devyani. It's good that I said all this. And please don't mind but I have to tell all this...I mean I had to,' he said. She looked discomposed and unsettled now. Some moments passed before he spoke again.

'Okay. Fine. I am perfect. And I am sorry. I never meant to hurt you Devyani and you know it,' he said calmly and his voice was full of affection and care for her now. She looked at him now.

'Tell me what you want Devyani. I will do whatever it takes,' he said calmly.

'Just promise me you are going to be happy Siddhant,' she requested calmly now. It irked him once again.

'Are you coming back in my life?' He asked boldly on her request of promise.

'What are you saying Siddhant. You know my answer. I am a married woman,' she grunted and looked down at the lawn pavement. He didn't say a word. The crickets chirping could be heard from the lawn's farthest corner, which had a massive mangrove. After a few moments, when it seemed to Siddhant that they both had nothing to say, she spoke very calmly in her articulated voice which she had regained now but it was still filled with utmost affection and more than that, it seemed to Siddhant, compassion for him.

'Till the time we are here, I want to relive the moments of happiness that I once lived with you. With a promise that there will be no arguments, no questions, no promises.' She was now looking at him with her shining, moist eyes. She looked like the same old Devyani who once had asked him to take her to her mother's house in the hills and he was once again as helpless and vulnerable as he was back then.

He looked at her with no smile but his countenance, his deep voice, as well his eyes exhibited enormous confidence now.

'Will you give these days of your life to me?' He asked her in the reciprocation of her question. What she had asked for were the happy moments engulfed with all the wedding gait and his companionship. What he had asked was the time in which she was to be with him like the girl he had known. They had asked each other without knowing what they had asked for from each other. She contemplated looking at him for a moment and then uttered in her soft but firm voice, 'Yes.'

VOLUME 2

CHAPTER 19

She tried to read with squinted eyes sitting on the table, which was in the center of the cafe at around one in the afternoon when he arrived. She didn't notice when he came and with a loving smile on his face for her, he settled down.

'Oh you are here,' she said smilingly when noticed him.

'I saw you cursing the book,' he joked.

'Oh I forgot to put on my lenses before coming,' she grumbled.

He swayed his head teasing her and mocked, 'So much hurry Miss Devyani. Forgot the lenses, eached here before time.'

'Come on Siddhant. I just wanted to read this book. I was too curious,' she replied.

'Okay okay, can we have something first? We'll deal with this shit later,' he answered, to which she gave him a loving smile as if she were looking at a cute toddler.

They ordered lunch and he was more than curious to know more about her life and everything else that she had had to tell him about the last thirteen years.

'Don't you think everyone's gonna look for you?' He asked first, to know how much time she had had.

'I told them I'll be in a local bazaar for some shopping,' she replied. 'And besides, they're not as fond of me as you think they are. They have their own people, especially today when a hell lot of people flocked the palace,' she added. She was so different at this moment he thought. Not a fake person like many perceived her to be. No pretentious smile and no use of words that represented her as an heiress of another class. She was as familiar as she was the last time, thirteen years ago, minus the relationship he had shared with her back then.

'What about your husband?' He asked.

'He had his flight this morning. Some priorities.'

'How did you meet him?' He asked her directly while starting to eat lunch, which had arrived.

'He was dad's friend's son,' she answered calmly.

'And what happened to that man...' he asked. She gazed and realised he had asked about Dhruv, whom her father wanted her to consider for marriage back then.

'Dhruv? I never met him' she told and then added, 'Dad too never asked.'

'So did *he* ask you to marry him...I mean your husband?' He asked and drank water.

'Oh Siddhant. Robin is a great man. I was never forced to marry him,' she answered positively.

He didn't say anything and again changed the topic. 'I didn't ask you by the way. Did you start something of your own?'

'No,' she said and drank some water. Never wanted to once I got married. I was happy the way life has been since then,' she added.

After lunch, they sat in a cafe where they could spend some time when she asked him about anyone in his life again. This time, more than asking, she wanted to know the answer. Siddhant couldn't lie.

'I've had people in my life. But no one was destined to stay forever.'

'Because you never wanted them to?' She snapped. He kept silent while half-heartedly turning the pages of the book she was carrying. He then handed the book to her to avoid the look on her face.

'I am not carrying my glasses,' she expressed.

'Oh, I'll read it for you,' he replied, as he didn't want the conversation to wander towards a point where it would upset her and would end with her departure.

He read the book for her for the next half an hour, which she listened with attention for the story and affection for him. She looked at him while his lips moved with full attention in the book.

He looked so incorrupt and blameless she thought. Nobody could tell looking at him right now how distraught his life could have been all these years, nobody could see how big a sin I had committed against this man who is sitting here for my happiness without blaming me even for a second for what I did to him, she thought. She had never seen a man in her life who was so responsive to her feelings; her love, her misery, her fears, her pleasure.

And then he finished the chapter of the book and looked at her while turning the page only to see her dazzled face.

'What?' He asked.

'Nothing. This book ...is really great,' she answered hiding what she was thinking.

He smiled and she said, 'I want to go somewhere. I want to sit away from these people. Not the palace. Somewhere we can sit peacefully.'

After a few minutes of taxi ride, they were at the hotel Siddhant was staying at. It looked like a three start hotel she thought where she walked with him via the foyer towards the elevator and went up to the first floor. He opened the door for her. While she entered and walked towards the balcony and he locked the door. She looked across the balcony and found the simplicity of the view relieving. 'Nice place,' she said. She walked inside and sat on the chair.

'You want something?' He asked.

'Oh no Siddhant. This is all that I wanted,' she said in a relieving tone still looking outside towards the road and listening to the roars of the vehicles, feeling the calmness of the room and the dying afternoon with sunlight coming inside the room. The room was neither too big nor too small. All that it had as furniture was a bed with side tables, a wardrobe, a writing table, and two chairs with the table.

'Are you happy Devyani?' He sat on the chair opposite her and asked after some moments.

She stayed silent for a moment as usual and then replied calmly, 'Why does one always has to be happy or sad. I am neither of those. But I have nothing to worry about. I have everything, my home, a caring husband. And peace.'

He stood up and made a call to the room service to order tea and again sat opposite her.

'I am becoming so boring *yaar*. I am upsetting you as well with my disgust' she joked now fearing his seriousness. He smiled.

'Robin always tells me I am a big bore.'

'Still he married you,' he snapped calmly.

'Marriage is not about that Siddhant. You know that there are a hell lot of other things. He is a good friend and a loving person.' He looked least interested in listening to it and she sensed it. She moved forward and kept her hand on his now.

'I always knew that I had wronged you Siddhant,' she said and her voice was real now, without any pretentiousness in it. He also looked at her now. Her deep eyes were apologetic although he never blamed her. He felt an uncontrollable urge to make love to her, which was more driven by the wish to get closer to her than to satiate the bodily needs.

'I never blamed you. And you don't need to tell that ever again either to me or to yourself,' he requested sensibly.

'I always knew it Siddhant,' she said and suddenly, changed the topic saying, 'By the way, I want to take a nap here. May I?' She looked relieved now after the apology.

'Of course.'

She stood up and went inside the washroom and when came, she made a call to room service to cancel the order of tea without asking him which he liked and which was surprising to him. He was developing a hope that had died years ago. She looked at him now and said casually while removing her sandals, 'Come sit on the bed *na.*' She wore jeans and a top with a green trench coat over it.

On the bed, she lay down with her face towards him and closed her eyes yet talked.

'I feel so comfortable here, away from those buzzing idiots,' she expressed.

'Will you come again to meet once we leave the city,' he asked.

'No,' she said very normally without opening her eyes.

'Why?' he asked complainingly but lying with ease, looking at her.

'Because I don't want the phantom of the past to horrify you.'

He didn't say anything to her. He had nothing to say for now and just wanted to live the moment with her on his bed, lying with her.

'I want to go for a boat ride in the evening,' she then said.

'Okay,' he said and then added quietly after a brief pause, 'Did you ever try to find...or contact me?' She didn't say anything although he wasn't sure if the reason was her sleep or she didn't want to disappoint him. He kept looking at her.

***

She took a nap for an hour while he looked at her and then they freshened up and headed towards the famous lake of the city for boating.

Amidst multiple boats riding over the not so clean but calm water of the lake, they were the only two on theirs. The sun was setting and the cold breeze made the surrounding beatific. People walking on the boulevard alongside the lake and the camels with people on their backs looked small and scenic. She was sitting beside him and in such beautiful surroundings, he felt like it wasn't a reality.

'It reminds me of my gondola ride in Venice. But it's much better here,' she said. 'It is so good to be here. Except for this rose fragrance. It would have been perfect had it been marigold,' she said sitting relaxed in the boat, looking in all the directions. 'I love marigolds that bloom in the monsoon, and their aroma,' she added. He didn't say anything and just looked at her.

She suddenly kept her hand on his while looking at the setting sun. 'Setting sun always brings peace to me,' she said. Their faces were just an inch away when she looked at him in his eyes. His deep eyes always said more than his mouth could. She touched his face with her hands but he didn't move. She kept on looking at his face and moved a bit forward and only when she could move further, her phone rang and she realised what was she up to.

She moved back and waited for a few seconds before taking her phone out of her bag.

'Hello,' she was back with her articulated voice balanced with softness and elegance. 'I was out for some shopping honey,' she replied to someone who he realised was her husband. 'That's great. I'll be waiting honey. Love you,' she added. She hung up the phone and looked at him who was now looking at the bank of the lake as the boatman was parking the boat at its place at the bank. He held her hand and helped her get out of the boat and they walked towards the boulevard.

'When is he coming?' He asked only to know what went inside her mind while they walked, as she was quiet.

'Tomorrow morning...Siddhant I am so sorry-'

'It's okay Devyani,' he said very calmly before she could complete herself. 'It happens. And I don't want it to disturb our companionship for the next few days okay?' He added and smiled, taking her hands in his. She felt comfortable and smiled and they walked again.

'And I always thought you hated sunsets,' he added while walking.

'No way. In fact I hate sunrise. It takes away all the beauty and peace that night gives us,' she replied. *"What if the dead silence of nights doesn't let one sleep?"* was what he wanted to ask but didn't. They walked and he remembered how they once stood on the edge of the cottage garden when she had said the words of her heart while the sun was rising; he didn't say anything about it though.

'Dinner at my place or somewhere?' He asked then.

'We can have somewhere in the city.'

The evening passed smoothly and they had dinner at a restaurant, which was not too far from the palace. After the dinner was over and he had paid the bill, they sat there for some time when she said, 'I don't know if I'll be coming tomorrow.' Her voice was not usual. She sounded unenthusiastic and he didn't reply for some moments.

'Come only if you can. Don't worry about me and don't get upset.' He smiled and tried to comfort her keeping his hand on hers, which comforted her and she smiled, but still looked dissatisfied.

After some minutes, he booked a cab and outside the restaurant, they waited for it. The streets were not so busy here and under the streetlights, they were standing on the sidewalk.

'I know the day was not too happening for you but I am thankful you came,' he said happily.

'It was great Siddhant. And I don't know after how long I have felt so...natural and free,' she expressed in a low voice. 'Will you be waiting for me tomorrow?', she then added after a minute of silence.

'Of course I will,' he assured.

'Even after knowing I am not sure.'

'Yes.'

She looked at him and then the cab arrived. She hugged him and he smiled. There was no complaint on his face she realised. She got inside the cab and the cab rode on the road to vanish after some moments. He stood there.

He had been hiding his disgust for many hours now. He was disgusted that she still felt she belonged to her husband and not him, that she found it to be a sin to come near him, and more than that, because he could not let her know how unacceptable it was for him that she was not sure of coming tomorrow because of her husband, that he could not show her how he felt when she controlled her feelings on the boat. Only if he hadn't promised her that he would not push his limits. But he had time to make her realise it the other way. That it was never right for them to live like this and they were meant to be together. He will wait.

CHAPTER 20

Robin Shah was a loving husband who was away from the ups and downs of life since his childhood. Hailing from a Mumbai-based business family, he never had anything too metamorphic in his life that could make him either overwhelmed or over distraught like Siddhant Mathur. Robin's father was a reputed man much revered in the society in which Mr. Sinha was much keen to find a suitable match for her daughter after the winter in which Devyani had told Siddhant they were not the right match. Ved Prakash Shah was a businessman who owned a media house and a textile mill. His son Robin was all that he could become as an heir apparent to Shah industries who lacked both the will to expand his father's business as well as the wish to add new achievements to his surname. For the type of girl Devyani was in her twenties–a beautiful maiden with an affluent background, well educated from a college in London, and an heiress of her father's wealth–many eligible men wanted her as a wife; not for the love for her beauty though. In the society of such a class, affluence, and influence, finding a match with a type of combination she possessed was not impossible but still rare to find. Many of the gentlemen were more than interested in making her their wife with whom they could take their family name further, beget children, and walk hand in hand to flaunt her as a beautiful shining trophy they had won. Amongst such men, Robin had been an odd choice as per Mr. Sinha.

However, Devyani had chosen him and Mr. Sinha couldn't deny. He had no major reason too, as even after having no wish to mint limitless money, Robin was a good match for his daughter. After a brief meeting at a party in Delhi, Devyani met Robin many times on his insistence and found him to be a genuine gentleman. One reason that could have been behind Devyani's decision to marry him could be the fact that she sensed that he was least interested in flaunting her as his achievement and was caring for her and liked her for what she was without her surname. After so many years of their marriage, it was clear that she was right in her assessment; he was neither a henpecked husband nor a controlling one. In fact, he was a loving husband who always stood by her side when she needed him, although she rarely asked for it. It was the first time in years when he wanted to be with his wife and hence had come to Udaipur; it was also the first time when *she* was away and not around him. Devyani, for a strong lady she was, had always been a support to her husband. More than support, it was Robin's dependency on Devyani, which compelled him to be there in Udaipur. From the smallest need at home to emotional support, she was always the one to be seen stood by him. From his anti-anxiety pills to the important business documents that he kept in home or office, she was always there when he needed help. It was Devyani's magnanimous nature that had made him more dependent on her and she was always more than happy to be with him with all her love and care despite his drinking habits in the initial few months of the conjugal relation. He very well knew that she was a perfect wife one could get. He never asked her to know what was it like from her point of view. Not that he never wanted to actually, but her sheer happiness with him with the absence of even a single complain since their wedding day had assured it to him how happy she was with him. He was not intact from the idiosyncratic tenet of many men towards their wives and had deduced that the absence of complaints made them a perfect couple; but he loved her.

***

For the last six years since the surname Sinha had turned into Shah, Devyani–for better or worse– had nothing much to do that could be called concrete on the part of a lady who once had professional ambitions. She was alright being a housewife. After their return from their honeymoon in Florence, she had thought that life would take a certain course but soon after her return, she realised that nothing could be done. Reason being, her keen interest in staying at home rather than getting occupied in any work. She had renounced her ambition of becoming a fine artist and all that she found most peaceful was to be at home and manage the household–from planting the garden that that she had redesigned according to her likes, to looking after the household chores, or travelling to different cities and keep experimenting with the interiors, especially the living area of her home with the handpicked antiques from across the world. After her marriage, she had designed the interiors of the villa, which was now her home and she kept on doing it after every six-month break. All the decor–recliners, wall plates, fireplace, chandeliers, sofas, figurines, mirrors, paintings, carpets and every other element would be replaced half yearly with a new one which would be in extreme contrast with the last one. All this was done to appeal to the aesthetic sense she had had but more than that, she liked to do this as it would help her pass her time and the whole process would take her to cities, bazaars, and different artifact collectors. But one more reason, and the major one, was that she liked to show to the world her aesthetic sense, her deep knowledge of art, design, beauty, and her sheer colossal lifestyle. It was especially for the in-laws she had had–two sisters-in-law Barkha and Hamsini, who were cousins of Robin, and their husbands–and a friend of theirs, Rita Mazumdar. They all would quite often visit Robin and Devyani's villa and were always keen–like the hero's sisters in the fairy tale or movies or novels–to make Robin realise how unsuitable Devyani was for him. The whole rendezvous that would have seven of them on the dinner table or in the breakfast area in the garden would have sarcastic statements on each other amidst the sugar-coated conversations insinuating how unworthy one was, towards whom the comment was being targeted. It was of course between the two sisters and Devyani and the others would just change the topic if the three ladies won't do it themselves. Despite such cold vibes, they would meet often and carry the sophistication that the family had associated itself with, without saying anything that could disturb the harmony of the good old family of Shah's.

But Robin always stood by his wife. No matter how good a brother he was, he loved and adored Devyani in all the ways a husband could. He was very well aware of how each of them felt about the other but also knew that it was a family issue everyone would envisage after the beginning of a nuptial relation.

However, the couple too had seen a ditch in their relationship the last summer when Devyani found something that could shock her or any other lady but surprisingly, she never behaved in any such way.

In the scorching heat of summers, the Shah's rarely perspired owing to their extremely comfortable lifestyle. In such a condition, finding a new kind of fragrance on Robin's coats and shirts was a bizarre thing to experience. Not only because it was not Robin's perfume or Devyani had renounced using any type of cologne or perfume for the last many years but because it was something she had never sensed in the house. It was Clive Christian's. Worse–It was having a strong and nice fragrance that Devyani thought could be made for women. All that it caused in the first few findings was a headache to her as she had found years back that she can't stand any type of artificial fragrance anymore. She thought that her husband was not a caveman to stay away from women and would meet women and men alike almost every day with formal hugs. She however, became alarmed one day when the fragrance moved downwards from the coat and the shirt to the Trousers and the underclothes. Not giving any importance to the laundry other than giving just the instructions, she now started sniffing everything he wore for the next few days. The fragrance remained. It could make her a bit disturbed but what was more alarming were the sleepless nights of Robin and his pale face since the last few days. She had stopped sniffing now. She thought she would confront him, but how to do that when he was already behaving eccentric and abnormal. One night, while she was in a deep slumber, she got disturbed from the scent of something familiar very close to her. It was Robin next to her in the bed like every night but was extremely close to her face. She got staggered and then sat on the bed asking him what it was. He looked depressed and told her about all that he had to, starting with creating a ground in the dimly lit room.

'What is it Robin?' She asked. He spoke after a pause in a low, resentful, but firm voice.

'You know Devyani. We sometimes do something out of just pleasure, something that we consider casual and regular,' he said and added after a pause, 'And trust me, all this is very normal in our kind of lifestyle.'

She didn't stop or console him. He who had done wrong could express all to feel his sins washed.

'But normalcy can't be blamed for infidelity,' he added.

He then told her everything and also about how guilty he was for his thought that any other woman could really become his second partner although it was for only a few hours.

'Who is she?' She asked very normally.

'Does it matter?' He asked, as he had told her that it was all over.

'It's okay if you don't want to,' she said plainly.

He said after a few moments gaining the courage and she waited for it as she felt that he would finally confess.

'Rita was my college friend. We knew each other since so long that people thought we would definitely marry but trust me Devyani, I never saw her the way I saw you in my life. And I realised it the moment I tried to see you in her. It was too late by then and...' he completed himself. He didn't say anything and she spoke after a brief pause.

'It's okay,' was all that she said to his surprise.

'Is that all that you want to say?' He asked sensing her calmness and lack of any type of aggression. She had never spoken in a loud voice in her whole married years but this time he had expected something, knowing her untamed and bold personality.

'If this is what is disturbing your life since the last few days, you don't need to worry from my side. Not because it's okay, but because it's okay as you've realised what happened,' she said plainly and added, 'This is the first and the last time we are discussing it.' That was all that she had said and seeing his eyes ignoring hers, she held his face in her hands and said calmly at last, 'I am okay. Will be more to see you happy and guiltless.' That was indeed the first and the last time the issue was raised in their home. Rita Mazumdar, who was a college friend and a socialite left the city later and was never discussed again. Devyani never asked him if he loved Rita before their marriage or if she was serious or if she left heartbroken or was just doing it out of 'normalcy'; it didn't matter to her as long as Robin was happy with her as his wife. And it was the first time since then when they could make their lives more happy with each other when Devyani was with her relatives and they had all the time they could spend with each other; this was what Robin had thought, and had come to Udaipur for her.

***

Devyani had reached the palace at around nine and was too tired to be spoken to or disturbed. After meeting everyone in the palace formally, she went to her room and tried to sleep. In a vast room that was in the corner on the ground floor, she looked across the lake from the window, while still lying in bed. She had stopped thinking over things in her life since long now. She lived in her own zone she had created where she lived without thinking much and living the way it was. She was the wife of a man and had thought that she would continue her life like this. She will have children may be and then she'll die normally without thinking much. She had thought all this but her own mind had betrayed her today without alarming her and was breaking the comfort zone she had created. How would she handle she thought.

CHAPTER 21

She wouldn't come Siddhant thought; it was already half past two in the afternoon and he hadn't called her as she already had told him the previous evening that she would call him if she won't come. He had her mobile number now but he had not used it since the day he had saved it. He was not hesitant to call her but was indeed cautious. On the banks of the lake where he stood outside a cafe in the sunny afternoon where she had told she would come at one, there were not many people now. He crossed the minor bridge across the lake and stood by the *ghat*–a berth like establishment with stairs leading to the lake–which was big, made of sandstone and had a huge series of mansion walls beside it, with *jharokhas*. The entrance to the ghat, which was on the opposite side of the bridge that Siddhant had come from, was a small one with a small pristine temple on its right. From there the ghat stretched till a long space and on the farthest part of it was a flock of pigeons which was flying in coherence and landing on the same area of the *ghat*. To the left of the entrance of the ghat was a man in a multicolour *Rajasthani* turban sitting on a mat and playing *Sarangi*–a traditional *Rajasthani* stringed musical instrument, to earn some pennies. Apart from him, there were only a few people to be seen there which included two men talking near the flock of the pigeons, a couple clicking selfies near the temple, a boy who was clicking pictures–of pigeons, the lake, its ducks, the scenic beauty of *havelis* on this side as well as the other side of the lake and the cafes that were on the street from where Siddhant had just now arrived–from his DSLR, and a destitute woman sitting near the stairs that led to the lake, with her children–a baby in her lap and a girl of eight or nine around her. The girl was actually crying and asking for food, which her mother told she would give her in some time. The mother looked really poor with a torn shawl with patchwork and a dusty saree over her body. The girl too was in a torn sweater over her frock and pyjamas. Mother's face was like most of the mothers with affection for its kids Siddhant thought and it was clear how poor they were, especially when she opened the knot at the end of her saree which had a small packet of newspaper which was wrapped around something and which Siddhant saw were actually two *rotis*–a flatbread of wheat flour–and some mashed potatoes and it all looked utterly stale and tasteless. She started feeding the girl who kept on saying that it wasn't tasty at all. Her mother kept on saying it was tasty and she will get good food at night which of course couldn't be true seeing their condition Siddhant thought. He walked towards them and the mother shied looking at him while the girl gazed at him while eating and moving to and fro near her mother. He took his wallet out of the inner pocket of his Khakee blazer he was wearing and took out a two thousand rupee note and offered it to the woman and said in Hindi, 'Please get her something good and healthy to eat. And yourself too.' She smiled and kept the money and Siddhant moved towards the bank of the lake so that the women wouldn't get embarrassed on being offered money. The folk artist who was playing *sarangi* started playing it louder and more fervently and started singing in his sharp voice the famous *Rajasthani* folk song *Kesariya Balma Padharo Mhare Des...*

He had seen Siddhant giving money to the poor lady. Within a moment a young girl appeared in the traditional *Rajasthani* dress and started dancing and swirling round and round clockwise and anti-clockwise with her hands moving up and down in a perfect coherence near the man. Her exquisite and colourful jewellery and dress glistened in the sunlight and she danced more speedily with the changing music of the player as he too played more speedily now. Siddhant ultimately moved towards them just to give them something, which they had started their performance for and stood near them and within a few moments, a bunch of people gathered around the artists.

The young girl of the destitute woman also came and enjoyed the performance and smiled to Siddhant. The photographer and some foreign tourists also clicked the pictures and shot the video now. The small girl took Siddhant's hand in hers and started jumping on the song seeing the young woman dancing so accurately with beautiful movements. He smiled and felt elated on such happiness of a kid as he had never associated himself with kids and was happy seeing such an innocent smile, laughter, and enjoyment on her face. And after a few minutes, the performance reached its climax and many people gave money to those artists. Siddhant gave a two thousand rupee note to the artist and just after a moment when he was smiling to the small girl who was now going back to her mother and the gathered people started getting scattered, *she* appeared crossing the bridge. Devyani was passing the bridge in her doe walk so delicately with an alluring smile that she looked extremely seductive to Siddhant. Her off-white chiffon saree with green and pink motifs waved in the wind along with her hair across her right shoulder. He walked towards her and they met on the verge of the bridge and he hugged her tightly to which she reciprocated affectionately and hugged him tightly which was a surprise to him and he kept on holding her for the next few seconds and as soon as their upper bodies parted a bit, he kissed her.

'I thought you would never come,' he said quietly looking into her big eyes.

'I knew you won't stop waiting,' she replied softly and smiled.

***

They were sitting in a rooftop restaurant on the embankment of Lake Pichola and the sun was all set to sink below the walls of the royal *havelis.* The lights of the restaurant were reflecting in the water of the lake and they could see that as well as the dazzling lights of the City Palace reflecting in the water. The hills, which were huge and far away from the palace, could be seen from where they sat. Amidst the conversation they were having, she spoke her mind.

'I don't know what would Robin think if he gets to know about me.'

'Where did you tell him you were going to?' He asked finally on his mention.

'I just told I needed to see the culture and art of the place and surroundings.'

'And he didn't stop you?' Siddhant asked.

'Of course he did.'

'Then?'

'What then. I said I need to and will be back in some time. He said okay,' she replied. 'He is a great man,' she added.

'Why did you lie and come here if he's such a great man,' he taunted and took a mouthful of baked macaroni that he was having.

She gazed at him and said, 'I'm not going to say what you want me to Siddhant.' He smiled. She smiled too. He ate some more and she kept on looking at him, sincerely this time.

'What?' he asked with his mouth full.

'I want you to promise me you will not continue like this once I am gone again,' she said keeping her hands on his. He avoided and looked across the lake now.

'Please,' she requested poignantly.

He looked at her and said finally, 'I will try...but no promise. And don't ask me to be happy and all now.' She smiled and then teased him when he continued eating, 'Okay tell me Siddhant, how many girls...or women you have slept with all these years.'

'None,' he said while eating some more.

'Look at you,' she said and gazed at him and knowing it, he said very quietly, 'Never counted.'

'*Viola!* I thought you were all woeful and all,' she expressed and laughed while sipping the red wine she was having.

'They were all the painkillers. To get rid of the drug that I am addicted to,' he said and was looking at her now with his deep eyes and was still. '... for eternity,' he added.

Her laugh too faded and with the same eloquence she had had, she said after a pause, 'I will be more than happy if you get rid of this drug as soon as you can.' She sounded sympathetic and now took his hand in both her hands and he laughed at her sympathy and looked the other way and then after some moments looked at her again.

'Will you come tomorrow?' He asked.

'Yes,' she replied.

'Will you be with me somewhere I can see you sleep once again?' He said while keeping his hand over hers now. He was eager she sensed.

She smiled and said, 'Hmm.' Her phone rang but she didn't receive or pay attention till he removed his hands and now they gazed at each other and then he stood up and left slowly. She took her phone out of her bag and received it.

'Hello.'

The society she was a part of had made her so vigilant that she could change her voice and articulation within a blink of an eye, he thought, while moving away towards the counter of the restaurant to pay the bill. It also comes to his mind that how she has become like people whom she lives around–fake and probably conceited–although not for him. She hung up the phone after speaking for a while with someone probably from the palace and looked at him. He was writing something on a piece of paper. He was signing the bill she thought and then looked across the lake and looked contemplating over something. She was thinking how in one such evening they were in the hilly area of Mussoorie. It was a good time. She was such a juvenile girl she thought. But he was as sincere he is today; then how is *he* supposed to suffer all that should've been endured by her alone she thought.

'Excuse me ma'am,' a waiter came to her and said when she was still looking across the lake.

'Here is a note for you. Sir has sent it,' he added. She got surprised and took it and the waiter left. Siddhant's back was all she could see when she looked at him and then she opened the note. He had written in his same old handwriting.

Tonight with me?

She looked at him in surprise and he was looking at her now with a naughty smile. She smiled and looked the other way.

***

Walking with her on the street that led to the road where her cab was supposed to arrive, he asked her, 'Will you come tomorrow?'

'Yes.'

He asked the question again, 'And will I see you sleeping like I saw yesterday?'

'Only sleeping,' she said and they laughed. 'But I don't like coming to the hotel. You know what I mean,' she expressed her concern.

'Yes. Don't worry. I will manage everything,' he assured her.

'You know...I want to stay at a place...I mean to be at a place which is very...very ordinary. Very simple and homelike,' she expressed her wish.

'Will a three BHK in Noida do?' He joked.

'Siddhant,' she complained frivolously.

'Okay. I will manage everything alright,' he assured her. They walked in the almost crowd-less alley, which had old buildings on both sides and street lights gleaming the surrounding. It was very quiet now in the street.

She then expressed quietly, 'Tomorrow is *Mehendi* ceremony. It is difficult for me to come.'

'I will wait. See if you can...' he said in a low voice.

'What I meant was that it's difficult for me. Not for you to be there,' she said.

They walked on and he added, 'I hate being surrounded by those people. In fact, I don't like people in general, I have realised lately.'

'But they love you really. And Rhea will be happy,' she said and added, 'Besides, we can spend more time together there. I will like it-'

'I'll be there,' he said at last and she smiled.

He then asked, 'Couldn't we spend this weekend together?'

She expressed her concern, 'You know the situation...'

'Yes, yes I know.' He hated her situation and reminders that she was someone's wife now.

'Besides, there is much fun this way with you in the daytime,' she said.

'Hmm...you will be free after this wedding?'

'Yes of course. I have become too tired all these days. I will be sleeping a lot after the wedding when Robin will be back to work.'

'That means you are free next weekend. We have time,' he expressed and walked on. Devyani had stopped he realised and turned to see why. She was looking at him.

'The wedding will get over next Wednesday...we will not be...' she mumbled.

He gazed at her for a second or two and then spoke realising what he had said, 'Oh...sorry I...I get it,' hiding his emotions. 'I just missed it,' he added. And they walked again. A few people could be seen now as they were reaching the main road where the cab was supposed to be waiting. As soon as they reached near the crossroad and faced each other, Devyani muttered, 'Siddhant.'

'Yes,' he said.

'There's been a question disturbing me all this while. Would you be honest?' She asked.

'Hmm...'

'Will you ever forgive me?' She asked. Hovering around that question, he had lived thirteen years of his life but had never blamed her. A child who has done wrong may look guilty but not punishable. The setting sun may bring gloom but can't be denied its presence in or right over the lives. True beauty can get barred but can't be parted with its purity.

He moved forward and took her face in his hands and kissed her forehead, kept his lips on her cold forehead for a while with his eyes closed, and then moved back.

'You are getting late,' he muttered and gestured towards the cab, which was now waiting behind her. She turned and moved towards it slowly.

'Hey Devyani,' he called suddenly. She turned readily. 'You didn't answer my note,' he said and winked with a smile.

She smiled with moist eyes and said, 'Good Night Siddhant', and got inside her cab. He stood there watching her cab moving and stopping and then again moving on the road, which had a few vehicles on the way to the palace. He knew it now that she was not coming back to him. Had it been some other girl, he could try; but it was Devyani and he knew her. She wasn't coming back to him and he had to live with this reality.

CHAPTER 22

The coldest day of December so far was cloudy with light rain and Devyani had a sore throat. Siddhant, even after her insistence had gone out of the cafe that they were sitting inside in the afternoon, to get her medicine. She was irritated at such cold weather and was having her garlic spinach soup when he arrived some twenty minutes later with an umbrella he had bought from an antique store on the street, which looked resplendent, and it was obvious that he had bought it in an emergency. His shoulders were quite wet with water droplets over his blazer.

'Oh god I told you not to go,' she bleated in worry in her croaky voice.

'Take these,' he said giving her an envelope and folded the umbrella. His face looked white because of the cold weather and he was breathing fast for he had come almost running in the low temperature with white vapour coming out of his mouth. She took the tablets while he removed his blazer and hung it on the back of the chair.

'I wonder why you don't listen to me,' she complained after having the tablet.

'Need I listen more?' He mocked and added, 'These orange capsules in the night too, they are four. The white one, once a day,' and told her which medicine was to be taken and when.

She didn't say anything and took the orange capsule and then laughed looking at his umbrella, which was now on the corner of the table.

'It wasn't good for you to roam in this weather,' he said.

'I am okay. I just need to take some rest,' she expressed.

'Should I drop you to the palace?' He asked quietly looking at her.

'Didn't you find any better place?' She said calmly. He smiled.

Last evening after coming to his hotel room, the first thing that Siddhant had done was a call to the room service. He had asked the attendant to send Hitesh to his room and asked him about rooms in the surrounding areas in the city. After telling him about some of the areas where he could find an apartment for rent, Hitesh had asked Siddhant indirectly the reason to leave the hotel.

'Is there anything you didn't like or anything less from our side, sir?' Hitesh had asked politely.

'Oh no. No, actually I am not checking out. I need a place where I can stay quietly,' Siddhant had told.

After a sigh of relief, Hitesh told him he would be back in some time with some more information and came back at around ten. He hadn't found any information as such but had come to tell Siddhant if it would be convenient for him to stay at his apartment which was vacant and only a kilometre away, as he himself was staying in the hotel's quarter. After thinking for about a minute, Siddhant asked him to clean up the apartment first thing in the morning and gave him a two thousand rupees note.

Not too far away from the bustling roads of the city was Hitesh's apartment. In a three-storey building, his apartment was on the first floor, which Siddhant had checked in the morning before meeting Devyani and had taken the keys from Hitesh. In the one-room apartment with an open kitchen, the whitewashed walls were neither too clean nor looked squalid to his comfort. It had one chair beside the entrance, one old queen-size bed with clean pillows linens and comforter on the bed, a small table with glasses and a jug on it, a chair near the window of the balcony which opened to a narrow street and had another apartment facing it, a wardrobe near the window, and a freshly cleaned washroom with everything necessary. The only thing Siddhant didn't like was the musty odour the house wafted, but that could be taken care of he thought.

Devyani entered the home hesitantly with folded arms and hands on her upper arms on the opposite sides. She felt cold all her way in her double-breasted trench coat she wore over her jumpsuit but now felt relieved inside the home which had a room heater which Siddhant had switched on, on entering. She felt relieved from sore throat now and although the odour of the home could have gone unnoticed by her, the new fragrance couldn't. While he closed the door, she walked to the table, which had a marigold bunch kept over it.

'Oh Siddhant.' She turned with a smile. 'Why do you do this?' She added. He just smiled and moved towards her keeping his coat on the chair and she hugged him.

'You are... amazing you know,' she sighed. They parted and he kissed her and she too reciprocated but then pushed him gently and walked towards the window and looked outside. She had noticed by now the marigold bunches that were on the bed and the kitchen countertop. The fragrance was comforting and she felt what she wanted to–a homelike surrounding–in an average apartment.

'I must say you haven't lost your sparkle. Had it been someone else, she would've ended up marrying you,' she said looking outside. The rain had stopped and the weather was much colder now.

'But you are lucky you got just the right kind of place I was thinking of. Like I read in the British novels.' She was speaking and didn't get surprised when he caught her in his arms.

'I would've stopped you had it not been so cold,' she said and smiled like she didn't have any feeling. Everything was alright till he kissed her neck removing the collar of her coat.

'Siddhant you know it's not...' she said and thought he would stop. He didn't listen and tried removing her coat. She turned now and moved away pushing him again.

She walked towards the side of the bed and saw his face, which had a deep affection. He walked and kissed her and she too kissed him for a while but pushed him again.

'You know there's nothing wrong in us being together,' he moved and held her by arms now. He kissed her again now and she pushed him with force.

'What's gotten into you,' she almost shouted.

He gazed at her and retorted readily, 'I can't play this fucking game anymore. You know I can't.' He was panting from anger and frustration now. His face looked contracted with raised eyebrows and he again held her arms and kissed her and was removing her coat when she pushed her with extreme force. They both were panting now.

'Is this the only thing that matters,' she exploded loudly and gestured for her body by opening her coat by pulling it apart. He didn't say anything and moved towards the window in anger and threw the water jug and glasses on the floor. Pieces of glass got scattered across the floor of the room. He was infuriated on his act as well as her reaction on it and now looked outside the window. He thought she would leave.

'You need to go. Just go...go,' he bewailed. He stood there and she walked to him. She hugged him from the back, which was more out of affection than to show any other emotion.

'I know how it is,' she comforted him softly.

'You don't know,' he mumbled.

'I should've never met you again.'

'And you think all would've been alright?' He asked in frustration. 'You neither left nor came back,' he added in a low voice and then continued in a frustrated voice, 'You have fucked my life since the day you've come.' He emphasised his last sentence with a hiss.

She moved and sat on the bed after a pause and he too sat beside her after a while. The room was silent and the noise of the kids could be heard from the alley.

'I am sorry,' he said but the anger still hadn't left him. She kept her head on his shoulder and said nothing for a while.

'I have wronged people all my life... but the only man who has expressed it to me is also the one who loves me the most... unfortunately,' she mumbled.

'I need to know what's in your mind,' he said in a deep, commanding voice. She got up slowly and picked the steel jug and kept it on the table. Then again bent down, picked the pieces of glass carefully and kept those in the corner. She opened the wardrobe to find if there's something to pick or brush aside the small pieces of glass and found another marigold bunch inside it. She looked at it and then closed the wardrobe and took the bunch from the table and removed the paper around it and bent again to brush the pieces aside in one corner. He was getting more irritated now; he stood up and took her by her arms suddenly.

'What the hell do you think you're doing,' he roared. She didn't say anything and kept looking downwards. He left her with a jerk and sat again and she, with a stoic face, resumed the cleaning of glass pieces till it was done.

'Ceremony will be over by evening. I will be waiting for you at dinner. Rhea must be waiting so I will have to leave now,' she said plainly while keeping the paper on the kitchen countertop and washed her hands in the kitchen sink.

'I will not come,' he muttered looking on the floor.

'I will be waiting for you by eight,' she continued in her calm tone as if she hadn't heard him but she indeed had, and he knew it.

'I will not come,' he said again.

'There might be some minute pieces on the ground. Don't walk barefoot.'

'I will not come,' he said louder now, looking at her.

She continued after a pause while combing her hair now after taking out the brush from her bag, 'It's too cold. You should go to the hotel now. It will be better there.'

'You think you are helping me by doing all this? By behaving like a good wife?' He turned towards her and growled. She didn't reply as always.

'What the fuck do you think is all this? A joke? You are meeting me like this and being an obedient wife warming your husband's bed?' He added. She looked at him. She didn't like it but still kept her silence.

'Will you utter something now?' He asked.

'Have some water. We'll talk when you are cool in the evening. I will wait for you,' she said calmly while calling the cab driver from the palace, with whom she had come today considering her health. She then walked to him and sat beside him. She kissed him on his cheek.

'Please take care Siddhant. I'll be happiest to see you happy.' She sounded serious and very firm now. He looked at her and she saw his eyes, which were still moist and he looked more vulnerable than ever. She kissed him softly on his wet lips.

CHAPTER 23

The long table in the dining hall looked longer today with more people. The family members of both bride and groom were there with other known faces Siddhant had seen the other day.

'Just two days and we will all miss this time,' said Mrs. Khanna, Rhea's paternal aunt in her heavy voice raising a toast.

'Of course Mrs. Khanna, and we will all miss our beautiful Rhea,' expressed Robin happily seeing Rhea's mother whose smile was filled with maternal love. Rhea sitting beside her mother kissed her shoulder on Robin's words and shied.

'And *we* are going to rejoice her presence as an addition to our family,' said Mr. Chopra, Raghav's father.

'Indeed,' said Mrs. Bedi who was sitting opposite Mr. Chopra beside Rhea's mother, 'What do you think Nalini?' she added asking Raghav's mother.

'Oh, I am sure. I have always liked Rhea,' Mrs. Chopra replied plainly with a smile to Mrs. Bedi.

'That's rare I tell you Anita. She has been so curious about Raghav's choice since he was a toddler that she would even suspect his gorgeous piano teacher would steal him from her,' said Mr. Chopra to Mrs. Bedi and everyone laughed.

'But is it true that you knew Rhea before you met her as Raghav's choice?' Asked Mrs. Bedi to Raghav's mother. Mr. Bedi was a good friend of Mr. Chopra and the Bedi family was there from both sides.

'Not really, I had some common friends with Mrs. Shah from whom I had heard a lot about Sinha and Khanna family,' said Raghav's mother telling about Mrs. Shah who was Robin's maternal aunt. 'And especially... the lady sitting right here,' added Raghav's mother looking at Devyani with an admiring glance to which Devyani replied with her usual smile full of ostentatious affection and her hand at her bosom.

'How did you know about Devyani?' Asked Mrs. Khanna.

'Not everyone needs to be in front of cameras to be known Bela,' taunted Mrs. Chopra with a smile and added, looking at Devyani, 'Her grace and looks compliment her aesthetic sense making her nearly perfect. In fact, I was spellbound for the very first time when I saw her at her art exhibition in Delhi, two years back. I mean I was not sure what was more beautiful.'

'You are just being modest Mrs. Chopra,' articulated Devyani softly with a nearly fake smile.

Siddhant who was till now sitting quietly opposite Robin and Devyani having his dinner while the stewards served the food and drinks, not paying any heed to what he thought was a shitty discussion, now looked at Devyani at the mention of his very own city where she had come two years back. She too looked at him and tried to maintain her smile.

'You are into art exhibitions Mrs. Shah? How come I never saw you before!' said an old man in *Khadee* Kurta who wore power glasses and sat at the far end, opposite Devyani.

'Oh I am just an amateur Mr. Dayal,' said Devyani softly with a smile.

'I must say Robin is a lucky man,' said the young woman sitting beside Mr. Dayal who looked like her daughter to which Robin gladly smiled. Her expression betrayed her words though.

'You know Gauri I always tell Aditya that I wish Devyani had a sister and I would've been more than happy to see them married,' said Mrs Khanna to another lady to which Aditya smiled and Siddhant looked at him with hidden disgust. 'I always love the way she speaks,' Mrs. Khanna added.

'But I wonder who this handsome gentleman is who's sitting quietly. I think I have seen him somewhere,' said a man of Mr. Chopra's age sitting on the far end opposite Mr. Dayal looking at Siddhant. Robin introduced Siddhant to Mr. Handa before Siddhant himself could speak, considering Siddhant to be unknown to most of the people sitting there. They greeted each other and then Siddhant spoke.

'Actually, I was waiting for my turn to eulogise Mrs. Devyani Shah, Mr. Handa,' said Siddhant sarcastically, with a smile, and everyone laughed. However, Devyani would've been thankful had Mr. Bedi not interrupted.

'Tell then Siddhant what do you like most about our beautiful woman,' he said to which Siddhant replied instantly, 'The way she uses her tongue'.

Silence fell over the hall. Everyone on the table including those who were not very vocal and participative in the conversation hitherto looked at him, and Devyani couldn't know which expression to show on her face while Robin's face had an impassive look.

'Oh I meant the way she speaks,' Siddhant said after a few moments while putting on a blameless expression. 'She is one of the most eloquent speakers I have ever met in life,' Siddhant said and then added, as if his words never had an equivocal nature, making an irreproachable face, 'Don't you all agree?' Everyone laughed and agreed to him. No more than a moment had passed in both the expressions of Siddhant, but it was more than embarrassing for Devyani but she hid it, something she was expert at. Robin too had a formal smile on his face.

'Why haven't you married Siddhant? I mean I am sure you must be having it on the cards. You are a nice gentleman I think,' said

Mrs. Khanna. She of course, didn't know about Devyani and Siddhant. Devyani got anxious. Siddhant took a pause. And then he spoke.

'In every man's life, Mrs. Khanna, comes a woman at a certain point who makes him go weak in the knees. Who afterwards makes him helpless, and who has all the powers in this universe to completely annihilate the man,' said Siddhant in his deep voice and everyone looked at him as if he was about to make a revelation. 'But I...still haven't gotten that lucky Mrs. Khanna, to find that lady,' he added with a playful smile and everybody smiled and realised that he was joking; Devyani knew he was not. He further added very casually, 'Oh Mrs. Khanna, not all of us are lucky. But I will definitely think about it the day I meet someone like you,' and they all laughed.

***

'What's wrong with you?' She asked him after the dinner when they were in the corner of the hall where the Mehendi ceremony had taken place before dinner, which was now filled with no less than hundreds of guests. He didn't say anything. They were standing there looking at the guests.

'By the way, you see that lady in red?' Devyani asked, talking about the lady who was sitting beside Mr. Dayal on the dining table. 'She's Laveena, Dayal's daughter. I got to know she was asking much about you the other day. Holds many art exhibitions,' she added. Siddhant had not noticed her the other day at the dinner.

'I find them all to be idiots. Actually not them only, I hate all of them. I've become a misanthrope,' he expressed calmly.

'You just need a break.'

'Maybe.'

'It's our milieu that we need as humans Siddhant,' she tried to pacify him for a better life.

'It's our milieu that's our biggest foe. That takes away everything from us to make us a part of their structure to behave like them.'

'We can't live without them. We always want someone to confide ourselves to.'

'That's our fear, not compulsion.'

'Even if so, how long will one suffer alone.'

'Better than being a coward.'

'Well in my case, I *am* a coward,' she said.

'You always had options.'

'Agree. But then I was a part of the structure you hate.'

'You chose to be a coward.'

'I still do. And that's what I keep telling you.' She had agreed and at the same time made him speechless by justifying. He had nothing to say.

'Did you not want to be with me?' He asked after a pause.

'We were too naive to know the basics of life,' she said quietly.

'I still am and happy being so.'

'Hope I'm not disturbing the philosophical conversation of you two,' interrupted Robin who came suddenly.

'I was just telling your wife you both make a great couple Robin,' Siddhant retorted to which Robin smiled.

'But seriously Siddhant, do you seriously not believe in love or it's just my opinion?' Asked Robin.

'Love...my friend ends after a time. It's a result of naivety,' Siddhant replied looking at both him and Devyani. Devyani had an impassive face now.

'You mean love comes with an expiry date?' Robin mocked.

'Many things don't come with an expiry date but people stop using them after a time,' Siddhant said poignantly.

'Then I am too lucky I guess for us,' said Robin and looked at Devyani.

'You think so?' Asked Siddhant to which Robin looked at him for a moment and then said, 'I know so,' keeping his arm around Devyani and smiled.

'Now I would request you to please excuse us, my friend,' Robin continued and added looking at Devyani, 'I need you to meet someone honey.' And they walked away giving a formal smile to Siddhant. He just watched them walk away and stop to talk to a couple standing away in the hall. He sat and was just having a drink when he heard a voice from his back. Mr. Bedi came and sat with him.

'You okay young man?' He asked.

'Of course, I am Mr. Bedi,' replied Siddhant.

'Oh, I know. But then we should never try to disturb the heart of a betrayed man. The deeper you lurk the darker it gets.' Siddhant didn't reply and didn't want to give him a chance to think about what he was thinking. But then he retorted, 'I haven't been betrayed.' They sat there looking at guests before the old man spoke again.

'You know Sid. It always happens,' said Mr. Bedi.

'Sorry?'

'Oh, you think I can't see? What you have in your mind for her. Hah...this is what happens. You think you must get what you want in life? Not necessarily,' Mr. Bedi expressed.

'You don't know anything. And I have no idea what you're saying.'

'Oh I know,' he moved his round bald-head as if he knew everything about Siddhant. 'You think I was never young? I never had any such thing called love. Hah...bullshit. I too had. Do you see them? Your aunt?' He gestured towards Mrs. Bedi who was talking to a man and woman away from them. 'Oh, I loved her. But you see me today?'

Siddhant still didn't want to talk to him.

'And there's one more bullshit about this love thing they say. They opine that money can't buy anything and everything. I say it can. Can't you see me?' Mr. Bedi sounded frustrated. 'You know when was the last time I had sex with my wife? Decades ago,' he added and continued, 'But I never had the courage you see. Courage to leave her, courage to move on.' He was in his sixties and Siddhant didn't want to know anything about his love or sex life anyway.

'Why are you telling all this to me?' Siddhant asked plainly.

'Because I can see you in the same situation I was in decades ago...helpless and hopeless in love. Only your situation is different,' he answered looking at Devyani who was still talking to the same couple with a fake smile on her face. Mr. Bedi was indeed an old man but he had seen life and had sensed what others couldn't about him and Devyani, Siddhant thought.

'But you have courage Siddhant. These women. Some of them... can never understand the meaning of love.'

'Talk about your women,' retorted Siddhant.

'Oh really? Is yours really *yours*? Well, I can't see that young man,' mocked Mr. Bedi.

'What do you mean?' Asked Siddhant curiously.

'Even I don't know. But I know one thing Siddhant and you should too,' Mr. Bedi said and then added after a pause, 'Women are only of two types as far as I have experienced them in my ripe old age. There are those who never know what they want in their life. Confused, unhappy, unstable, craving for love... but will always be seen happy and jovial. Because? Because they want everyone to respect and love them...even if they are least desirable.' He had expressed like a philosopher. He paused again while looking at his wife.

'And?' Asked Siddhant when he didn't continue.

'Sorry?' Said Mr. Bedi who was drunk as usual and would often irk others with his forgetfulness.

'The second type?' Siddhant reminded him. He was irritated.

'Oh yeah. Yeah, there are some others too. They know...what's to be done. When they love someone, they love without instability... without being confused, without anything at the back of their minds. They can demarcate right from wrong. They live in black and white,' he said and added after a brief pause, '*Such* women deserve love and respect.' He had completed himself and his glass of whiskey too.

'Just because they have a better conscience to demarcate right from wrong?' Siddhant asked curiously. He seemed interested in talking to Mr. Bedi now.

'No. No. Because when they love someone, they have the power to love them till the end of time,' Mr. Bedi said quietly.

'And what about those who...leave someone they called they loved?' Siddhant realised that Mr. Bedi might have had good knowledge of ladies of at least this family.

'Oh my boy my boy, you still haven't got it, have you?' Said Mr. Bedi, which irked Siddhant.

'What?' He asked conceitedly.

'Love...Siddhant...is not about leaving or staying, is it? It's not even about sex,' Mr. Bedi said moving his rotund body a bit forward and continued, 'Actually to a certain extent, it is. But it's not about time and age. Not about living together or leaving someone for their happiness. Yes, it can't be controlled but one is always free to leave the other for the happiness of the one they love.'

'Then why leave? Be with them if it's true,' Siddhant argued as if Mr. Bedi had all the answers to his worries.

'Is that all my friend? And what do we do when we get it? We pour champagne. We disgrace it and then make it wretched. Making it a mere union,' said Mr. Bedi in a complaining tone.

He continued, 'It's easy to get love. It is indeed a challenge to sustain its aroma, to understand your own love and your very own heart. And it's not about people and their bodies or being together or sex after a point. It's only about love and the loved one. It's painful to leave...indeed, but it's equally pleasurable to test your love.' He talked in a whisper now.

'So is it good to leave even if you both suffer?' Asked Siddhant.

'Oh I haven't written a treatise on love my young friend but let me tell you one thing,' Mr. Bedi spoke normally now and relaxed his back and added, 'The purer the love gets, the more mystifying it becomes. For the mind and heart of a woman can never be understood. No matter how close you both are or how many times you have had sex or how many kids you have and how many years you live together.' Siddhant sat there and listened to him while gazing at him.

'And now with your kind permission I would request you to excuse me, my friend,' said Mr. Bedi while getting up.

'Where are you going?' Asked Siddhant.

'Oh it's time to masturbate,' he whispered and winked at Siddhant.

The good old man, as Siddhant saw him, who was presumably a nut case and never knew what he spoke or ended up always contradicting himself, had given him a lecture, which Siddhant hated. Wasn't he aware of all that? But he still felt good. He had seen more of life as compared to Siddhant. Siddhant now at least could see his view on women and see the world sometimes according to it, if needed. He was still thinking when he heard a voice.

'Thank god he left,' said Laveena and sat where Mr Bedi was sitting with her glass of wine in her hand. 'Hi, we haven't been introduced. I'm Laveena,' she added.

'Siddhant,' he replied. Laveena was the same age as Siddhant was and looked alluring and attractive, although she had looked average to him when he had seen her the first time this evening.

'I know. Devyani told me about you,' she said.

'I hope all good things,' he joked.

'Doesn't matter if she says bad,' replied Laveena.

'Really?' He exclaimed.

'Of course, I'm not judgmental. I don't trust others till I examine a person closely,' she replied. Her voice was very soothing and so was her personality he realised.

'Examine? So what did you examine about me?' He mocked.

'I love those who speak less. That's why I am here with you.' Siddhant, sensing where this conversation could go wandered from it by asking, 'What else did she tell you?'

'Doesn't matter. But seems you are much concerned. Are you people...?' She tried to know.

'We are nothing,' he said plainly.

'I was sure. She's too stuck-up to be with someone who doesn't belong to her bureaucratic or business family background.'

'Sorry?' He expressed to know if she was talking about *his* financial status.

'I am sorry. What I meant was that...leave it,' she stopped.

'Oh please. You can open your heart with someone who speaks less,' he comforted her with a smile and then added, 'And is not from this league of people.' He did it on purpose.

'Nothing much Siddhant. I know I shouldn't say but there are some extremely opportunistic people you meet in life,' she said looking at Devyani who was now speaking with a woman in her usual way, making facial expressions and laughing in a completely controlled way.

'How fake one can get I think sometimes,' she scorned with a smile.

'Oh too fake,' said Siddhant in a flippant manner and sipped his whiskey.

'Are you making fun of me?' She smiled.

'Oh no. I just want to hear some more,' he jested.

'I know I know. I can never forget how she sidelined my exhibition that was organised in Delhi when a great Italian artist was on his visit to India,' she said and then added, 'The same exhibition that people spoke of in front of you. That was a big opportunity for me.' He didn't believe her but then had a mixed reaction.

'Your dad too is in the same business. Didn't he know about it?' He asked.

'Dad isn't much active since last few years,' she replied. 'He wasn't even aware she was the one behind my show being hijacked. I just told I cancelled my show,' she added.

'And?' He asked curiously now.

'What do you mean and?'

'Anything else you want to tell me about her?' He smiled.

'Too many people are here you see. Besides, I am more interesting when alone with wine and a good company,' she looked into his eyes with a smile. She had deep dark eyes.

'You think so?' He asked quietly in his deep voice.

'You may try,' she replied in her soft voice, which Siddhant didn't know was this seductive usually or was practiced occasionally. Siddhant gave a confused look to which she said, 'I don't think anyone's going to look for either of us at this time.' Siddhant looked at Devyani who wasn't there now.

'She won't come. Women of this family know how to make their men happy,' she said with her raised eyebrow and a movement of the head. Siddhant looked at her and was just about to say something when a man from hotel staff appeared and said,

'Excuse me, sir.' Siddhant looked at him and he extended an envelope saying, 'There's a note for you.'

'For me?' Siddhant asked taking the envelope.

'Yes sir,' said the boy and left. Siddhant opened the envelope, read it, folded it again and looked around for Devyani, who wasn't there. He said to Laveena who looked lost now but still was looking at him, 'My bad luck dear, I would've loved to spend some time with you but I need to go now.'.

'It's okay,' she said after a pause with a smile and then took out her card from her bag and handed it to him. 'Use it when you want,' she said.

'I would love to,' he replied and kissed her hand.

He left the hall and came out of the palace as there was no point sitting there anymore. He was confused. What was wrong with *that* woman he thought. Just when he didn't want to trust her, still wanted to ask her why she still meets him if she has turned so impassive over the years, when he was getting to know so many things about her and was about to go and spend a night with a lady who had just now called her too fake and an opportunist, she had sent a note that almost made everything else look null and void. He stood outside the palace for some moments.

Sense of guilt enveloped him now; he had loved her he thought after some minutes elapsed. And no one including gods could change that fact. She herself had told him that she was a coward if that is what one is called when one fails to take challenges while coming out of the comfort zone. He then took out the note from his pocket and read it again.

I am sorry. I never meant to hurt you. You know that.

Nothing will change the beautiful bond we share between us and I am sure of that.

Too difficult to speak to you at the moment..

At the flat. Tomorrow afternoon at 12.

Go straight to the hotel. It's too cold outside.

Sleep well!

P.S. You are looking too good today. :)

DS

CHAPTER 24

The coldest day of winter–which was the previous day–had been shifted to become the second coldest day and the current day had replaced it for the title. Siddhant still slept in his bed when a knock at the door disturbed him and he couldn't guess who it could be when he saw his phone and it was still eleven. He got up in frustration and opened the door and the frustration turned into a surprise to find her standing there.

'It's so cold outside,' she said while shivering and got inside immediately. 'You take too much time,' she added. She blew air from her mouth out of coldness and the white vapours could be seen. Her nose had turned red he noticed.

'Why are you here this time?' He asked. He was still in half sleep. She gave her a complaining look when he added, 'No I mean you were coming at noon.'

'You are a limit sometimes,' she whispered and then answered, 'I didn't want to wait for the rain.'

'Hmm...I am just gonna freshen up and come,' he said and went to the washroom while she sat in front of the small room heater kept beside the bed. There was no room for formalities in the relationship which was going to last for both of them for just next few days and he was going to continue to live in the same state of mind again while she was going to live her life the same way as before, again.

'I asked you to go to the hotel. You never listen to me,' she spoke loudly. 'You were mad last night. It's good everyone was high on the celebration,' she added loudly getting up after getting enough warmth and started making the bed. She took off the woolen cap that she wore and kept it in the wardrobe. He didn't reply. He came out just when she was done ordering breakfast on the phone after making the bed. She sat on the bed after taking her boots off. He saw her in the bed sitting with the comforter up till her waist and said, 'Seems you're a bit too ready to spend some quality time with me.'

She didn't say anything and he sat on the bed and kept a cigarette in his mouth. 'Many people asked about you last night,' she said while pulling the cigarette out of his mouth in a sudden movement as if it was a very normal gesture for her. He looked at her with annoyance but she didn't see him and kept on saying, 'It's good you shocked them but they're not gonna stop. There's gonna be much discussion...and gossip about you,' she continued normally.

'And you're worried?' He asked.

'They wish,' she replied.

'Did he say something?' He asked about Robin.

'He would never say anything,' she replied. 'He knows me... trusts me,' she added after a pause. 'You not feeling cold?' She asked suddenly seeing him sitting in only a t-shirt. He nodded his head in no and took the cigarette from her hand.

'He flew back to Mumbai today,' she said getting up and tiptoed to the wardrobe. 'Some urgent work you see,' she continued taking out his sweatshirt from the wardrobe and walked towards him. She folded it vertically and helped him wear the sweatshirt and then peeped through the curtains outside the window before tiptoeing again to sit beside him.

'Would you tell me something?' He asked. She looked at him.

'Did you ever have any relationship after me or before Robin?' he asked plainly and she gazed at him for a while before replying.

'Not really,' she replied. 'I've had people who came close to me and I tried to stay with them,' she added.

'After me?' He uttered.

'No. Before Robin.'

'It's all same.'

'You may say so if you wish to.'

'Means?'

'Means nothing,' she said and added while covering herself well, 'Did someone say anything to you?'

'No. Just asked. Why?'

'Just like that.'

Someone knocked on the door and he went to open it to receive the breakfast she had ordered.

'Why did you order? We could go out,' he asked after keeping the packet on the side table next to her side of the bed and opened the wardrobe and then its drawer to get the envelope.

'I didn't want to go out,' she said. She looked lost.

'Have it,' he said after getting back to the bed and handed her the envelope of her medicine and added, 'You forgot it here.'

'I don't feel like eating.'

He looked at her and sighed and after a pause, took her hand in his and said, 'Don't think that I asked you to deduce or prove something. And stop finding meanings in everything I say. You know me. And you know we are here for just a few days.' He poured water from the bottle into a glass and gave her saying, 'Nothing's gonna change. Neither your decision to live with him nor my wish to stay with you. We are humans. And I know you wouldn't have judged me if I were at your place.'

'You could never be,' she said.

'Who knows? One never knows.' He tried to convince her.

'I was always scared to be left alone,' she said taking the glass.

'I know.'

'How?' She asked after a pause.

'I know you,' he replied and she gazed at him while he opened and served her breakfast.

They ate the white sauce pasta she had ordered and then were out in the balcony. It was cold.

They saw a couple taking a selfie there and she laughed at the pose they were making in the street. They seemed to be tourists.

'I never understood this. Taking selfies and telling the world on social media what you were up to,' she spoke her mind.

'And you like standing here judging people,' he mocked while smoking.

'It's true. It's all about showing the world what you were up to. They're competing with others to show they are no less than them,' she argued and added, 'On social media of course.'

'That's why you're not on social media,' he said.

'I'm not on social media because I don't feel the need to fight the identity crisis that almost all of them are fighting,' she retorted. And then she asked him in a surprised tone, 'How do you know I am not on social media?' He didn't say anything.

'Oh god. You mean you were searching for me all this while?' She asked with a smile. 'To meet me?' She added.

'Kind of,' he said after a pause while still smoking.

'What do you mean?'

'Nothing. I just searched you on social media many times in last many years,' he said.

'You know a random thought came in my mind last night. A bizarre random thought,' she said.

'What?' He asked.

'I thought how life would've been had it all happened otherwise.' She added after a pause, 'Did you ever think that way?' He again didn't reply instantly but spoke after a few seconds.

'I've been thinking that way since the last thirteen years,' he told her plainly and then added looking into her eyes, 'And yesterday too. And then I landed in the realms of my reality and thought that I might never see you again after the next three-four days.' He turned to go inside the room and asked her too, 'You'll catch a cold again. Come inside.'

He was just walking towards the bed when she came inside locking the door and hugged him from behind to his utter surprise and then murmured, 'Don't. I like it like this,' when he tried to turn. He turned, after a few moments, when her hold loosened a little.

'Are you-' he was about to say something when she locked his lips with hers with more fervency than he did the last day and they stood there inspecting the intensity of their estranged love it seemed. They parted after some moments.

'Are you sure?' He asked once they parted for a moment.

'More than that,' she looked into his eyes and whispered while panting for breath and pushed him against the wall beside the bed and tested their long lost warmth once again after years. The sweatshirt that she had helped him wear had been taken off too, by her, but with more rush, and along with it, his t-shirt too, while he removed her coat and then her top. He couldn't know if he was in a trance or it was happening in reality, but didn't want to lose whatever it was. He lifted her and she locked her legs around his waist and clenched his butt while holding his head from one hand. He walked and plunged in the bed and removed all that stood in the way of their union after years of yearning.

'I missed you like this since an age it seems,' he said. She pulled him closer over her and whispered, 'Make me forget everything I've ever known apart from you.' She kissed him and added, 'Take me into the realms of your reality.' She clasped his lips and then added finally, 'Show me how much you missed me Siddhant,' and the sweltering temptation vanquished the chill that covered the city, overwhelmingly.

***

They were lying in the bed and the darkness had embraced the city while they both were on their quest to explore their realms that longed for each others invasion, since last many hours. Sheer affection had taken over the frenzy now and they both felt as if a burden had been lifted from their hearts.

'You have changed a lot,' she said with a smile without looking at him. Her head on his chest with his arms around her made her feel relieved. Not only because she had her oceans of desires toured completely with all the torments and typhoons getting over. Not because the soft ups and downs on the surface of the softest marbles he ever knew were squashed by his raw hands and his build. But because she had thrashed all the walls, had destroyed all the citadels, broke all the locks hanging on the doors of her chastity and there was nothing more, that she could offer to the devil of love she had unleashed.

From the tip of her soft finger with long nails painted in red, she was circling around his brown nipples and was playing with the small hairs around it while he lay down with his eyes closed and his flawless grip around her.

'You have become harder with same barbaric actions,' she teased him but with the fact that she had encountered it for hours. 'Especially from some parts,' she added. He smiled laying in the same way nodding his head.

'But the tricks have still been the same, with only an improved coarseness of a brute,' she said looking at him now with her face on the back of her palm which was on his chest now.

'You can't tell new tricks to an old bastard,' he said with a smile looking at her now.

She laughed and looked into his eyes with her smile fading away with a few seconds that passed.

'I have to go. They will look for me after some time,' she expressed her apprehension.

'Not so soon,' he said and tightened his grip. She smiled and closed her eyes keeping her head again on the chest.

'You haven't changed. You could tell the whole building what we were up to,' he mocked.

'Dont lie.'

'Hmm. Didn't your husband tell you.'

'Hmm.'

'Or he could never make you feel so.'

'He is a good man Siddhant,' she said affectionately.

'Why are you ruining a good man's life? Loving someone else and living with him as a wife,' he said calmly.

'I might be ruining. But reason is that maybe I was never destined to marry anyone,' she said softly.

'Still, you're ruining.'

'Some people are born to ruin others life in marriage. I might be one of them,' she said with a smile.

'I too.'

'Then I want you to ruin someone's life like I am ruining his,' she mocked.

'We shouldn't. We have no right,' he said and added, 'It's better to be with someone who we know is ruining us. We should be with each other. You know you love me.'

'I don't love anyone. I can't love anyone.'

'Your husband?'

'I love him but not like you are saying. Love is different for me than it is for you,' she said. 'I am living with him and he is happy. What's more? He has everything he wants from me. I respect him as a man. I care for him. I can't see him sad,' she added.

'Is that all what it takes to be married?' He asked.

'Marriage isn't about theorems. It's like humans. Each one is different yet none is perfect. Almost.'

'Do you really believe in these bullshit ideas or just telling me.'

'Of course I do. I'm a married woman,' she laughed.

'And are you happy in it?'

'I don't see any reason not to be.'

'Why are you with me here?'

She answered him after a pause, 'It's my guilty pleasure. Didn't you want it?'

'I hate you,' he replied.

'I know you hate me. I left you,' she said plainly.

'I hate you coz you never left me,' he said calmly.

'Hmm...I need to go now. Rhea must be waiting,' she said and got up.

'You coming tomorrow?' He asked, now looking at her while she walked.

'Hmm...' she said while getting dressed up in front of the small mirror outside the washroom wall and he watched her.

He was very well aware that this consummation after years did not suggest anything that could advance the relationship he wanted.

CHAPTER 25

They sat in a cafe the next day, not too far from the palace.

'I'll tolerate those people for you,' he told when she asked him to come in the evening.

'It's for Rhea,' she smiled.

'Anyways. I've someone I can sit there with,' he grinned.

'Who?' She asked and then said instantly, 'Mr. Bedi?' And laughed. He gazed.

'Okay okay. Some girl?'

'What's her name. Laveena?' He exclaimed.

'Oh!' She exclaimed.

'And she's quite revelatory,' he mocked and sipped his vanilla latte.

'I'm sure. Exhibition. Her husband. What else?' She expressed.

'Husband?' He exclaimed.

'So she talked about the exhibition only,' she mocked.

'Hmm...' He hated that she always knew almost everything.

'Her husband was a bit too much interested in me, before their divorce, of course. Then I didn't know how my husband managed the exhibition when I expressed my wish,' she told. 'I never knew it had anything to do with her,' she added while eating the fettuccini.

'I am not asking,' he said.

'I know. I just don't know why she can't get over it. But I wish god bless her. Telling just to get rid of the ounce of guilt I had for the exhibition issue that I got to know about later.'

'I am sure,' he said sipping the vanilla latte.

'What else did she speak about?' She asked.

'Nothing much, just a glass of wine and some good time.' She looked at him in annoyance and he avoided her glance.

'Anyway,' she said at last. 'What's the mark on your upper arm?' She asked.

'I had a fistfight in a cafe in Madrid last year,' he told realising she was talking about the scar she might have seen yesterday that he had had on his upper arm.

'You were in Spain last year?' She asked in surprise. 'We too were there last year. Granada. I didn't like it much. I liked Pinions there though,' she added.

'Can't you stay tonight?' He asked looking at her.

'Not at all possible. It's Sangeet ceremony today. Everyone will be looking for me. Wedding is in two days. The countdown has begun,' she expressed and ate some more. He kept on looking at her.

'Indeed. It has begun,' he expressed after a pause and she too looked at him now.

***

The colossal hall looked stupendous with huge flower hangings and all types of chandeliers that glistened the ambience. The only thing that could be seen in all the directions was prodigious decor, all types of champagnes, whiskies, and wines, accompanying the people from affluent families.

'I had asked her to get married in Cinigiano. This place is good though,' said a boy–who was some cousin of Rhea–to the men sitting with him on the table which included Siddhant too.

'Cancun too could've been great,' said a man looking at Siddhant.

'Never been to,' said Siddhant.

'She's like Devyani. She too didn't marry abroad. Exotic Indian feeling and all you see,' said Aditya.

'Where did they marry?' Asked Siddhant gulping down the whisky.

'Don't know brother. Some hilly area it was. I wasn't there,' told Aditya.

'Twas Simla,' said the man.

Devyani hadn't yet arrived with Rhea and some other women of the family and to Siddhant's surprise, his phone rang and it was Pooja.

'Excuse me, gentlemen,' he said and went to the lobby of the hotel.

'Where have you been?' Pooja bleated.

'I was just busy.'

'Busy? It's been two days and you haven't even received my call.'

'I know. I know. I'm sorry I was just...enchanted with the beauty of this place.'

'Are you sure?' She asked surprisingly. 'Sorry...enchanted... beauty...am I getting some surprise when you're back?' She asked jovially now.

'Don't know. It's a surprise for me too.' He sounded this genuine and humane for the first time to her.

'I don't believe it Siddhant. I can't wait to see you,' she expressed.

'Okay Pooja, I think I'm getting a call. Will talk later, take care,' he lied about the call.

'Sure. Love you,' she said and they hung the phone.

Siddhant was back in the crowd of guests and the jubilance and merriment could be sensed in the air now with the tunes that the women and men were dancing to on the ornate stage which had LCDs hung at its edge which showcased the bride and groom dancing a few moments later. Siddhant stood and saw the women and saw Devyani at last, dancing less, and just accompanying the others when asked to. When her eyes met Siddhant's, she felt shy, although she was never shy in her disposition. She danced for some time and looked at him quite often while he watched her with a grin.

She then was coming to him when a woman started talking to her and it seemed she had something interesting to tell and Devyani listened to her and soon they were joined by another lady of Devyani's age. He, however, couldn't wait to meet her and see her closely. She looked ethereal to him in her white thread lace and pearl embroidered *lehenga* and seemed as if she was breathing a more rarefied air; she looked esoteric. She was talking while giving him a flirtatious smile on seeing him waiting for her. A wine waiter arrived after a minute carrying a note to her which she took and read after asking the women to be excused.

'Meet me in the archway at the backside.'

She looked at him and nodded her head subtly in disagreement while still in the conversation with others. He grinned and moved his lips–'I am waiting.' She looked at him and he walked away towards the archway.

She didn't move and kept on talking and kept looking for him and found him nowhere now. Moving slowly, she walked towards the archway, which was silent and no one was around.

When she reached near the end of the archway where a passage on her left lead the way to the lobby, she felt his hands pull her with a sudden jolt and she felt herself in his arms the next moment, pressed against the wall of the passage. 'This is mad. Leave me,' she whispered with the thumping heartbeats while he grasped her body and fondled her waist and back. He, however, didn't listen and she could still feel the wet softness of his lips and the roughness of his stubble on her neck and all over her décolletage.

She pulled his hair after a while and whispered, 'Someone could see us. Please let me go.'

'I need you,' he whispered with panting breath looking at her face.

She gazed and then locked his lips with hers and then murmured, 'Let's go to my room,' and led him to her room which was not far from the archway at the back of the palace.

Their spooning began the moment they got inside her room with incessant fondling. Without waiting to get on the bed, he lifted her and put her on the table, which they came upon on the entrance to the room, while she undressed him and made him topless.

The liberty from the fear of moral acceptance from the milieu she belonged to engulfed her and all reason had left her this moment and kept on leaving with each sudden breath she exhaled with each thumping she very much felt.

'Don't. Please not now,' she whispered with eyes still closed when she felt the touch of his teeth on her bosom and then his mouth gasping her soft skin; he didn't do that again. The extreme grip they had had on each other's body however loosened after a while which they realised were some half an hour since they were copulating.

'You are magic,' he was panting and sat on a wing chair nearby buttoning his trousers while she kept on catching her breath and then fixed her clothes and covered her bosom which was covered with a sheen of sweat and his dribble. The huge room that was filled with the hues of white and blue had the best of furniture and a huge mirror in which she now was looking at herself and fixing her makeup.

'You are brute. What have you done,' she complained seeing the scarlet bruise-like mark on her cleavage which she implied towards. 'Seems big,' she added with a slight worry while touching up her makeup and brushing her bosom with a makeup brush.

He caught her from the back. 'Craving for you makes many things bigger and harder in my body,' he said ribaldly and kissed her earlobe.

'God. You're bleeding,' she said suddenly seeing his shoulder in the mirror, which had a scratch she had left. She turned to see it closely. It wasn't bleeding actually but had some small drops that had just appeared on the skin.

'Hmm...this is what I had been craving for,' he said and locked her lips.

'You need something before you wear the shirt. Let me get something,' she said and walked towards the washroom but he held her by arms and embraced her.

'Let's stay like this,' he muttered.

'You are mad,' she said and walked into the washroom and he lay down on the bed.

She had adhesive bandages in hand when she came back and she covered the scratches on his shoulder and stood up to move and he again pulled her over him.

'I need you more,' he said

'I can't Siddhant. Try to understand.'

'I love you,' he said looking into her eyes and sounded resolute.

She looked into his deep eyes and kissed him and then said, 'I'll come early tomorrow',

CHAPTER 26

The apartment was locked it seemed. He didn't open the door after she knocked many times and the calls made in the last fifteen minutes went in vain. She decided to visit the hotel at last where he might have gone last night and asked for him where she was received as if she was being waited for since long.

'Oh yes. Yes ma'am,' said the man at the reception when Devyani enquired about him. And after that, it all looked extremely gloomy to her although he was sent to the hospital in time.

'Actually, we didn't know whom to call and sir wasn't in the condition to tell anything,' continued the man. 'But we have sent him to the hospital and hope he's fine now as told by one of our personnel. We've called a lady too from his phone whom he had spoken to the last night,' he added.

'Which hospital?' Asked Devyani in a hurry suddenly and went out promptly.

***

He slept in the bed with a blanket up till his chests and she sat beside his bed.

'There's nothing to worry. He's been given a painkiller,' said the nurse who had come to check his state.

'Thanks,' replied Devyani who had already met the doctor who was on duty when Siddhant had arrived in the hospital. She had a word with the doctor to know the exact state and medication for his problem. It was a case of appendicitis and the only good news was that the abscess had not been ruptured although the pain he had experienced this morning was acute and could result in acute appendicitis she thought after knowing the issue. She didn't know if he knew about it. The diagnosis of it called for the dispensing of antibiotics post which the abscess needed to be drained with a tube inserted through the skin. But the need for a good doctor and facilities was the primary concern and he would have to fly back to Delhi soon for that she thought. But how? He has no parents or siblings. He has no one to look after him. She watched him sleeping and the effect of the sedative could be seen from his face. In the small room of the hospital, she sat on a chair beside the bed and not on the couch, which was behind her, parallel to the patient's bed, when he began to come back to consciousness and she got up as soon as she realised it.

'Relax,' she said. 'You are ok.' He took some seconds to sink in the situation before he spoke.

'When did you come?' He asked lazily.

'Just now.' He watched his wristwatch and it was half-past twelve. His eyes looked tired.

'You should go. I'll be back when I'm ok,' he said getting up and she kept the pillow at his back.

'I am not that sick,' he added seeing her gesture.

'Your body needs rest.'

He spoke after a pause. 'When did you arrive? And how did you get to know?' He asked to which she replied now and told.

'I'm such a jerk. Ruining your time too,' he sounded irked.

'Hmm, you're right. I so wanted to enjoy there, you should've fallen sick after I was gone,' she said plainly and sat on the bed.

'Come here,' he said and tried to pull her but she resisted and sat back again.

'Siddhant you are sick. You know that?' She sounded serious.

'Yeah, yeah. They were telling me and to each other about appendicitis and something when I came,' he said lazily as if he didn't care.

'You need a good doctor.'

'Of course, I know, but I need to hug you right now,' he pulled her again and she resisted more this time.

'Siddhant! Listen to me. The doctor said that they need to treat you with antibiotics and then the abscess needs to be treated,' she roared. 'And then you'll have to go through laparoscopy to remove the appendix.'

'Oh, these doctors just blabber to make money. You know them,' he ridiculed.

'Will you get serious?' She warned.

'Okay, okay I'm serious.'

'You are not going to behave casually about it okay?'

'Okay I agree, but can we get out of this place?' He affirmed.

'Hmm.'

He pulled her gently and said, 'Thanks.' She kissed him.

'I don't know if I'll be back to normal today. My head is killing me. You should go to Rhea and not ruin her day,' he uttered to her.

'I'm here,' she said and he kissed her again.

A sudden thump at the door, which was in front of the patient's bed, opened it and they looked towards it. Devyani, still bent over him with his arms around her, turned and found a lady coming inside with stress written all over her face which turned into surprise after seeing them. Devyani suddenly stood up but not in the gesture that could show any fear from anyone. Pooja walked to Siddhant and hugged him.

'What's happened to you?' She sounded concerned and relieved at the same time.

'Nothing to worry. It was just a little pain for some reason,' he told. 'Will be outta here in an hour or two,' he added.

'You nearly killed me,' she said in a low voice and stood again, knowing the presence of a third person in the room.

'Pooja she's Devyani,' he told Pooja and added looking at Devyani, 'She's Pooja.' He too was confused if not alarmed as to how to introduce the two females who had the most important roles to play in his life for the last thirteen years. Devyani, who although had got to know from the hotel personnel that a certain lady had been called from Siddhant's phone, had forgotten in the ordeal that someone could be on the way and appear anytime.

'Hi,' said Pooja plainly. She knew Devyani from her name as a past that Siddhant had had.

'Hello,' articulated Devyani in the same way as she would say to any other stranger. Neither of them said any word of being pleased or elated to meet each other.

'Thanks for the bills,' said Pooja who had got to know from the hospital reception about the payment of the bill and medicine that Devyani had already paid and Siddhant too got to know about it at that moment.

'Don't mention it please,' replied Devyani with a smile.

'I met Devyani here a few days back,' told Siddhant to Pooja and also to Devyani. 'She's the woman I've been heavily dependent upon for many years.' They both could not say anything, just smiled formally. No sooner than a minute passed when Devyani spoke.

'I think I should be leaving now. And since Pooja is here, I don't think I need to worry,' said Devyani, giving them both a warm smile. 'I'll be expecting you fit and at the palace tonight,' she added.

'I'll see you at night,' he replied.

'And don't forget to bring Pooja. I'll be expecting you too Pooja,' she said to both of them and hugged Pooja before leaving.

CHAPTER 27

'Why didn't you tell me?' Pooja asked after an hour in the hospital.

'I didn't know it was important,' Siddhant replied.

'Siddhant do you remember what we spoke about before you came here?' She asked.

'I do very well.'

'Then?'

'I didn't know back then she would be here.'

'And that makes a difference?'

'No. She is married and leaving the day after the wedding,' he made the revelation after a pause and she looked worried about this news for him yet a bit relaxed now for herself.

'Will you be okay?' She asked quietly after a pause.

'Hmm. I need to sleep now.'

He slept and she sat on the couch parallel to the patient's bed contemplating over what would happen as the turmoil of his life which she had surpassed to some extent with her love had resurfaced and even if she knew now that the cause of it will be leaving soon, the effect won't. The scar had been cut open.

***

The three of them sat on a table in the palace at night. All the guests had landed in the city and the wedding gala had begun in its full splendour with people dancing and drinking and savouring the exotic cuisines from all over the world. Pooja's phone rang and she excused herself to talk in silence.

'Why didn't you tell me about her?' Devyani asked with a smile. She wasn't complaining.

'You know the answer...' he replied and added, 'And you know why.' She knew he wasn't hiding but might have had a hope.

'You love her,' she said with a smile.

'I'm done with loving in life,' he said.

'You're marrying her. Aren't you?' She asked.

'Hmm...I told her I can think of it before I came here. It's just marriage though,' he told. 'And like you said, all are not perfect,' he added after a pause.

'But she is a good girl isn't she,' she expressed.

'That's why I'm afraid. I don't wanna ruin her life.'

'You told me we are both meant to ruin others life in marriage.' She smiled now with relief on her face.

'I had also said we should have ruined each other's lives,' he said. They both sat and looked at others. He spoke after a pause, 'Why are you making me commit a sin?' She looked at him.

'You already are a sinner,' she mocked.

'Then let's sin together for the whole of our lives.'

Her countenance changed. 'I am not the girl you are looking for. I am not that old Devyani that you're looking for,' she told him firmly but sincerely.

'I can see that. I still love you.' He sounded adamant.

'It is the good old memory that you miss. And you can't deny that we are no more than two strangers who once shared some good time together. That's all.' She wasn't mocking anymore and sounded resolute. He hated the remark she had just now made. Pooja came back and sat with them. 'Sorry,' she exclaimed.

'Siddhant you are really lucky I must say. You could never find a girl like Pooja,' articulated Devyani and Siddhant watched how perfectly she had mastered the skill to hide the real side of her in front of others.

'Thank you Devyani. Actually I'm lucky. I wonder how could any girl lose him on any ground,' replied Pooja. She never hid it from Siddhant that she wasn't judgmental but had envied Devyani for the reason that she had made his life miserable for such a long time.

'I'm sure,' Devyani replied. He felt a hollowness inside him after all this convincing and tutelage from her about love and society.

'Excuse me ladies, I just need to use the washroom,' he said and left for some fresh air as it was getting sick for him to see both Pooja and Devyani together. He neither had guessed nor had any wish to see them together in his life. The two sides of his life which were poles apart had come to the same point and made him feel extreme psychological nausea and he felt as if nothing was inside and everything he had in him struggled to come out. He was out of his realm of reality since last few days and was ignoring the day that would cause him this sickness but never expected it like this, suddenly. The arrival of Pooja had plunged him into the reality he was dwelling into since years. He was again the same sick, dispirited man now.

'When are you both getting married then,' Devyani asked Pooja amicably.

'Hopefully soon. And I hope meeting you won't disturb him again,' she said casually with a smile, though her intentions were clear.

'Sorry?' Devyani said softly with a smile.

Pooja didn't look at her instantly and then spoke in a serious tone, 'He's really ruined his years for you Devyani. I just request you not to come close and ruin his life once again. He just doesn't know what to trust and what not.' She sounded cold and Devyani gazed at her.

'I don't know what you know about us Pooja but...I really don't think you could understand our situations let alone be mine.' She was sincere.

'I don't want to dear. Understanding you won't concern me. It's him and his life you ruined that I care about,' Pooja retorted. Devyani smiled.

'But now he's happy with you isn't he?' Devyani sounded as if mocking at Pooja's opinion although she had no intention to.

'Maybe not, but he has someone now who won't throw him once desires get fulfilled,' Pooja countered.

'I wish that'll make him forget the old memories.'

'Please don't mind but your memories just became a burden for him. Like a prey that was feeding off his happiness.'

'It might be an addiction,' Devyani jeered. Her smile made Pooja feel disgusted.

'It's filthy and sick. And you know what Devyani, no matter how rich you are and how wide is the gap between your economic status and either of us, sleeping with men doesn't make you great no matter how beautiful you are,' replied Pooja with hatred that she tried to hide.

They saw Siddhant coming to them and saw him greeting someone who just came across him.

'Oh, that brings one more thing,' said Devyani and continued, 'Have you slept with anyone else before...ever?' Pooja gazed at her in utter hatred and disgust and Devyani moved a bit forward to prevent anyone else from hearing them and scoffed quietly with a piercing smile, 'If yes, then I'm afraid I'll always be the one to lose my virginity to him no matter how many men I sleep with.' She added, 'And you'll never be the one to have that moment no matter how many times you sleep with him.

The pride and pleasure he took in loving me won't be there...it will only get diminished.' She moved back and sat again in the earlier position.

Pooja still gazed at her and grumbled in extreme disgust, 'I wonder what he saw in you. I'll not deign to argue with you. You are nothing but a sick woman.'

Siddhant came by then and sat with them. 'I'm sorry ladies I was away,' he said.

Devyani looked normal while Pooja said immediately yet normally, 'I'm not feeling well Siddhant. I need to sleep I guess. Will you please take me to the hotel?'

'Of course, but we could go in a while if you could wait', he said and also looked at Devyani.

'No I can't sit anymore,' she replied instantly.

'It's fine Siddhant. She needs rest. You should take her to the hotel,' articulated Devyani. Siddhant who didn't want to go away from her although there was no point sitting there, looked at her and said, 'Okay.'

'I'm waiting outside,' said Pooja and walked to leave the palace straight away.

'What happened to her?' He asked Devyani.

'Nothing,' replied Devyani, seeing her walking away and added, 'She must be tired.' He just gazed at Devyani and then stood up to leave.

'So you leaving?' She asked.

'I think so.'

'Will be at apartment tomorrow?'

'Hotel I guess. She'll be there.'

'You can come there. Half past eleven I guess I'll be there.' He looked at her in partial amazement and partial curiosity as if he never knew her. 'You still want to meet me?' He asked.

'What makes you think I don't?'

'You know I may get engaged with her in some months. And she's here and still?' He asked.

'I want to smell you,' she whispered coming close to him in his ears and added, 'One last time.' Her face couldn't be read. It had the expression of both affection and longing for carnage knowledge he thought when he tried to read it from both the viewpoints. He was once again bewildered by her expression. The woman who avoided coming close to him a few days back was herself asking for his time and intimate companionship, and that too inside the walls of the apartment, without any bond or attachment after their departure from the city after two days. There was no question of refusing, even if it was for one last time.

CHAPTER 28

He had reached the apartment before Pooja woke up. She had told him the last night she had a meeting today and she had to be there although she didn't want to leave and had expressed it to him.

'I don't think I should leave you here,' she said.

'You must go. I'm fine now. And I have people here,' he replied and she gazed at him. 'The hotel staff is here Pooja,' he added convincing her that he didn't depend on Devyani although he had meant the same.

***

She stood at the doorstep of the apartment at around twelve, knocking at the door and he opened the door after a few minutes.

'What are you doing here?' She asked in astonishment. 'The guy at the hotel told me you stay here too,' she told about Hitesh.

'I just come here for some peace and solitude,' he said while walking inside again and sitting on the bed. She too entered the apartment.

'Siddhant, don't do this to yourself. Life isn't about running away from people or behind them. It's about finding peace with people you are with,' she said and he listened half-heartedly. 'And why are you not wearing a shirt?' She asked him who sat in his shorts.

'I just felt warmth here,' he replied gesturing towards the heater, which was switched off.

'Just wear something,' she said and gave him the t-shirt which was kept on the bed. 'And take care Siddhant,' she said and kissed him. 'I have my flight in sometime, I'll have to leave. Just take care and take medicines on time okay.'

'Okay,' he said. She kissed his forehead and left after hugging him and he locked the door.

Devyani came out of the bathroom and sat on the bed. 'I told you she loves you,' she said sitting on the bed behind him.

'This is all wrong Devyani,' he said.

'What's wrong?' She asked.

'This. What we're doing.'

'Why you think so?'

'We can't play with others' feelings.'

She came close to him from his back. 'But you never said anything when I came to you leaving my husband,' she said calmly in his ears with a smile, looking at him from behind.

'I'm talking about both of them. They're good people.' He explained himself in his deep voice. She laughed now and lay down on the bed behind him.

'Seems I'm the only one who's not good and upstanding' she mocked.

'Don't get me wrong. I never said that,' he uttered. He sounded genuine and serious.

'Doesn't matter. No beauty is perfect till it's tainted with scars of judgment,' she said calmly looking at the ceiling of the apartment now.

'You know how upstanding you are in my opinion,' he said looking towards the pillow of the bed which was beside her, without turning back to look at her.

'I know. That's why I'm here.'

'But I can't ruin anyone's life anymore,' he said and added after a moment, 'Especially yours more than anyone else's. Even if it's the last time.' She didn't speak. He sat there and neither of them spoke for a while.

'What are you thinking?' She then asked in a concerned voice. He replied after a brief pause.

'Thinking that how worthless a man I have become,' he said in a low voice. She now looked at him although she could only see his back. He now looked downwards on the floor.

'Years ago when everyone would tell me I was such a bright young man, I would look down upon others who were around me. Who were not very good at academics or not very talented or not very well knew things that go around the world,' he expressed in a low voice. 'And today, how far behind I have been left in this race called life,' he added. 'In this time lapse of life, I never realised how fast others were moving and I was just...seeing the time slithering away from my grasp...bit by bit.' He stopped and she didn't say or ask anything to him. Neither of them spoke for the next few minutes. What he had expressed was both about the absence of professional proliferation as well as personal and moral descent in his life. He didn't know if she had understood what he had said. He didn't even intend to, as more than to her, he had told that fact to himself. And he did not want to fall deeper in a ditch of decadence. He spoke again.

'You should go. If I am meeting you the last time today, I want to see you as his wife and not like my...' he said intensely. 'I'm your culprit. Our meeting like this could ruin your relationship,' he added and then stood up to walk towards the door. He reached the door and turned to look at her. She was lying on the bed in her beige t-shirt bra looking at him while he looked at her, tensed and concerned. He was disturbed and her face looked as if her heart was devoid of any feeling. She then spread her hand out towards him and looked yearning now and he couldn't help. He gazed at her for a while and then walked to her to sit beside her. He took her in his arms and forgot everything he had just now said for a while, to see her happy.

CHAPTER 29

The family stood under the huge *mandap*–the pillared pavilion–and with them stood many others. Numerous others sat and looked at the bride and groom from outside the *mandap* which looked exquisitely pleasing with delicately carved pillars draped with silk and flowers. The white and red flower strings could be seen hanging from the edges on the top of the *mandap.* The light emanating from numerous chandeliers and beautiful traditional lamps glistened the surrounding. The huge floral hangings and the pious fire of the *mandap* filled the whole environ with an aroma that was magical. The setting sun made the evening seem enchanting. Rhea looked beautiful as a bride and so did Raghav as her groom. Siddhant looked at Devyani who was closer to Rhea and stood with Robin. She looked like she never did before; he would always say that while seeing her, he thought. But she indeed looked different today. She looked all that a married woman could look like, not only because she wore a blood red bespoke silk saree with her hair tied in a bun with a jasmine flower garland and completed her look with heavy neckpiece and earrings but because her face looked ethereal and pure in the artificial light mixed with that of a setting sun when she stood beside Robin as his wife. She watched Rhea and Raghav take rounds of the fire with ritualistic Sanskrit chants being recited which made the surrounding even more beautiful and serene. She was smiling and her face looked nothing like it looked in the day today when they were at the apartment.

He would never love anyone the way he had loved her.

***

They sat with each other in the garden that had multiple tables with scarlet settings and were alone when Robin was away to meet someone. He spoke to her after having a normal conversation.

'So, it all ends, Mrs. Shah,' he said but without any grievance or despondency and with a smile. She smiled.

'It's all a new beginning. Like they have begun a new life,' she said talking about Rhea and Raghav.

'Hmm, they married someone they wanted to,' he expressed casually.

'They got someone who loves them more than anyone else. And that...is what matters,' she articulated.

'Love,' he muttered and added, 'Let's not talk about that today and leave in peace.'

'But why? She loves you more than anyone else could.' He gave her a questioning look. 'Hmm,' she expressed.

'She'll never get it back I'm afraid,' he replied.

'She will. I know you. You'll love her one day.'

'You don't know me.'

'You're closing your eyes to the dawn in your love for the dark nights. I'm not the girl you had loved. I'm not that Devyani that you're looking for.'

'Indeed,' he expressed.

'Don't be mad. You are being ignorant of a love that's there.'

'Have you seen a cremation?' He asked calmly.

'Why?'

'You may take a person to thousands of places for a cure, yet once reached the grave, there's no cure that works,' he said then added, 'And unfortunately, it's always the people whom one had loved the most who cremate them. People who hate don't even try to break the bonds of the dead with the world.' He stood up looking dejected and dispirited like this for the first time since he had met her here.

'Come with me.' She stood up and said taking him in a quiet corner area of the palace which had no one around.

'Our chapter got over years ago Siddhant,' she convinced him.

'Some chapters decide the fate of a book,' he argued.

'I am not that one.'

'It is I who'll decide that,' he said hiding what went inside him; his face and moist eyes betrayed him though.

'Don't make me feel guilty before leaving.'

'You don't need to,' he said. 'Unrequited love is the only sin that exonerates the sinner.'

'Why all this now? We parted ways on a good note. And you were okay back then.' She sounded as if all was normal.

'Okay. If my silence convinces you.'

'And there's nothing like unrequited love. It's just psychological. The more something goes away from you, the more you look for it. This girl loves you more than anyone ever could,' she said and then added tenderly, 'Life is too precious to ruin for someone Siddhant. I just wish I could make you understand.'

'Fair enough.'

'You'll never understand,' she said quietly with a tense look on her face. He didn't say anything for a while and then said holding her face, 'Don't you worry. I'll not hold grudges. Just became a boy for some time that I had been years ago Devyani.' He sounded deep, firm, and resolute now. 'I give you my word I'll try to be happy and forget you,' he continued and added, 'But don't expect me to be normal. For I can never forget you.' She kept gazing at him.

'Why can't you be a little practical?' She grumbled and it exasperated him now.

'Oh really? Really? Practical? Like what should I do?' He roared in frustration leaving her face.

'Siddhant-'

'No tell me what should I do. Should I leave someone to die like your father did?' She looked at him in surprise and didn't say anything. She then tried to hold him by his arms and say something but he pushed her back holding her arms.

'You know what? You have no right to tell anyone how to live and I know it doesn't even matter to you. I know all this is just a fucking small part of your life that you'd forget about the moment you leave this place.'

Her eyes looked moist now yet she didn't say anything. They both didn't say anything for a while and then he sighed and his phone rang. It was Pooja. He received it.

'Yeah I'm fine,' he said and hung up the phone after few moments and looked at her again.

'Can't you be happy?' She asked quietly after a moment or two and he looked at her in surprise.

'I am going Devyani. I am just scared of that day when I'll be successful in my attempt to hate you. And I don't want that to happen,' he said while breathing heavily and added, 'I wish you a great life and everything else you desire.' He kissed her forehead and turned to leave the palace.

She stood there watching him go.

CHAPTER 30

The day was cold and cloudy unlike yesterday and became chillier as the evening grew. It was three and he was still lying down in the bed in the apartment. He wasn't sleeping but just lay there and found no spirit to get up. It was a dream or a bad dream in a dream he thought. But the crease in the bed was still there that was made when she was there. How could some of the pieces of glass still be there if she hadn't swept them in that corner? Maybe it was someone else. Or may be he just hallucinated it all. He was neither sleeping nor awake for the extreme pain in his head didn't let him do either. He was dazed and no sense of reaction could be felt. He, however, had it in mind that she had her flight at around five. But what if all this was not for real and what he was seeing and feeling since last few days was just his imagination and he was getting demented with a psychotic disruption. Lying sideways, he looked towards the side table of the bed, and saw the medicines he had got from the hospital and realised it was all indeed true. He needed a medicine he thought, although not for appendicitis but for his headache. He got up slowly as if lifting the burden of his body and thought that he might be having some in his coat, which was in the wardrobe. He searched the inner pocket of his coat that he wore three days back. The medicine was there. It had something else too which he thought he didn't keep there. He inserted his hand and felt something cold and metallic and took it out. It was hers; a sterling silver pendant with engravings–which made an image of a Hindu goddess–that she would sometimes wear and always remove while in bed for some superstition she had believed in and he very well remembered it, for he had asked her about the same only three days ago.

'*What are you doing?*' He had asked when she was removing her pendant while he was disrobing her and removing her boots.

'*Nothing. Can't wear it while doing this,*' she had said with heavy breathing and he had not asked her again.

He watched it and took out a note too which he had felt inside the pocket. It read-

Have a blessed life,

Devyani.

It reassured him that all of it was indeed true and not a hallucination. He sat on the bed and looked outside the window in the balcony where she stood with him three days ago. He also saw the parts and corners of the room where she stayed with him. Nothing was there and he sat there alone. Of course, the kids who played in the narrow street could be heard playing and shouting. It was half past three in the evening he realised when he looked at his watch. He groped his coat pocket once again and then all the pockets of his coat. All were empty. He again saw the room and the balcony and realised that she was gone. He sat down for some time and realised that she still would be in the city and had her flight at five thirty. He could at least see her at the airport for the last time he thought.

***

It was hard to stand in the chilly weather with cold breeze in the open parking. Only a few people were there and he was right on time. No more than ten minutes passed when a car stopped outside the entrance to the main edifice of the airport. A man with a woman and a toddler stepped out. It wasn't them he realized, although another car followed which he hadn't noticed and stopped beside the car that came first. Someone stepped out of the car but he couldn't see as another car and people who stepped out stood exactly in front of her. The car moved eventually and he saw them standing there taking some of their luggage along with a handbag that hung in her hand. In her loosely fitted pink fine gauge sweater and jeans she looked as beautiful as she always did he thought although he couldn't see her eyes which were covered with glasses. He wanted to see her as much as he could in those few seconds in which she walked with her husband towards the entrance and entered it eventually. She looked so normal he thought. He put a cigarette in his mouth and lit it. He saw the entrance once again. No one was there now. He turned.

***

Weather was extremely cold with the night getting darker, however, the bar had some warmth partially with people in it and partially because of the cognac that helped him in feeling so. His body felt good after he had much of it. All his way from the airport to the part of the city where the bar was located, he saw many buildings decorated with colourful lights and all the bars, restaurants and hotels seemed to be packed with people who were ready to celebrate. Many people hustled around him too in the bar where he sat and the cacophony was relieving for him. 'One more,' he said to the bartender, sitting on the barstool, to feel good and drain the coldness from his body. The jostling crowd kept on getting swelled with each passing quarter of the hour. The city was ready to welcome the New Year..

VOLUME 3

CHAPTER 31

Six months later, Delhi.

'Do you think I can be a perfect man for you?' He asked Pooja casually when they sat in a restaurant in Connaught Place, at a weekend, where people danced on the dance floor but there wasn't loud music and the softness of it helped them have a good time.

'No one can be perfect. I am not perfect,' she expressed while having a small mouthful of her wine.

'No philosophy today,' he said.

'But there is nothing known as perfect Sid. *Life* is not perfect. We make it perfect with our little happiness and with people we love, we care for,' she emphasised casually.

'Love? You believe in it?' He asked and had a mouthful of wine.

'Not like others do.'

'How do you know what others think?'

'I don't know. But I know that love is not something that needs to be felt all the time or to be seen in our actions. It's just there. When we love someone, we love them. And that's that. No one including you and I can emphasise it over and over again to express it,' she said while he ate his meal.

'All that I know is that I can't imagine someone as a man in my life but you,' she said. ' And I can say with all my heart that

I can try and be the most suitable lady of your life if not the perfect one,' she added.

'Seems only I have the wrong definition of love,' Siddhant mocked after a pause and they laughed.

'And besides, I think my kids won't get a better father than you.'

'Oh, I don't think so.'

'But I know so.'

'All parents are good. I mean they always do best for their children.'

'Maybe. You'd still be the best.'

'If they take after you, then sure.' She gazed at him with happiness.

'I see such a great change in you for the first time. And I can't thank god enough for that.'

'I was always normal,' he argued but very normally unlike he would do earlier.

'You wish. I can't remember when was the last time you were so open.'

'What bullshit! You're the only woman I ever opened my heart to,' he flirted innocently.

'I wish that was true.'

'But it's true.'

'Well, you ain't got a chance not to open it. I'm anyway getting married to you,' she said and he smiled.

'You are a wonderful human Pooja,' he said sincerely. 'I don't know what would have happened to me had we not been together.'

'Glad you understood it finally,' she said playfully.

'Hmm...I only couldn't see you in the mess of life.' He expressed in a low voice.

'What's done is done. It's this day that matters,' she tried to make him forget what was over.

'Exactly,' he said in enthusiasm now and added, 'And that...calls for a celebration.' He spoke and got up and took her hands to take her to the dance floor. She was overwhelmed and exclaimed, 'Oh my god!' and stood up to go to the dance floor where the couples did whatever type of half-known dance they knew that could be called a concoction of Rumba, Tango, Foxtrot and others but looked amusing with their joy. He looked happy and she too was happy for a great beginning at last and danced with him.

***

He dropped her home and kissed her in the car. The evening was a good one for them after the load of the weekdays. The last six months proved to be metamorphic in their lives and she nonetheless hadn't expressed it to him but had thought and been satisfied that may be the confrontation with an addiction often had the power to make it less efficacious. Not that he didn't realise that but the reason for him was different from hers as it was not the only reason.

He didn't live in a gothic era or an earlier century where unrequited love–or at least that's what he called it–would make it necessary for a lover to suffer till his last breath. Besides, he had convinced himself that what if Pooja was the person who was always destined for him. After all, she was the one beside him while he underwent the surgery a few months ago. Partly in a process to convince himself about Pooja and partly while realising that past events of his life were his reality, he had begun a new life, or at least had embarked on his journey to live it. The hollowness inside him was leaving slowly with a new approach towards life. Although it was all difficult but he, at last, had started to convince himself that he can't let his condition affect others around him anymore and acted as normal as he could in front of Pooja hiding inside himself what was left.

He avoided the fact that he could do all this because he knew that *someone* was happy in life. He did all this but was never sure if he will ever love someone else.

CHAPTER 32

Months elapsed since he had underwent the surgery for his appendicitis although the routine checkup was necessary for him and he didn't want to take a risk for health anymore and was in the hospital for the same after which he was going to take a sigh of relief as it was one of the final checkups he needed. Reports were alright but his head was not, as he needed to sleep badly and was going to spend his Sunday the next day alone, sleeping and spending some time with himself. Not much people were in the hospital at this hour in the evening and specially near the main door which had a reception on its left from the entrance and two ways in front of it from where one led to the OPD and the waiting lounge whereas the second one led to the wards as well as the departments of coronary care unit, intensive care unit, cancer centre and others amongst the surgery and urgent care departments. He just passed across the reception area and came out to the outer area of the hospital where he had parked his car and opened it to sit in it. He waited for a second, started the engine and then stopped it. He came out suddenly, anxiously walked fast inside and tried to behave normally. He sat there waiting for some time to make sure if he had seen someone he knew although it was just a glance and he could be wrong he thought. But he was probably right he thought and then waited. He was walking near the reception area normally and after more than half an hour when he realised he was right, he behaved normally again as he wanted to make it sure to her he was not waiting for her. He walked to go out as she was going too and suddenly he realised from the corner of his eyes that he had been seen but still waited to be called and if not, then he will talk himself. That wasn't needed though as he heard a voice.

'Siddhant, is that you?' Rhea asked. She finally called him and he reassured it to himself that he wasn't mistaken in recognising her.

'Rhea, what are you doing here?' He turned and exclaimed and they hugged each other.

'Nothing. Just a friend of mine was here. Was in the city so thought to visit,' she told plainly. She was a sincere woman and didn't hate Siddhant for his background.

'Oh,' he said and added, 'Anything serious?'

'Kind of,' she said.

'Who is it?' He asked.

'Just a close one, I hope she'll be okay,' she said anxiously and added, 'How come you're here?'

'Just...just a routine checkup,' he said and added, 'So how's Raghav and everyone back at home?'

'Everyone's good,' she replied but seemed less interested now and he realised it instantly. He didn't want to ask anything about the person who was a common link between them and didn't need to as she was here for a friend and he wouldn't ask anything to look very eager and desperate.

'Okay then Rhea,' he said.

'Okay Siddhant,' she said and they hugged each other and she bid him goodbye and he came out. He got inside his car and didn't start it for some moments. He behaves mad and does unnecessary things sometimes he thought. He then took a sigh of relief. The engine of his car roared and he left the precinct.

***

He took his medicine for headache but couldn't sleep which was a normal occurrence with him in case of headaches and watched TV in his living room but still thought about Rhea in between and how annoying such a situation becomes sometimes when you have to face it. He said to himself quietly and very calmly lying on the couch, 'How fucked up your life is. The more you run away from something the more it haunts you.' He watched the movie till half-past two and then another show, as sleep had still not knocked on his door for the night. Weather is so humid he thought and went out in his balcony and saw lights of the poles outside each tower of the society and other society adjacent to his own. He loved this view and especially at night when no one could be seen but some dogs and their pups from the ninth floor. Keeping a cigarette in his mouth, he lit it and thought that she must be somewhere else, and god knows what I thought when I saw Rhea outside another entrance that was adjacent to the OPD. She must be in Mumbai. Or maybe London. How does it matter and why am I guessing here at this hour he thought. He enjoyed the cool breeze and felt relaxed. He then walked inside and watched the comedy show again. He didn't realise when he began dozing and woke up again, both by the loud laughter of the audience of the TV show that was running and a wild thought that came to his mind out of nowhere. What if that *'She'* from *'I hope she'll be okay'* was her? No, it can't be he suddenly thought then. Such thoughts come so often to me these days. Sometimes they are logical and sometimes rubbish. And why would her cousin lie to me? I never had any ill feelings for that family or even Robin. And even if I have, why would she lie if her cousin was really serious, he convinced himself. 'You think too much sometimes Siddhant,' he sighed to himself and then tried to sleep lying there while the TV was still on. What if it is her? He thought in his sleep and this time, he was serious and it seemed that the phantom he was hiding inside himself was now taking a form once again and he got irritated at himself. He got up and kept another cigarette in his mouth and then kept it aside and cursed himself. 'You can't mend your ways.' He walked to the kitchen and drank some water from the bottle and saw his car keys hanging from a hook near the wall of the kitchen. He stood there for a while holding the fridge door open. He stood there still for some more moments and then suddenly closed the door of the fridge, put on his jeans and t-shirt, took the car and apartment keys, and left the house.

***

Humidity was less suffocating at this hour and he also had turned on the AC of the car while sitting inside it, parking it on the road opposite to the hospital. It was five now and as nothing could be seen, he was dozing sitting inside and waking up to see if any known face could be seen entering or coming out of the hospital. He woke up after the dawn broke with the noises of the buses and cars. I should be watchful he thought and now saw vigilantly at the main gate of the hospital. Nothing could be seen and it was all in vain he thought for a moment but thought to wait at least till seven. If there's anyone really close to Rhea, she should be here early. He waited. Stepping out of the car, he went to a roadside tea vendor and asked for a cup of tea and lit a cigarette keeping it in mouth.

'Are you waiting for someone sir?' The vendor asked Siddhant in Hindi. He must've seen him waiting there since long he thought.

'Hmm,' he muttered.

'Rain hasn't arrived yet sir. Humidity keeps on increasing. It's *Shraavan* though,' said the tea vendor while making some tea, talking about the month of monsoon according to the Hindu calendar. Siddhant didn't say anything and he too didn't say anything for a while.

'Are you from here sir?' He then asked Siddhant. Siddhant wasn't paying heed to his talks.

'Hmm.'

'I've come today from home after a week,' he said. 'From UP,' he added.

'You from UP?' Asked Siddhant at last who also had his hometown in the same state.

'Yes sir,' he replied.

'How's it there these days?' Asked Siddhant without really wishing to know the answer.

'It's good sir,' he replied and asked, 'Have you been to UP sir?'

'Hmm,' he replied. He was just about to say something else when he saw a car getting slowed down near the gate of the hospital which then entered it. He couldn't see or recognise who it was, but before parking the car, someone would come out he thought. He crossed the road walking fast and then looked from outside, hiding himself behind the wall and the pillar outside the hospital. He was right he thought when he saw Rhea coming out along with her mother. It definitely was someone close. He couldn't go back now and had to know whoever it was. He should wait he thought.

***

He was a bit casual too as he thought it could be someone from their friends only. The reason was that he had realised that why Devyani would be admitted to a hospital in Delhi–although it had its name amongst one of the best in the country–when she could get better treatment anywhere across the world especially if the 'patient' as told by Rhea was serious. And he didn't see Robin too. The effect of sleeplessness at night had made him feel bizarre things he thought but still thought he should go inside to check one last time. And he walked inside. He took an appointment just to pass the time over there. He was outside the OPD just expecting someone he could see from the family and every time the elevator would open, he would turn his back and walk in the opposite direction and see from a distance who it was. Half an hour was passed and it was ten now. Why was he here he thought. He went inside the chemist store in front of the reception area on the right to the entrance and bought some toffees. He counted the coins that the storekeeper had given him when his mind got interrupted again with a known voice with an addition of another and he turned and watched for some moments to convince himself that the people he was seeing were really there. The anxiousness was overtaking his mind yet he behaved as normal as he could and walked as if he had seen him but was in the hospital for his own cause when Robin saw him.

'Siddhant?' Exclaimed Robin.

'Hi, how are you doing Robin?' He asked normally.

'I am doing good. What are you doing here?' He asked in a bit amazement and looked at Rhea.

'Nothing. Just came to collect my reports. What about you?' Told Siddhant convincingly.

Robin looked at Rhea who looked a bit uneasy and then told Siddhant calmly, 'Devyani is here.'

'What happened to her?' Siddhant asked firmly. Robin looked glum and looked downwards now.

'She's just...too ill,' he said calmly. 'A haemorrhage,' he added.

The three of them stood there while Siddhant grasped what he had heard from Robin. He didn't look at Rhea to ask why she had lied to him the previous day, which she thought he would. He looked calm. Contrary to what many people think, the human mind can get unresponsive in such a situation instead of being agitated. He looked indifferent from his countenance.

'Can I see her?' He asked quietly after a few seconds.

'Sure,' answered Robin. 'Just wait here for a moment. I just need to take a pill for myself,' added Robin after a moment and went inside the chemist store. Siddhant stood there with Rhea.

He gazed at her now and she didn't say anything yet felt less uneasy now and looked elsewhere.

'Why did you lie?' He asked.

'Coz I didn't want you to know,' she replied readily.

'Know what?'

'That she's here.'

'Why?'

She waited for a few seconds before answering. 'Coz she didn't want you to know,' she told.

'What you mean?'

'She didn't want you to know she was...ill.'

'What rubbish. She didn't know I would be meeting you here.'

She didn't speak anything. And then Robin arrived before she could speak. 'Come...Siddhant,' he said and walked slowly towards the staircase instead of the elevator.

'Meet me in the hospital cafeteria after you are back. I'll be waiting in half an hour,' Rhea said and walked away. He stood there tried to comprehend what she had said and then walked towards the staircase where Robin had walked.

She was in a ward on the first floor and he followed Robin to the door and saw Rhea's mother when Robin opened the door. She was sitting on the couch in a small and well-equipped ICU ward. He greeted her with a nod to which she replied conceitedly. He then saw her on the bed on the right side where she lay down on a life support system with an oxygen mask on. He still didn't want to be seen as affected as he was really. He moved towards her but didn't get too close and saw multiple wires on her body that were attached to multiple machines that he might have seen the last time when his mother was in the ICU years ago, along with the cardiac monitor which was on her left side. He moved a bit forward and saw her face, which was mostly covered with the mask and her skin looked extremely pale. She wore the hospital gown and her pallid arms in the half sleeves of the gown looked extremely thin with noticeable veins. His legs felt too weak to carry his weight and his hands, too cold, although he felt his face and the area near his ear to be extremely hot as if due to imbalanced blood circulation in the dead silence of the room, which had an extremely negative aura he felt. Turning back, he sat on the couch beside Robin.

'I will be back in some time,' said Mrs. Khanna and stood up and Robin too stood up and she hugged him with warmth and said, 'Don't lose hope. You are strong.' He didn't say anything but gave a formal, dull smile. She left and Siddhant watched Devyani. Robin again sat beside him on the couch. They sat there in silence for some moments before he spoke.

'What happened?' He asked firmly in a low voice.

'Haemorrhage,' Robin sighed. Siddhant didn't speak readily then and waited.

'How?' He asked after a pause.

'Some inherited issue.'

'What did the doctor say?'

Robin didn't say anything. Siddhant too didn't ask it again. He then asked, 'Why don't you take her somewhere else?'

'No use I guess.'

'When did she come?'

'Yesterday morning.'

'And what did the doctor say?'

Robin again didn't reply. Siddhant didn't ask anything and kept on looking at her again.

'How did it? I mean how did it happen?' He asked after a brief pause.

'She was in the washroom when I heard the sound,' told Robin. 'Came here immediately but she was...comatose by then,' he added after some moments. 'Thought of taking her somewhere else. Doctors told me I can if I want to just...convince myself,' he added glumly.

'What you mean? We can't just sit here and wait,' he groaned.

Robin said after a pause, 'Thanks Siddhant.' 'Coming here wasn't a good idea for us I guess,' he added. Siddhant knew what he meant to say. 'When did you?' He asked.

'Two days back.'

'You people have been here since then?' He exclaimed.

Robin's phone vibrated and he went out. Siddhant watched her, as he had never expected. He stood up after moments and got closer to her. He looked at her hands with something attached to it which he thought was pulse oximeter and touched her thumb very lightly from his finger which lay down there as if it had no life. She was cold and he got a bit uneasy as if someone was watching over him and he felt a bout of jitters.

Robin entered again and Siddhant turned and walked towards the door just to hide his countenance from her husband without wishing to leave.

'Thanks for coming,' expressed Robin despondently. Siddhant just nodded and asked for his card, 'Could I have your contact number or card.' Robin nodded and handed it to him taking it out from his wallet. Siddhant took it and walked out and stood near the railing that stretched on the four sides above of the corridors of the courtyard, which was on the ground floor where some chairs could be seen and some staff members too. He felt as if life came to him after a bout of smothering experience. His head was not paining anymore and he felt as if he was having a nightmare in a dream and was still lying on the couch in his apartment.

He kept his palm on his face for some time resting his knees on the railing. His face was warm and hands, cold, he felt.

He then walked towards the hospital cafeteria.

CHAPTER 33

'Do I need to ask Rhea?' Siddhant asked calmly yet firmly as soon as he sat in the cafeteria of the hospital where she sat on the corner table. She spoke after a while, 'She asked me not to tell you. And I'm not guilty of it so please...'

'What did she ask not to tell?'

'That she was never too easy to be understood by either you or by her husband,' Rhea expressed calmly.

'Don't play with words. I need to know,' he groaned. 'Please.' She gazed at him.

'Okay,' she said. 'She was one mad girl. And as if it was not enough, cursed by an unwanted disorder. If you know what I mean.'

'No I don't,' he snapped.

'I told you, you could never get it.'

'What rubbish?'

'You think that because you didn't know about her mother.'

'What about her?'

'That's why I say you didn't know.'

'Tell me what's it?'

'She wasn't...sound. You know what I mean. Her mother.'

'Like?'

'She had some issue and it seems she kind of inherited it,' Rhea expressed softly.

'That can't be.'

'You may call it so coz you don't know it.'

'She never told me.'

'What did she tell you?'

He didn't say anything.

'She told you what she had in her heart for you. She hid what she had in her heart, *for* you.'

'So? What has it got to do with her illness here? Why didn't you tell me yesterday?'

'She didn't want you to perish for the love she had had for you.' He listened and didn't speak for a few seconds. 'And?' He asked quietly and then waited vigilantly.

'I don't know exactly but what I heard since my teenage was that her mother, my aunt, wasn't sound. Especially when she left,' Rhea told and then continued, 'And what I think is that not only the relationship between the parents but the illness of her mother too enveloped her. And I don't know if that is the exact reason or she had reasons of her own that she always felt the imminent doom on you whenever she was with you.'

'Wait. You mean she left me coz she was scared for me?' He asked and his face looked disgusted and surprised.

'That's what I know,' she said. 'She always had some serious issue with relationships,' she added.

'But she was happy with me,' said Siddhant who still thought of it as another rubbish by another of her relatives.

'Of course she was.'

'So?'

She gazed at him. He looked disturbed to her and that's why he could not understand what she tried to tell him, she thought. 'You still don't get it. She left you for she always had a fear of losing you.'

'But I was with her. And she knew... and knows that I very much love her.'

'That's what I am trying to tell you. She feared to lose you not *by* you...but by certain doom that could strike you had she been with you. A kind of phobia you can say...of losing people she loved.' He kept on looking at her even after she had finished.

'Why should I believe you?'

'Coz you have no reason not to...and I am sitting here just because of her and telling you all this that she never wanted me to tell anyone.'

'Did *she* tell you all this or?'

'She expressed it to me when I myself realised it and asked her.'

'When did you get to know?' He asked after a pause.

'Sometime after your break-up,' she replied. 'I just saw her seeing your profile on a social media platform and asked her. God knows in what state of mind she told me. But she also asked me never to tell it to you if a situation arises.'

'Was she...is she *so* superstitious?' He asked.

'It's not just superstition. It was also her mental state about you. And the confluence proved to be fatal for her...at last.'

'What you mean? Did she...' he tried to ask if it was she herself who was responsible for her state.

'Not at all. See I am just guessing here so don't ask anything to Robin for her sake,' she asked and added, 'After she returned from my wedding, her behaviour had sort of changed as he told me.'

'Like what?'

'I don't know exactly but she seemed to be...vexed with people. Don't ask about it to Robin. He just told me.' He didn't know what to say. 'She had told me she had taken an oath and had promised herself she will not be in touch with you again after leaving you years ago,' she added after almost half a minute. They both sat without saying a word after this.

'Anything else you want to tell?' He asked at last firmly. His behaviour looked sick and glum to her now.

'I told you what I knew,' Rhea replied. They sat for some moments and then she added, 'I think she had become like you Siddhant...or was becoming. From what I know about you from her.' He gazed at her now and then stood up.

'Did you really love her?' She asked the moment he stood up. This question had defined the lives, and only the defined lives could answer this question. Others had no meaning for the answer that the question had had. He just looked at her without answering and then left the cafeteria.

CHAPTER 34

Thinking was unworkable at all, with realisation and cognition being out of the question right now; the process of sinking in what was known went on. "How could it be?" was the only question, if any, that was passing through the mind and consciousness now, and emptying the second glass of whisky in the afternoon could not help it. It was all too bookish the mind said. Not that he didn't trust Rhea for she had no reason to tell what she did. Numerous questions haunted him now looking for answers but the will to find them was leaving him gradually when everything was near an end and they could never see each other like before. He could never confront her for what she did and she could never confess what went inside her mind that made her do what she did. So sickening such a faith is he thought; if *this* is the reason behind her decisions in life, then what were the cognitive abilities for, in a spirit and its existence. She had left him for she had a phobia of seeing him in pain with her presence in his life. Turning him into an indifferent soul years ago, she had this time turned him into a stoic whose face could not reflect what went inside him even if the poignant mnemonic was showing everything to him from a completely novel viewpoint; this time, like a newborn. The questions which disturbed him the most with a sense of being betrayed a few hours ago regarding her mother, her condition, and her own condition were all vanished and all that was left was a silence that resonated more than a sound that a man could make.

He walked out of the bar quietly and sat in his car in the parking and didn't realise when he dozed and woke up after what he realised was an hour later. Waking up while going through such a condition often makes a man doubt his own cognitive ability he thought and gave himself some time to realise what had happened. All that he could do now was nothing but talk with Robin if he would not be rigid, not for the sake of knowing what he didn't but getting close to and then getting an entry in an establishment where he could never dwell–her reality and purpose. He took out Robin's card from his pocket and called him to ask if he could meet him, and to his surprise, Robin agreed.

***

Siddhant saw him standing and looking outside from a huge window in the area that was on the left on getting upstairs on the way to her ward, which was on the right. Siddhant walked to him.

'Sorry I came again,' Siddhant murmured standing beside him.

'Oh it's fine,' replied Robin realising his presence and said, 'Sit,' gesturing towards the couch that was there and added, 'Rhea's mother is there so I came here.'

'It's okay. I just came to see you two,' said Siddhant sitting with him on the couch.

'Thanks,' he replied and then asked formally, 'How's your work going?'

'Very well.'

They sat without saying anything for a while as Robin didn't have anything to talk to him and Siddhant didn't want to sound inquisitive.

'What's the time of doctor's visit?' Siddhant then asked.

'In the evening,' replied Robin. Siddhant then waited to initiate the conversation about her.

'You were saying she had inherited something. The reason for her health,' said Siddhant carefully not to sound too interrogative while asking a personal question.

'Hmm. Something AVM,' he said. 'Some malfunctioning in her brain's artery and veins,' he added. Siddhant listened to him and then added quietly, 'I didn't know.'

'Even I didn't know,' said Robin and Siddhant thought he might not know about her mother or her faith and decisions. He sat there. The will to ask more had died in him there where she was only a few yards away in her last, and may be a peaceful slumber.

'Can I see her?' He asked. In this phase of life when she was not going to speak to him again and had sacrificed all that she had had in the name of an oath to save *him*, he didn't have anything he realised to feel hesitant about. Robin gazed at him and nodded. They walked towards the ward where Mrs. Khanna sat on the couch.

She was surprised to see him again and he didn't nod or greet her or even look at her this time. He just found the woman lying in the bed in the same state that she was in, a few hours ago.

'I am just coming in a while,' Rhea's mother said when they entered the ward and Robin too came out with her leaving Siddhant inside alone with Devyani. The stoic he had been was not there at this moment and the vexation and psychogenic imbalance left him like the ghouls are believed to leave the man inside the house of god. He got closer to her than he was in the morning. He spoke after moments of seeing her, grasping all that he knew now.

'So I found your lie,' he mumbled plaintively looking at her. 'I don't know if you are listening to me. But this... this will of yours to save me isn't gonna help me,' he added. 'You need to come and see that I am nothing without you.' She was lying there still and he kept on gazing at her.

'How could you lie to me...' he continued sorely. 'All that while when I was here and thought that you...' he was speaking agonisingly now till he couldn't speak anymore and she lay still.

Robin entered the ward. He turned and tried to hide his moist eyes. He didn't want Robin to have any ill feelings for her regarding himself.

'Siddhant, I am going home for some time. Rhea and Mrs. Khanna will be here in some minutes,' Robin stated. 'Will you come for a drink?' Asked Robin. Siddhant didn't want to leave but couldn't say no as well and wasn't surprised too that a husband was leaving for a 'drink' leaving his wife. His sense of judgment was not very sentient this moment and he was the last person to judge anyone anyway now.

CHAPTER 35

Robin's ancestral home in Delhi was not as huge as his villa was in Mumbai. A small bungalow that was some minutes away from the hospital consisted of a few locked rooms and a study that they sat in for a drink after coming from the hospital. The pristine looking study looked maintained though it had an aura that conveyed that it wasn't much in use since the last generation. Among the furniture of the old generation, the only contemporary additions were the two wing chairs giving the room a bit of a modern touch.

'Please sit Siddhant,' said Robin getting a bottle of whisky kept on the top of the fireplace that was on the left of where Siddhant sat. Robin took a deep sigh while sitting and keeping the bottle on the table that was there between them, an old one with carvings that were in fashion back then.

'How've your life been Siddhant?' Asked Robin flatly in a low voice. 'You seem to be a serious guy,' he added.

'I'm no special to be talked about. Just one of those you come across,' replied Siddhant in his deep voice.

'Oh, I don't think so. People I come across are...hateful and conceited,' he replied. Robin had a flat voice, which always had a pinch of warmth in it. Yet he sounded dull and tired now when they were at home. Siddhant didn't speak.

'You know that's the reason I asked you to come,' he added. 'I wanted someone to speak to who knew us and still is not from us...conceited and formal.'

'I'm glad,' replied Siddhant. The maid brought the ice bucket and glasses in the dimly lit room and Robin made the drink. The light was enough though as the sun was still bright and was glowing the room from the French windows on the right side even with a veil of white curtains.

'Twenty-one years old,' said Robin in his tired, toneless voice as if speaking to himself. 'Dunno where would we all have been back then,' he added talking about the Glenlivet archive single malt scotch whisky which had written over its label '21' in large fonts. He looked lost yet conscious now and for the first time. Siddhant thought that what this man must be thinking right now, although the thought didn't ebb away his own plight. They sat for some time without saying anything.

'You want me to do anything?' Asked Siddhant in a low voice.

'No. No, Siddhant. You are already a great help. You know I was just thinking of the time when the family will be united by evening today and the claustrophobic situation,' Robin replied and added, 'I needed someone to dole out my this time with.' Siddhant listened to the man.

'And after this? I mean will you be...living well after a time... without her?' Siddhant then asked plainly.

'I've no idea mate,' he said quietly. They sat and had a drink and Robin uttered after a while as if he was realising it before speaking it, 'What a wonderful soul she was.' He added after a brief pause, 'And what an annoyed lady she had become.' Siddhant was told the same by Rhea. Something he could not ask about in the hospital with his mind somewhere else. He could ask now though.

'As in?' He asked quietly.

'Nothing,' Robin replied quietly looking at his glass. 'I don't know what ruined us,' he added.

'What do you mean?'

Robin looked at him and said, 'She was quiet...solitude from some time. Because of her health, I had thought.'

'What had happened?'

'Nothing much. At least that's what I had thought. She already had a blood pressure issue.'

'Blood pressure?' Asked Siddhant. He didn't know about it. 'Since when?' He added.

'Last two-three years. But that could do this...I didn't know.'

'You said her inherited illness...'

'Oh, ya. That too, of course. It all leads to what happened.'

'You never talked to her?'

'What could I? She was always good to me.'

'And with others?'

'Who doesn't talk to housemaids that way? Even if it was new for her,' he said. 'And I never thought it could be as worthy as to be worried about.'

'Was everything good?' Siddhant asked plainly. Robin looked at him seriously for the first time now and waited before saying anything.

'Yes. Indeed,' he said.

'I shouldn't have asked a personal question,' said Siddhant gulping down his whiskey. His tone controverted his words.

'Doesn't matter. Anyone would be surprised on such behaviour from *her,*' he said and added, 'You were her friend she told me. You must be aware of how she was.'

'Hmm,' expressed Siddhant.

'Need to go Siddhant,' said Robin suddenly after a moment. They stood up and Robin stretched his hand out to shake with Siddhant and said, 'Thanks Siddhant. You were the only one I could speak to about her at this time.'

'Anytime,' said Siddhant quietly.

They left the house.

CHAPTER 36

More than thirteen years had been passed since the sense of bereavement had enveloped him from such proximity and had landed him in a hospital in the winter of that year. More than a decade had passed since the time when his mother had got a cardiac arrest and he had taken her to the nearest hospital where she was admitted in the ICU. Not that he had not seen such a situation in the family before. His father had expired from the same heart ailment but he was never admitted for long and was declared lifeless sooner. His mother, however, had spent two nights in the ICU after which she had been declared with the same result. The disparity, however, had been there in both his stays in the hospital; he had his mother to look up to when his father was there and whom he could call a family. He still remembers *her* words when she sat beside him when his mother was in the ICU.

'She'll be fine,' she had said holding his arms when they were sitting on the bench outside the entrance to the ICU wards.

'I know she'll not,' he had said grimly in a low voice.

'Don't say that please,' Devyani had said to which he hadn't replied and sat there still.

'You should go. It's quite late,' he had expressed then.

'I am staying here,' was the answer.

It was after half an hour when the doctor had come to them and broke the matter to him with an apologetic expression. He just stood there and then completed the formalities to get his mother back to home where some of his aunts and uncles were staying back then. He clearly remembered how he hid his emotional state in front of Devyani and in public, in the corridor of the hospital when she had held his arms and had muffled in her choked voice looking into his eyes, 'I am here. I am here,' and then had said hugging him, 'And I will never leave you I promise. For I love you...and will do till I last,' and she had cried more while he just wept with tears flowing down his cheeks.

In the coming days of mourning that followed, she was the one who took care of him like a mother when he would not eat and would share his sorrow like a wife.

'Life doesn't end. It goes on,' she had said keeping her head on his shoulder to which he had not replied.

Did the fateful occurrence convince her to take her decision back then, he thought. Had she held herself responsible for his grief and loss? For she had told him her decision only after a few weeks of this occurrence. What else could make her take the decision for his good? It might have been her take. Who knows. He can just guess now.

Another moonless, dark night was getting darker with time while he sat in the bar not far from the hospital. He already had lost the count of drinks today, which had happened after a long time. His stupor reminded him of many incidents from the past today, another of which was that when she had met him for the last time years ago in a cafe. Was she deliberately portraying herself that way that day? Maybe that's the reason she had left him that pendant. And why not, he had come from the hospital only a day ago. The contrition in the heart was plunging the capability of understanding into pitch darkness making him feel the brewing of an empty hollowness inside him. Was her existence so much engrossed with superstitions he thought.

The LED screen on the rear of the bar counter displayed some music concert that he looked at now. It was live from Spain, the place he had been and she had been some time ago. And he had not told her when they spoke about it that he had wished she was there with him when he himself was there.

'Sir your phone,' said the bartender and he suddenly looked at him and then towards his phone, which was on the bar counter, vibrating. It was Robin and he received it.

'Hello,' he said.

'Hello, Siddhant?' Robin asked.

'Ya Robin, tell,' he said in a wobbly voice. Robin waited for a few moments before speaking.

'She passed away,' he told then.

Siddhant too waited for some moments and then said calmly, 'I will be there Robin. Coming.' They disconnected the call.

He sat there for a while and then asked for another drink to the bartender.

VOLUME 4

CHAPTER 37

The prayer meeting on the final day of mourning was held at the ancestral bungalow after almost two weeks of the cremation. The hall, and the lawn too, was overly occupied with family and friends. The petrichor that emanated from the lawn ground and the plants surrounding it in the evening was somehow relating the rain with her very existence Siddhant thought; getting vanished in the earth leaving behind the fragrance that lasts and the foliage that thrives. He sat outside the entrance to the hall, in the garden near the flower bed and didn't speak to anyone there but had greeted Rhea and Robin when he had arrived. Seeing him sitting alone for quite some time, Rhea came to him when many of the people had left and the sun was ready to sink in a while. She sat with him.

'What are you thinking?' She asked after a minute or two.

'Nothing,' he replied plainly looking at the flower bed.

'I shouldn't have told you Siddhant. It's all my fault,' she expressed.

'I'm thankful you did.'

'I shouldn't have delivered this agony.' He didn't say anything.

'She would never want you to be like this.' He again kept his silence. She kept her hand over his.

'You okay?' She asked.

'Hmm. I'm fine Rhea.'

He added after a while, 'You think she was mad?' To which she sneered.

'Only a fool could call her that Siddhant,' she said. 'In the world of our rationality, some may call her that though. In the world, however, where true bonds are more important, she was a girl no one could hold a candle to,' she added.

'Are you sure of everything you told me Rhea?' He asked.

'You still doubt me?' She asked in astonishment.

'I am not doubting you,' he said plainly. 'I just can't believe what you told me,' he added.

He then asked if she knew what she went through at his mother's demise or was that the reason.

'Might be. I can't be sure,' Rhea answered. 'She would never tell anyone, would she?' She added.

'Not even her husband?' He asked. 'Or couldn't he get to know?'

'Only if she told him which I don't think she did,' she replied. He too thought that Robin won't be this cordial to him had that been the case. A question then came to his mind that he had not yet asked any of them.

'What were they doing here Rhea?' He asked.

'He had some work I guess. He told me that,' she replied. He looked at her now and asked, 'Are you sure?'

'Why would he lie to me?' She asked looking confused herself now.

Siddhant sat there thinking of that and then contemplating that what could bring them here and how Robin is going to tell him if they were really here for his work or not.

CHAPTER 38

The ancestral bungalow was almost uninhabited two days later with only a bereaved husband and a maid or two living inside of its premises. Robin was sitting in his study when Siddhant arrived and he asked him to sit. The room looked gloomy with only a table lamp giving off a yellow-orange light. A bottle was already there when he arrived and Robin asked Siddhant too to accompany him when a maid arrived with another glass.

'Have a drink.'

'No thanks,' Siddhant replied. Siddhant had called him some hours ago to ask if they could sit together for he had some work in the same area for which he would anyway be there. He had lied, though Robin sounded pleased to be visited by him.

'Won't you give me a company,' Robin said in a wobbly voice. The feeling of loss had overtaken him it seemed. Siddhant realised that Robin was more despondent today in comparison to the other day. His countenance was dejected and not emotionless like that day.

'Sorry I have to drive back home,' Siddhant replied although it was never an issue with him. Robin didn't say anything. The man Siddhant had hated the most in his life since last many months sat there but the hatred was missing. It wasn't replaced by any compassion though.

'You should take care of yourself Robin,' he said formally.

'I could never take care of myself mate. It was she who did that for me,' he said looking at the ceiling resting his head on the back of the chair. He then added, 'Thanks for coming Siddhant.'

'Don't mention it Robin. I too am grieved,' Siddhant said.

'Oh, I'm sure,' Robin said and added quietly, 'A good man always feels others' sorrows.'

Siddhant couldn't ask him directly why they had come to the city.

'You shouldn't be that distraught Robin. You have work to look after and manage,' he said. Robin didn't reply.

Siddhant had never expected to see Robin in this state.

'You okay?' He asked after a brief pause.

'Ya...I am okay,' Robin replied and sounded a bit firm now.

'How's your work going on here?' Siddhant asked. He looked at Siddhant.

'Who told you I had work here?' He asked.

'No one,' Siddhant lied. 'I thought you must be having some work here so you came,' he added.

Robin didn't reply for some time and Siddhant waited, expecting him to answer. He then spoke.

'Should I tell you Siddhant,' he murmured and then added, 'I know I can't tell it to anyone.'

'Of course you can share if you want to Robin. You know me,' Siddhant stated carefully.

'Hmm. I know,' he uttered.

'What is it that's disturbing you, Robin?'

'I don't know,' Robin murmured. Siddhant kept silent. The surrounding had utter silence and the moment they would stop speaking, it seemed the silence would start enveloping them. He then added, 'You know...since last few days...it seems to me that I never knew her.' And he was quiet again.

'What had happened?' Siddhant asked plainly.

'She was so...so annoyed all the time. And with me too.' Siddhant didn't interject at this point with a point that he had stated that she was never vexed when it was concerning him.

'Did she say anything?' Siddhant asked.

'No no no...never. I had asked her. But she was just...' he sounded full of emotions now.

'What?'

'Senile.'

'Why?'

Robin didn't reply again. He then said, 'You know why I was here?' He was asking what Siddhant wanted to ask.

'No.'

'We were coming back from Mussoorie.' It surprised Siddhant.

He held himself up and asked quietly, 'Why were you people there?'

Robin gulped the whisky down his throat before answering and then spoke. 'She told me she wanted to go there. I could never say no to her,' he said and looked as if was about to say something and Siddhant waited.

'But she changed when we were still there. From her body to her mind. She transformed from what she had been. She went to see some monk in a monastery there. I was out when she was inside the temple and...' he stopped.

'And?'

'And she was changed when she came out. I just thought she was having a look at things inside it.'

'What was she doing there?'

'I did not know back then,' he said quietly. 'And then she fell ill. And a monk had come to see her.' He stated the last sentence in a low voice.

'For what?' Siddhant asked.

'Some blessing,' he said quietly. 'At least that's what she had told me,' he added.

'What type of blessing?' Siddhant asked. 'I mean what was he there for?' He added.

'God knows. I couldn't ask her. She was too ill to be disturbed.' Robin looked irked now, though not by the question but the time that it had reminded him of.

'That's all? Is that what disturbed you?' Siddhant asked when Robin kept silent. Siddhant was getting annoyed by him for not telling as to what exactly had made him call her senile or god knows what else he was under the impression she had become. Robin made himself another drink and gulped it down and asked Siddhant for it once again in case he had changed his mind. Siddhant had the same answer. Robin continued.

'Then one night...of the same day when the monk had arrived at the hotel...she wasn't on the bed. It was hours after midnight had passed. I got up and looked for her and got out of the hotel room to see where she was,' Robin told and as he was telling, the cadence of his voice changed. Siddhant didn't intervene when he took a break. He found Robin to be willing to share. He was right and Robin started again looking at the empty glass kept on the table.

'She was out. In the frosty night...she was out. She stood near the steep of the hill where the boundaries of the hotel garden ended,' he said. 'And she looked like she was not Devyani anymore,' he added.

'What do you mean?'

'She looked...when I called and she didn't turn to me, I pulled her by her arm and she turned. And she looked...so pale and...

so...skeletal. As if she had turned into someone else in just some hours.' He stopped.

'What do you mean? She was ill wasn't she?' Siddhant asked.

'Siddhant, you won't believe me...she looked like...living dead,' he said very quietly and Siddhant heard him as the home was extremely silent. 'So cadaverous,' he added and looked not towards Siddhant but in the emptiness beside him, in the air, as if he could see her in the room as clearly as he could see her that night.

'Then?' Asked Siddhant quietly. The nothingness in the room felt to be uneasy to Siddhant.

'She didn't look like Devyani. My Devyani,' he said. 'Her eyes were moist and I asked her what it was. And she just...hugged me and said that she missed her mother,' he added.

'That's all?'

'Ya,' Robin said and still looked dazed. 'Ya,' he said again and looked firm now, looking at Siddhant. The rain had started outside and they looked outside the window sitting there. The curtain was not there today and the water droplets could be seen. The sound of the raindrops falling on the leaves and plants made Siddhant feel he was still in the mortal world.

'And you just came back and then...?' Siddhant asked about their return and her final steps on the earth.

'We left the next day and she was...on the bed the next day after we reached here.' The rain was falling fiercely now. Siddhant asked him for a drink.

'Oh, of course, my friend,' he said and Siddhant made himself a drink. 'After all, you proved yourself to be the only confidant I could share all...this with,' Robin added. 'You must be thinking about my mental imbalance Siddhant,' he then said.

'No. Not at all,' Siddhant said.

'Hmm...I know you can't understand how it feels when someone loses a better half...a companion like her. But...you are decent and genuine....AND helpful my friend,' he said and now looked at Siddhant. Siddhant just looked at him amicably.

'Tell me one thing Siddhant,' expressed Robin in a very normal tone now. 'Have you been with women. I mean...you know what I mean right.'

'Hmm...not with many, Why?' Siddhant replied.

'I think they are...leave it,' he said but then added glumly, 'Sometimes I think that...I always thought I knew her so well...which I still think I did,' he said the last part with more emphasis. 'Yet sometimes, since the day she was there in the hospital...I thought that did I ever know her...I mean the real woman she must have been,' he added. Siddhant gulped down his whisky and spoke.

'You are just thinking because all this happened. I think she was a...she was your wife and you knew her more than anyone else could,' Siddhant said quietly and calmly in his deep voice.

'Hmm you are right Siddhant,' Robin replied. The rain had stopped the way it had started, suddenly and noticeably.

'What was that monastery you told me about Robin?' Siddhant asked.

'I don't know the name. There was one over there. I think people know it, it's quite famous,' Robin expressed. 'Why?' He asked.

'No nothing, just like that,' Siddhant replied.

'Hmm...you are a good man Siddhant. I am glad I came here and met you. At a wrong time though,' Robin said. 'I wonder why we didn't talk much in Udaipur,' he added. Siddhant didn't say anything on it and they sat there in silence for a while.

'I think I should leave now Robin. And you too should stop and get some sleep,' Siddhant said.

'Oh yes. Yes, my friend,' he said and Siddhant stood up.

'I am glad we met,' Robin said and they shook hands and Robin added, 'If alive, we'll meet again. In a better situation let's hope.'

'What you mean? You leaving?' Siddhant asked.

'Yes, my friend. I am leaving for London. As far as I can, as long as I can.'

Siddhant nodded and said formally, 'Tell me when you're in the city. Whenever you are.'

'I don't think so,' he said quietly looking outside, still sitting.

'What you mean?'

'I am never coming back to this city mate...this city just...' he didn't complete himself.

'I understand. God bless you, Robin,' Siddhant said and gave him amiable look for the last time.

'God bless you,' said Robin looking at Siddhant.

The night was dark and cloudy and it could rain anytime again. Siddhant walked slowly on the gravel that led to the main gate of the bungalow and felt again the petrichor emanating in the dead silence of the garden and lawn that was filled with trees and plants and obstructed light from coming in the vicinity making the surrounding more gloomy with only a few lights glowing the gravel up. He stopped for a moment to see on his left where darkness had enveloped much of the lawn. He stood there for some seconds and walked again. When reached outside the bungalow where he had parked his car, he put a cigarette in his mouth and lit it before getting inside the car. He, however, thought of something and threw it aside. He turned towards the bungalow to have a look. The bungalow looked gloomier than it looked from inside. He stood there still for some minutes with his hands in his trouser pockets. This was the last place, he thought.

VOLUME 5

CHAPTER 39

Strings of prayer flags were still. The rows of the strings with colourful small flags stretched from the golden dome of the white edifice of the monastery to a hill on the opposite side of it that was some two or three hundred meters above the ground of the temple complex and had a slope to scale over it. The courtyard of the monastery was big and only a few people could be seen who were the tourists. The grand ditch that had monastery on one side had another hill on the other and the temple looked hidden behind another hill as it was between the hill and the ditch. On the front side of the monastery was the hill where tourists or monks could scale over and where the prayer flags were fluttering on the top. Siddhant stood in the courtyard and looked towards the ditch resting his hands on the railing of the complex. He had arrived Mussoorie this morning and had come to the monastery that could be reached driving down the slope of the hill where Siddhant had his cab parked. He was waiting for the monk to meet for whom he had sent a word. However, the monk didn't come before half an hour had been passed. He waited and thought that he must be busy in his diurnal rituals. The mountains looked unyielding and strong yet serene. They always looked protective, better than the chaos of the city. City, where life made man blind to the divinity that could only be seen in the deepest part of the consciousness. The divinity that resided in that heart that lived in the chaos with others but hid the uncontaminated love for him.

He saw a monk in maroon robes walking towards him after half an hour though he didn't know if he was coming to him. He was also skeptical as to how the monk will react to the message he had sent him. Instead of going inside the monastery, he had asked a young monk to help him find and meet the monk who had come to a hotel nearby to see a sick lady a few weeks ago. He made clear to the young monk the profound nature of the issue. The monk was the one he was waiting for.

'Hello,' he bowed his head down slightly and greeted the monk when the latter came to him and stopped. The monk reciprocated his greeting with a nod of the head. He was a middle-aged monk with almost no expression on his face.

'Actually, I wanted to talk to you about the sick lady that you had come to meet a few weeks back in the hotel,' Siddhant said meticulously and politely for he didn't want to offend the monk and not wanted the latter to have any wrong impression about him.

The monk looked at him and scrutinized his face and asked, 'May I know who are you dear?' His voice had politeness yet his face looked indifferent.

'I am...from her family...' he said.

'And who told you about me?' The monk asked calmly.

'Her husband,' answered Siddhant. The monk gazed at him.

'And what do you want to know?' The monk asked.

'I wanted to know if she had some issue regarding...her health. That she spoke to you about,' Siddhant said.

'What is there to tell my dear. The lady I met was not well. She came to me and told how much she believed in god,' he expressed coldly.

'But you went to meet her.'

'But that is between me and the person I met,' the monk expressed stringently yet tonelessly. His mouth moved as if it was not the part of his face and his eyes seemed to be devoid of any communication.

'See I don't know what are you thinking about me sir but...I really *need* to know,' said Siddhant.

'But I don't see that I have anything more, that I have to tell you dear,' the monk said softly now.

'She is dead. She is no more,' Siddhant spoke readily in an exasperated tone but in a low voice.

The monk's countenance got softened. Siddhant looked the other way and looked tense. The monk stood there.

'Who are you?' He asked then.

'How does it matter? Can't you understand that no random man would be coming here asking you about her?' Siddhant said in his deep voice.

'What's your name?' The monk asked.

'Siddhant. Siddhant Mathur.' The monk didn't say anything.

'Are you the one she met many years back on her return from another country?' The monk asked. He had surprised Siddhant but very slightly. The indifference towards almost everything had become a part of his very existence now.

'Yes,' Siddhant looked at him and replied. He looked at the monk in hope now. She told him about their meeting he thought.

'Then you knew her. Why do you ask me?' The monk again sounded stringent.

'You know why I ask you. She met you and she told you everything. Don't you think I need to know and if no then why not?' Siddhant asked.

'Because if someone tells me something and doesn't ask me to share it with someone, my conscience doesn't allow me to tell,' the monk said.

'But you know me now. You know everything. I know that,' Siddhant said. They stood there in silence for a while till Siddhant spoke again. 'This is God's house. Do you think your duty compels you to hide something from me after knowing who I am?' Siddhant said quietly in his deep voice. The monk stood there and did not say anything without any emotion on his face. There was no sign of him doing any revelation. Siddhant could wait for he had a bigger cause. However, what he had experienced all these years had made him intolerant towards almost everyone.

'You know what? I don't believe in god and you have proved me right in doing so,' Siddhant said calmly yet stirringly. 'No faith is bigger than faith in love. Be it with human or be it with your god,' he added. It looked from his face that he was sure that the monk would not tell anything, until the latter spoke.

'I will meet you in the evening. Not here,' the monk said finally and told him he will be meeting in his hotel room in the evening. Siddhant looked relieved yet exasperated for his needless formal delay but agreed.

***

He was sitting in the hotel waiting for his visitor but had been dealing with time with whisky. This is the place he had been to thirteen years ago he thought while sitting in the small room of the hotel near his bed. Multiple thoughts ran in his mind. The change couldn't be seen when tried to be seen, change was all over there when he did not try to see. The ride to the small village and the drops of rain of that day were there he felt. He had reached the monastery passing the whole market and also the road where a fast car had moved uncontrollably years ago and a thumping of heart was felt on his chest on a sunny day. The heart, however, had stopped its working and had gone for a long...a very long vacation. The emporium still had multiple shawls and stoles hanging outside the store door and girls and women still touched and checked it; the *touch,* however, was gone. Or it was there but couldn't be felt from the senses a man possesses. And in the bustling crowd of the evening, the sun was sinking the same way it sank that time; away from the crowd, far away, yet a part of lives. Like it played a part a few days ago in the life of a woman who had loved him and was ready to enter his life officially.

***

Pooja had come to meet him on a river bridge on the evening of the day of the funeral when he stood there, bereaved.

'Why this urgency? And where have you been?' Pooja asked while he looked towards the sinking sun. 'Why are you not receiving my calls since yesterday?' She added and waited. He looked at her and she was aghast. With heavy stubble on his face, he looked cadaverous at this moment. His eyes looked lifeless from the extremity of alcohol and his skin, bloodless.

'What had happened to you?' She asked in surprise, touching his face, which felt cold. He gazed at her and she just looked at him as if examining.

'I am leaving,' he said. His deep voice sounded as stirring as it never did before.

'Leaving? Where? What has happened to you Siddhant?' She asked hysterically. He gazed and expressed glumly, 'She loved me.' And then he added, 'For all her life...and I couldn't see it.' Pooja tried to understand what he had just stated.

'Who?' Pooja asked. 'Did you...meet her?' She added quietly after a pause.

'I couldn't,' he said.

'Where is she?' She asked. He was silent. Her eyes were wet by now from disquiet.

He looked glum but not devastated. He had seen *her* on the pyre a few hours ago.

'I am leaving...for my life now has to endure what was destined for both of us,' he said in a low yet firm voice. Pooja somehow had an idea now what he spoke about. She had known from his expression whom he spoke about. She was not ready though.

'Don't...please don't,' was all that she could mutter while her eyes were filled with tears ready to roll down her cheeks. He looked tensed yet resolute. He took her face in his hands and kissed her forehead. Tears rolled down her cheeks now.

'No man can run away from his destiny. And I can't leave her looking at me like this,' he said. 'Not this time,' he added. She kept gazing at him. In the evening breeze, her hair waved.

'You can't do this to yourself if she loved you,' she said quietly in a choked voice.

'She endured all by herself. Now is my time Pooja,' he said. And then he added, 'For she was the only woman I ever loved and will always...god bless you Pooja.' He just looked at her for some moments while she looked into his eyes and then he turned to leave her forever. She sniveled as soon as he turned he realised but walked on. The sky appeared dark blue now as the sun had sunk completely and the lights of the bridge substituted its glow. He indeed, had his time left.

CHAPTER 40

The door knock made him alert and he walked readily to open it. The monk with a yellow shoulder 'monk bag' stood there and Siddhant welcomed him and asked him to sit and kept the bottle away beside the bed on the floor. He sat on the sofa that was on the corner and Siddhant sat opposite him.

'Thank you for coming,' said Siddhant to which the monk nodded. 'Would you like to have something?' Siddhant added.

'No thanks. Tell me what do you seek?' Asked the monk plainly.

Siddhant after a pause asked, 'I want to know, what was it that she came to you for. And why had you come to see her exactly? For she was not like the way she had been after that meeting.'

'I will surely answer. But I need to know who you are first. And how were you related to her?' The monk asked. Siddhant looked at him before he could speak.

'I was her...I loved her. And if I am not wrong, she loved me,' said Siddhant coldly in his deep voice. The monk took a brief pause before speaking again.

'The lady you are talking about was an ardent believer of destiny. She was sick and her mental state was going through extreme turbulence when she met me the first time in the temple,' the monk said and Siddhant listened.

'She was disturbed, for she was under the agony of extreme guilt, the reason of her extreme pain,' he said and again took a pause as if trying to recall although his expression didn't tell the same story.

'She told me that love...was something she was not destined to have in life. And the doom of her life had affected someone she had loved...someone she had loved to an extreme vehemence,' he said and paused again, this time for some more seconds. Siddhant asked him quietly, 'What did you tell her then?'

'I told her it is just her imagination. And nothing can make the doom of her life befall on someone she loved. Then she told me how she had experienced it and how someone's life was destroyed because of her. Someone for whom her love was so intense that it could challenge the gods and challenge the destiny...which I realised...later,' told the monk.

'What did you do then?' Asked Siddhant. His hands were cold and so were the fingers of his feet inside shoes he felt.

'I could not do anything, for I am no magician but a firm believer of god,' the monk said and added, 'She then told me to pray for her, the prayer I could not.'

'What did she ask?' Siddhant readily asked.

'She asked me to make a solemn prayer to the god, to let her love dwell in flesh and blood on the earth, even if it needs a life to be sacrificed.'

'As in?'

'Her love should remain here, even if she...is to be embarked on a journey to the eternity that we call an end,' the monk said plainly. Silence fell over the room and Siddhant waited for him to complete himself.

'I could not do that. But it was my duty to ask her to be calm.'

'And?'

'She beseeched. Like it was an inexorable calamity that was about to reach out to the one she loved. And I did...pray for what she sought. And she sat with me until I was done doing it.' The silence again enveloped the environs. Siddhant sat there thinking if this was what he wanted to know or if this really was the truth he needed all his life. Or if the truth that he had been believing till a few weeks ago was more satisfying. He sat there as the only living man in the room as if waiting again to ask something to someone who had no relation to either of the lives–or death–of souls who were concerned. He asked finally the last question that he had had in his mind that had been disturbing him the most since last many days.

'And why did you come to see her again?' Siddhant asked quietly.

'She had asked me to,' answered the monk. He added, 'However, I was there for only a few minutes and she had asked me a weird question I did not expect. She asked me if my prayer was going to be accepted by God, to whom I have dedicated my life.' The monk took a pause and then said, 'I told her. Indeed.' They both kept silence.

'And?' Siddhant asked. The monk did not say anything now and just looked at Siddhant's face for almost half a minute as if examining. He then searched something in his bag that he had kept on the table between them, from both his hands and took out what seemed to Siddhant like a journal. He extended his hand towards Siddhant but when Siddhant tried taking the journal, he didn't leave it from his firm clutch. Siddhant gazed at him. The monk looked at him with his shining piercing eyes and asked in his deep voice politely yet with such an authority to which no one could lie, 'Are you the one she spoke about?'

Siddhant did not say anything but looked at him with such an expression that needed no words. His deep eyes not beseeched but testified more than what was needed, and the monk loosened the clutch and the journal slipped from his hands. Neither had she told him about the person she spoke about nor the relationship she had shared with the soul, yet the monk did what seemed correct to him at the moment. Siddhant untangled the black string that was around the brown leather of the journal that looked like the skin of an animal and had motifs on it. He opened the journal. The pages of the journal looked old and yellow both because of time and the material it was made from. He just flipped the pages and asked the monk, 'What is it?'

'I don't know. This is what she had given to me to keep. When her husband had gone out for a call,' the monk told. The evening was dark now as the sun had sunk. They did not say anything to each other anymore. The monk then said, as if waiting for Siddhant to ask any more questions that he had the answers for, 'I have told you what I knew.' He said and kept his hand on his who looked down towards the journal and looked numb. The monk it seemed consoled him for he now knew that he was the person, he was the man she had spoken about. Siddhant looked at him and said very quietly, 'Thanks,' to which the monk nodded. When the monk moved his hand and seemed ready to get up, Siddhant asked him, 'Do you think your prayers were heard?' Siddhant looked firm again. The monk did not move and replied calmly, 'I do not know. Yet after what you told me today about her...it is up to you to believe in it.' Siddhant gazed at him for a while and he too.

'Does it happen?' Siddhant asked.

'I never heard about or seen it happening in front of me.'

'Do you think it happened?' He asked again.

'From what you told me, I believe what she had told me had some arcane truth in it. Maybe a true bond between souls can sometimes change the course of destiny.' The room had a silence now that resembled the silence that falls over the part of the earth where turbulence has made its presence eminent and has left the lives restive.

'Is it not a sin?' Asked Siddhant.

'What is acceptable to God can have no shadow of sin over it. A soul esteemed enough to forgo the bond of life for someone, I believe makes the bond with the Almighty,' the monk replied and then added, 'It makes the bond immortal. Not with flesh and blood, but with the love that resonates forever.' He then put his hand on Siddhant's shoulder and got up. Siddhant too got up but didn't move. The monk took his bag and moved towards the door and touched the doorknob when Siddhant asked suddenly yet slowly, 'How did you know I was the person?', gesturing towards the journal he held in his hand. The monk looked at him, standing in the same position and said not loudly but in a voice that could reach the mind and graze the heart, 'If a man apart from my husband, whom you know now, ever comes to you asking about me, give it to him for it belongs to him...like the words of yours belong to the god.' The monk stood there after telling him and then added, 'These were her words on her bed when she met me that evening. They were as potent as they were capable to be remembered.' The monk looked at him and Siddhant nodded as if no more questions were left and he was thankful to him. The monk opened the door and left the room closing the door behind him. Silence fell over again.

CHAPTER 41

19th January,

I met a monk today on the road outside the school that had only a few people when the snowfall began. I got scared. People were leaving really fast and I could not know how to reach back to school after it would be dark. But thank god, there was a monk who was there. He was under the canopy of the same store that I was standing under. I was so scared of him. They always scare me. Their robe, their facial expressions and their chants, although I know it is for good and god. But he came to me and said, "No need to worry child, I will help you get back to the school," as if he knew why I was worried. But he must have seen the fear on my face. But it's good snowfall stopped for a while and I got back here. Mrs. Brown would've killed me had she been aware I was out.

The squiggly handwriting was readable. The diary although had stains which could have been there since the beginning or after the time when the monk had kept it with himself. The journal that Devyani Sinha would maintain with some important events of her life was on the writing table beside the window and Siddhant sat there reading it. The first entry was of January of some year that he didn't know about as the year was not mentioned. But it indeed was from the time when she had gone to the boarding school away from her home for the first time he thought. He ran eyes through the following entries, which were more about the exam results and the times when she would miss her home. Some were as juvenile as any kid can be while some expressed the psyche of a child who was away from family.

The next entry that Siddhant read with some care was from a few years later it seemed.

29th March,

Neither dad nor Ma came this vacation to take me. Nay, Ma never comes. It is dad who says she will. But this year he didn't. I miss them. When they were together. Will I relive the time when I was with them...even if they fought. But they loved me and I love that time. My love for ice cream too is well known to them. But do they know my love for them? I wish they do.

Then, the "*I wish they do*" was cut with the fountain pen ink that was being used by her all those days, and another line was added after the cut.

I know they do.

Pamela told me today in the church that she had asked God to give her the passing marks and she will go to the church for the next five Sundays, and she giggled. It was her fifteenth birthday. I didn't ask anything. I never do. Maybe I would like to ask for the reconciliation of Ma and dad. If God does that, I will surely go to the church every Sunday.

The entry was over. And it was over till the time her mother lived. The unsettled childhood peeked out of the journal and seemed as if it made him realise how incapable he was to do anything.

Her next entry was in her fifteenth year and Siddhant knew it from the fateful incident she had told him about years ago at a place away from the city, witnessing the setting sun.

15 July,

I am back. The funeral of Ma got over days back. I could not see her though. Dad told me she was cremated in Delhi and he had taken her from her home to our home. My home did not look good to me for the first time. Especially when I saw my mother in my dream. She was calling me. Am I going mad? I do not know. Dad was busy with his family members and friends and then work. I although felt good with

Rhea. She is young and a nice girl. She pestered me to play with her some stupid game she was having. She is my aunt's daughter. I don't like her mother. Or should I say the feeling is mutual? She is good though. But I did not like her when she said something about my mother this time when Ma was not even there. God bless my mother!

Then it seemed that there was no entry for years till she was back in India. But then there were some torn pages too he realised. What was there in those pages that she wrote and did not want others to read if the diary ever fell in someone else's hands. Or did she do that before handing it over to the monk, he thought. He felt an emptiness as if she had again taken something from him. He continued reading again.

17th February,

Hello, my friend!

We've been away since long but my heart missed you. I am back in India and this time, till the time I want to be here. Of course, I will reside here and would love to spend time and life here. I have to see my mother's house where I am longing to go since long but couldn't ask dad to. He wants me to meet some guy who's his friend's son and will be here in some weeks. He is not forcing anything though and is not in any hurry. He is happy. So are my aunt and Rhea as I am in Delhi and staying with them. Aunt has changed, she is cordial and good to me. Let's see how long do I take to start off my work. But before that, I need to meet my long lost cousin Tanya, a girl of dad's foster brother whose father was adopted by grandpa. I met her years ago when I was here and was working for homeless people. Dad asked me if I would like to meet her if I'm getting bored. Not bored, but going just to see the people here, nothing special. Au revoir!

Tanya never told Siddhant that her dad was an adopted son of her grandfather, nor did Devyani. Just that she was her distant cousin and his grandpa considered Tanya's dad his second son. But knowing Devyani now, she surely would have done so to save Tanya from any question by me in any case or to save her from humiliation that she might have felt, he thought. Maybe that was the reason Tanya had increased the distance between them and herself when they came into a relationship. Doesn't matter. He never discussed anything else than themselves with Devyani anyway. The journal now had the mention of his name for the first time in the next entry and he read it.

19th February,

The party was okay. Same like those I never liked. Drunkards who muster the hope to be liked by people, and last night, they hoped by me. Poor they! Some of them were good and Tanya, as I expected, was cordial; nothing more, nothing less. However, there was a guy. Siddhant was his name. He was neither drunkard nor sleazy, yet I think he was trying hard to hope for something. Not like others...but god knows. He was interesting. Likeable...may be. I liked his manners.

The weather too is good here. Much for now!

This was the first impression that he had had on her. He didn't feel anything. But what went inside her when she met him the second time was unknown even to him; the old as well as the present Siddhant. He continued the reading.

23rd February,

I met Tanya again today as she wanted to talk about aunt's interview. Siddhant was there. Initially, I did not like it but he seems to be a good man. He is nice and can be trusted I believe. What to say...am I being too fast? Nay, I think I have rarely met a person like him. Don't know why I say so but there's an urge to know more. Meeting him tomorrow over brunch.

P.S. I have felt familiar with only this man apart from Dad. Safe and comfortable. Wonder if there's more to come.

She had not clearly mentioned what exactly she had had in her mind but she was indeed feeling familiar with him he thought. He read about the next day, which was on the same page.

24th February,

I love him. I am afraid that I do. The way he touched me is something I always longed. From the most vulnerable part of my heart, and my soul. I was skeptical till last night but when I met him today, I was sure. I told him I have other commitments. Will I stick to my resolution?

I can't forget his piercing eyes that he looked at me with. The most haunting thing is that those eyes remind me of Ma. The same innocence. I can't let him meet the same fate.

I will no more be fortunate to see those eyes again. I am afraid!

Let him live with no more attachments. Let it be his infatuation... which I am sure it is not.

It was not something that came between them later on he thought. It was there since the beginning, her fear of losing the people she loved the way she had lost her mother and did not even see her the last time. The mention of how she had told him about her mother on that day was totally missing from this entry and it was all about him. That's why she had wept that day. He now knows why she had told him that day that she was committed; not because she was concerned about her father, but because she was concerned about him.

The bottom of the fate that they could not escape was unfolding to him as if happening again in front of him but this time, from her point of view. And he recalls now how she herself had told him a few months ago when they had met again and were talking about her husband, '*Only once have I felt a selfless love after my mother.*' And I neither asked nor she clarified who she was talking about because she was a married woman by then, he thought. Only if he could ask he thought now. He continued the reading.

10th March,

I got to know that Tanya is going to Mussoorie. I have been asking about him to Tanya all this while but then stopped a few days back. The course of destiny shouldn't be disturbed.

But this is the last time I will be seeing the people I feel for. My Ma... her home is no less than her own existence, where she lived in her last days. And He will be there.

Don't I have the right to see him again...only god knows when will I see him again or will I ever...?

I thought this urge would diminish...but it seems the more I suppress the more this fire gets fiery. If only once...

And the entry was over. So she came for me he thought...and she wanted to see me. And she was as helpless as I was. She didn't make any entry for a long time after this. It was this time after which she had seen some best days of her life he thought, and he was sure about it. Because those were the best days of *his* life. The next entry brought to the surface the issue that had been deeply rooted in her psychology, in a very manifested form. The liberty of accepting the life that she was living was gone forever.

15th September,

The gravity of my sin costed him. My aspiration brought the grimness in his life that will never be gone. How will he cope I thought. But then it may not be the end...if I keep the ties intact with the man I love and need, like the flowers of marigold need the sunlight to blossom and the night needs the moon to shine it.

My moon is grim these days...I will leave him to shine once he is ready...soon.

The telephone ring of the hotel phone kept on the side table brought him back to the present. The night was getting darker now he saw from the window and didn't get up from the chair for a few seconds. He stood up and received to know that it was from the room service asking him if he had any order for the dinner as the kitchen service was about to get over for the day. He said no and put the phone receiver down. The people in the hotel seemed to have slept by now and the silence was complete and throughout the corridors of the hotel. He walked slowly towards the table and sat again.

So she had decided to do what she did next some weeks after his mother's demise he thought. He turned the pallid page of the journal and the next entry was of the day when she met him for the last time before she tied the knot.

5th October,

I confessed to my world that my world doesn't have any space for him. I am sure he didn't doubt my intention.

But thank you, God, for it was all easy for him it seemed to me. He didn't stop me. He didn't stop me, and he didn't fight. He didn't call me back when I walked towards my car, and I am more than happy for that lord. For the type of man he is, he could know seeing my eyes what went inside my mind and my heart when I walked away.

And could the creation of Yours justify what it had uttered? Indeed no.

One question from him, one word of convincing me to walk back in his life...and I could never leave his arms...which You destined to be for someone else...and I had rebelled against You to find my space in it.

He behaved easily though looked disturbed...it is common isn't it?

I hope he will find the creation you created to inhabit his world...soon. He will be happy, for I have left forever.

Bless him, my lord!

What could be the turmoil in the mind of a teenager who made this journal her friend? A teen who was overtaken by a girl who now spoke to *Him,* who had created her. It was God who she referred and spoke to now.

And the hollowness inside him grew. Had I been brave enough to call her back...the life, and death could be something else, he thought. Had I been less of an egoist in life...which ultimately had affected my subconscious. It wasn't god...it wasn't her...it was *I* who left her...and plunged her into the pit of gloom.

With thoughts running in his mind and a feeling as if centipedes ran all over his face and inside his brains, he sighed deeply and closed his eyes. The ultimate weakness he was feeling inside him was suppressing the sheer urge to cry that was brewing inside him. He kept his palms on the face while resting elbows on the table. He tried drinking some water but couldn't, and coughed. His heart was thumping now with cough and he rested his head on the back of the chair for some minutes before resuming the read.

The next entry was days after she met Robin but had nothing more than a few normal occurrences. He still read each and every entry he had in front of him. Then there were the torn pages again and the journal had only some last few pages left now. And the second last entry was there. It was after they met years after their breakup. It was after the day when she and Robin had left Udaipur.

2nd January,

Was it You or was it I who did this to him? Is this what I had left his life for? Is this why I was destined to be away from him? What have I made of that soul...devoid of life and love that both You and I know he deserves. And when I brewed in my mind a doubt for Your arrangement and felt him once again...in that apartment...where I felt him and his odour...with the fragrance of marigold...You again showed him on the threshold of annihilation to me. To tell me You cannot be wrong and it was I who brought agony to his life?

But...If it has to be someone, let me be the one. For I have left him once again. For I did not confess to him what we know.

Each of her days that she suffered because of him were unfolding in front of his eyes. How wretched her love was in her eyes for he was suffering. The love that he took pride in. The love which he thought was pure from his side and which–in a subliminal way–had convinced him that he and only he knew what true love felt like.

Threshold of annihilation...was she talking about him getting hospitalised? A mortal ailment he had suffered or what he had suffered all this while he thought.

And while he saw her at the airport under the impression that he had suffered while she had rejoiced, it was *she* who was so swelled up with the turbulence inside her mind that she had to resort to her old friend and later, her way to liaise with 'her god'–her journal.

And the last entry was there. And it was just a few weeks ago when she had for the last time conversed with 'her god.' When she was here.

23rd July,

And he was drowning in the realm of darkness and I stood there seeing him. I could neither move nor call for help. Though it was a dream, I do not know what You seek.

Is this what I think it is? I am sure it is. Or why else would You bring that upon me? Trust me, I will not let him suffer and I will supersede his space with mine. I am here where our love consummated...when I told him I had loved him...and the eyes...his eyes that moment...and I could never see those eyes like that.

I am here and I seek Your counsel...to take me into the realm where I belong...for his happiness and life are to be here...

And I trust You that you will not dishearten me, for I will not doubt You this time, and for You know that his soul is not his soul alone and my soul is not mine. His life is not his life and mine, not mine. And if one needs to enter Your realm while the other rejoices Your creation, I confess to You that it is I. And after that, nothing would be between me and him, not even You. That will be another time, another world, where I will reunite with my love.

Bless him for he is the one for whom I can sacrifice the bonds you created when you created a man and a woman.

I love him.

Bless him.

And the pages were blank after this entry. The pale pages with some marks were there and then there were none. So there was something ready to befall him she believed. And she believed it was the arrangement by someone she called god and who had, after her prayers and beseeching superseded her life with his. She believed it. He had finished reading that journal like her life was there in its pages and ink. He sat there, still, with some thoughts coming in his mind. All that while, when she loved me and I loved her. When I cursed her and she suffered it, and I didn't understand her and she sacrificed her existence for me.... she was loving me like a...

There was nothing that could be thought of after this. He always believed that thinking could be the practice done to fathom out what could have lied in certain missing links that a man could join. He didn't have to think now. He had all that he needed to know. He stood up slowly and opened the second door of his room that opened in the garden of the hotel from where the hills and the deep mountain valleys and steep could be seen. Walking slowly towards the flower bed where the lawn ended and the ditch began, he reached the boundary and now looked towards the hill that was there in front of him. The secret tryst between the night and the dawn could be felt in the frosty environ and in its absolute silence. The wind was making a whoosh and was making it hard for anyone to be there. The darkness of the hour made the hills and the steeps look stupendous and surreal. This was the place she had told him she didn't want to leave the last time they were here. Who knows if she felt safe here...in the mountains.

He always thought that the ability to think in man is always supported by the cause that needs to meet an end. He had none. For he had reached the end that had no end and no way to go.

The stalemate he had reached to had only one way, to be where he was, and live, for the wish she had had for him. The unending sufferings of their love that she alone had endured had seen the end that she had thought would bring an end to his misery with the end of the pulsation of her heart.

It was, however, his time. It was now for him to make this 'creation of His' the purgatory for himself. The wretchedness of love had been experienced by her. It was a beginning for him to endure it this time, with more vehemence though.

The dawn drew on and the different hues of the sky could be seen; the silhouette of the trees and rocks of the hills and the steep valley were visible. The flower bed too could be seen clearly now. He stood there and saw the slightest hues of the flowers that were there. The golden hues of the marigold flowers were clear to behold now.

About The Author

Shekhar Srivastava is a Gurgaon based writer who has been working with media agencies for the past few years to add value to brands and surge their online traffic. Shekhar also worked as a freelance journalist for newspapers before taking an interlude in his professional life to accomplish his much-coveted aspiration of writing his first novel. Always keen on seeing life from others' viewpoint, Shekhar tries to find stories across every social strata—while being involved with NGOs and welfare groups—to weave them in a tale that readers can love and relate to. Shekhar has also been writing on online platforms and can be reached on his social media handles and blog page through the links given below.

Mail — authorshekhar@gmail.com

Instagram — theauthorshekhar

Blog — travellingkrishnaite.wordpress.com